Floating Underwater

D0926171

Shawn, Tracy,author.
Floating underwater :a novel

2021
33305252101591
ca   05/02/22

Floating Underwater

a novel

Tracy Shawn

Turbulent Muse Publishing
California, United States

This book is a work of fiction. The names, characters and events in this book are the products of the author's imagination or are used fictitiously. Any similarity to real persons living or dead is coincidental and not intended by the author.

Floating Underwater

Published by Turbulent Muse Publishing
California, United States

Copyright © 2021 by Tracy Shawn
All rights reserved. Neither this book, nor any parts within it may be sold or reproduced in any form or by any electronic or mechanical means, including information storage and retrieval systems, without permission in writing from the author. The only exception is by a reviewer, who may quote short excerpts in a review.

Library of Congress Control Number: 2021933578

ISBN (paperback): 9781736664902
eISBN: 9781736664919

Contents

Chapter One

Paloma smiled at Reed as she clenched the sides of her chair. They sat at their usual spot—a small table outside their favorite deli. Pedestrians slogged by through an unseasonably humid June. A heat wave had intruded on the small town of Sunflower Beach; even the window-box geraniums were wilting in defeat. Paloma doubted they'd survive the summer.

She directed her attention back to her husband. She had to tell him. But she kept her mouth shut as she caught sight of a small bird flitting by and out of view so quickly it could have been her imagination. She swallowed down the murky taste of dread. Maybe it would be better for Reed not to get his hopes up. But he had a right to know—and besides, she *wanted* him to know.

He cocked his head, grinning. "What is it?"

"I've got some good news." She reached over and held his hand, knowing he had already guessed.

"We're pregnant," he said.

She laughed and nodded in confirmation.

"Honey, that's great." He squeezed her hand and smiled as if loss were never an issue. "This time will be different. I just know it." He got up to hug her. She stood and received his embrace, the glow of his positivity radiating through her body.

"I hope so." She sat back down, wishing she could catch sight of the bird again. She didn't tell him how two days earlier, as she was mindlessly driving to work, one of her visions had struck. With both hands fixed on the steering wheel, she had managed to pull off the road. She'd tried to will the image away, yet it grew even more vivid. A corpse of a baby sparrow floated down a creek. With its thumb-sized frame and bruised eyelids, it looked like it had plummeted to its death before it even had a chance to breathe. She waded in and scooped it out of the water, but its translucent form had slipped through her cupped hands. She watched, paralyzed, as it tumbled toward the waiting mouth of the ocean—lifeless, distant, gone.

When the vision ended, she had eased her car back onto the street, shutting out the message. But, as before, she could not forget it, even here with Reed. Especially here with Reed.

"Of course it's going to be okay," he said. "Wait just a minute."

He went into the deli and walked up to the counter. Paloma held her stomach as she watched her husband point to a row of Russian tea cakes. He beamed at droopy-eyed Manny behind the counter, who never changed his just-give-me-your-order expression. With Reed's tall, robust frame constrained inside his Oxford shirt and his brown, grey-flecked curls brushing his collar, her husband's bouncing-on-his-toes earnestness made her want to cry. Even though his optimism could be annoying, it also saddened her in its naïve vulnerability.

He returned and handed Paloma a crisp white bag with two conjoined butter stains already seeping through. "Just a little treat to enjoy later," Reed said, "for my wife—and baby." He flashed his big-toothed grin as though nothing bad would ever happen again.

Paloma opened the bag and inhaled the sugary aroma.

Reed chuckled as he folded his large body back into his chair and leaned in, eagerness lighting up his face. "When's the due date?"

For some reason, she couldn't remember. She knew the date marked something else, something that made her nervous. "The doctor says I'm due…" She stopped and took a sip of ice water, trying to shake off the apprehension.

"If we count the months from your last period, wouldn't it be around April?" Reed drew closer, the lunch-crowd noise closing in around them.

She nodded, her memory jogged. "The baby is due April twenty-first." As soon as she said it, she remembered: April 21 was her mother's birthday. Paloma gagged; the smell of a pastrami sandwich the ponytailed guy at the next table was wolfing down eliciting sudden nausea.

"You okay?"

"Yeah," she said. "Just feeling queasy." She picked up a napkin and wiped her forehead. "I guess my hormones are kicking in."

Reed's eyebrows shot up. "They are? That's a good thing. You never felt any morning sickness before." He beamed at her, his conviction reeling her in.

"You're right." Maybe her vision of the dead sparrow was about something else—or maybe it meant nothing at all.

"Sure I am," Reed said with utter finality.

Manny's impatient voice burst through an open window as he called out their number and rang the counter's bell five times in a row—then, impatiently, five more times. Reed stood up and raced back into the deli. But as he brought back his tuna on rye and her turkey sandwich, he gripped the bright orange tray like a little kid who was afraid everything might crash to the ground at the slightest misstep.

Paloma held her sweaty glass to her forehead. "Thank you." She ignored the foreboding that sank into her gut.

Reed bit into his sandwich and chewed with gusto. Paloma watched him, envious of—but also heartened by—his ability to believe in the future. She reminded herself that happiness was not going to turn into tragedy the second she allowed herself to trust it. Noticing a dab of tuna on Reed's chin, she smiled as she reached over to wipe it off.

"Don't worry." Reed winked. "Our kid can't ever be as sloppy as I am."

"I wouldn't bet on that. Your messy gene runs pretty deep."

She had missed their silly bantering. They hadn't been this playful with each other since the last pregnancy, but his jokes and her bursts of laughter had dissipated over time. She wagered, though, that most couples eventually lose sight of what first brought them together.

Reed patted her hand. "It *is* going to work out this time, Paloma…"

Paloma smiled, then took a bite of her sandwich. Maybe Reed was right; everything would be okay—the future did not have to be defined by the past.

And then, out of the corner of her eye, Paloma saw her. Bone-thin Serena raced across the street and planted herself next to the bumper of a parked car. In her ragged skirt and barely there T-shirt, Serena could be mistaken for one of Sunflower Beach's many homeless people, who tucked themselves into alleys, behind bushes dotting the hillsides, and around trash-strewn paths by the railroad tracks. Yet the bedraggled Serena lived with her family, who tried their best to care for her in their own, private way. Serena stared at Paloma with her mismatched eyes, one blue and the other an unnatural shade of milky green. Slowly, Serena shook her head as her gaze misted over with what looked to be pity. Even though she had followed Paloma around ever since she'd moved into town, when she was in sixth grade and Paloma in fifth, Paloma's heart raced now, and the nausea returned.

Reed leaned away and averted his face from Serena's scrutiny. "She's been showing up even more, you know."

"I know," Paloma whispered. "I think she's trying to tell me something." Paloma shoved her plate away. Eating would be impossible now.

"She's not trying to tell you anything." Reed sighed. "She's just more unhinged than usual."

Paloma dared to look again. Serena pinned her down with those unnerving eyes, and then her mouth suddenly twisted into a grimace. Not knowing what else to do, Paloma waved. Serena turned abruptly. Passersby shook their heads and stared as she skipped barefoot down the street. Paloma watched the last coiled ends of Serena's long, tangled hair as it floated out of view.

Chapter Two

One month later, Paloma lumbered to the bathroom on an unbearably hot Wednesday morning. Her stomach clenched like a fist fighting to hold on to a lifeline being wrenched from its grip. Yet there was nothing she could do but let go. Nothing. Holding back tears, she tried to block out the ugly sound of the flushing toilet. The pipes echoed the last gurgle. Paloma knelt in defeat. After several breaths, she made herself get up and stepped to the sink. She twisted the cold-water faucet, avoiding eye contact with her reflection. Repeatedly drenching her face with cupped hands, she tried to wash away the sticky shroud of grief. She then jerked her head up and shut off the water. Her fingers gripped the counter's edge. How could it be so easy for her body to reject what would have been her child? And why did this keep happening?

She escaped the bathroom's yellow walls. Her legs felt hollow, like the limbs of a ghost. This had happened with the two other miscarriages, and she wondered if it was a sign—but of what she didn't know. Knotting the long, curly mess of her auburn hair into a bun, she wished for a life that would wash away her lonely childhood, a life jam-packed with giggles and toys, siblings and friends—a life filled with joy. But as she stepped forward, she wondered if that could ever be. Then she paused, momentarily blinded by the July sunshine spilling down the hallway. She narrowed her eyes and watched dust motes swirling like oblivious planets in a separate universe. Maybe she hadn't really miscarried. Perhaps she'd wake up tomorrow smiling in the morning light, knowing that her belly was tight with life.

Her cell's insistent buzzing from the bedroom snapped her back to reality, and her body sagged with emptiness. Like a sleepwalker, she ambled forward, the raw pain of loss cramping throughout her core. Yet inside her room, a surge of adrenaline made her heart race; she *had* to find her phone. She knew it was irrational, but if she had misplaced it, then what else would disappear? Telling herself to take deep breaths, she searched under the bed, inside the closet, on the windowsill. She became dizzy with dread. Then she let out a shuddery breath—and finally saw that the shiny, black screen was in plain view.

It sat innocently on top of her latest stack of baby books. She grabbed it, peering at the screen. Her best friend Justine had called, and Reed had left a voice mail. The thought of telling the ever-ready-with-advice Justine made her head throb. And she didn't have the heart to tell Reed over the phone. As stressed as she was to find her cell, she was now just as frantic to push it out of sight. She powered it off and wedged it under the books. One day soon she would lug them to the nearest thrift store. But as she stared at a cover of a wide-eyed baby swaddled in a lavender blanket, a strange and wonderful stirring at the bottom of her stomach told her to save them. She placed a hand across her chest, knowing this fleeting guess of future happiness was her way of shoving away the grief of the here and now. And as she slumped onto the bed, she wondered who her child would have been? What would have been her favorite color? Her favorite subject in school? Would she have loved swimming in the ocean like her mother? Would she have enjoyed bursting out in song like her father? Would she have inherited Paloma's shyness? Or take after Reed and go out of her way to chat with strangers?

Though she and Reed had been volleying names back and forth, they hadn't yet agreed on any. Maybe if they had named *this* unborn child, the baby would have felt that they had acknowledged her existence, and then, somehow, she would have held on. Paloma clenched her mouth tight; she couldn't share this with anyone—not even Justine—as she knew how irrational it sounded. So, she pushed down the guilt, told herself that she'd have to get on with her life. But then her mind immediately landed on the past. Like thousands of times before, Paloma also pushed that dark emotion away. What good would it do to focus on events that could never be changed?

Paloma forced herself to stand. She squinted at a slice of sunlight landing on her bed. No matter what may or may not happen in the future, all she wanted to do in that moment was withdraw into a cool, dark place. Yet it was impossible to hide from the Southern California summer within the walls of their upstairs unit, with only thin cotton curtains on the window for cover. The best she could do was curl on the bed and bury her head under a pillow. Then Serena's wailing began.

"I will return from sea once again." Serena's words shot through the window. Paloma sighed, knowing from experience that Serena was swaying on the sidewalk below while she stared up at Paloma's unit.

Though the heat had grown even more oppressive, Paloma kneeled on top of the pillows to shut the window. She could only force it down a couple of inches. Within moments, though, Serena's wailing stopped. Relieved, Paloma collapsed back on the comforter. Over the floral print of her T-shirt—the one she had picked out thinking that it would somehow bring good luck—Paloma caressed her lower belly, hoping to diminish the continuing pangs.

Then the odd, singsong yelling kicked in once more: "I will return, and you will know. You will know, know, know. You will all know."

Paloma gritted her teeth. Usually, Serena's ominous words were merely background noise, but now they bored into her. Paloma held her breath, trying to understand Serena's most recent message. Like so many times before, she wished she knew how to help Serena, connect to her in a meaningful way that would not only stop her from following Paloma around all the time, but also help ease her agitation. But no matter what Paloma did over the years—from trying to engage Serena in conversation to inviting her for a cup of coffee—Serena always backed away and then resumed her shanties as though they were the only thing that kept her tethered to the earth.

Still trying to deflect her grief, Paloma wondered—like she had so many times before—why Serena's mother, Anca, refused to get her daughter any professional help. Having worked for Anca for more than ten years at the florist shop, Paloma knew her to be an otherwise practical and intelligent woman. And yet Anca continued to ignore her daughter's tenuous relationship with reality. Serena lived in a fairy tale, a world in which shipwrecked sailors and imaginary sea creatures were more real than neighbors and family—but, still, her dedication to her art remained definite.

A breeze unsettled the curtains and Paloma's mind drifted away from Serena. Watching the curtains' listless sway, Paloma listened to the coarse rhythm of a skateboarder's wheels scraping down the street. She closed her eyes and breathed in the smell of sunbaked pavement and briny seaweed from the beach a few blocks away. A wave of loss caught her. Would she ever hold the hand of her child as they splashed in the tide? She bit her lip and blinked back tears, but they came anyway.

Without knowing why, her thoughts went back to Serena. Since Serena's wailing had ceased for several minutes, Paloma figured that she must have headed to the beach, as she did almost every morning, stomping down the street in her ratty clothes and twisted-mouth expression. She recalled how Serena's mother used to buy her daughter new clothes and shoes, but how Serena would have none of that. Instead, she nabbed swimmers' clothes off the beach, believing they were gifts sent on the tide by her "real" mother, a mermaid who, she said, "was as faithful as the sunrise." According to one of the neighbors, within weeks of moving to Sunflower Beach, Anca had given in. She headed to the beach before dawn every few months with a bag of used clothes as she played the role of Serena's mythical mother, later celebrating the beach garb they used to "find" together by holding hands with her daughter and skipping over the sand. By the time Serena was eighteen, though, she somehow learned to steer clear of Anca's offerings and only picked up the unattended clothes of beachgoers.

With palms resting on her lower stomach, Paloma told herself that it wasn't productive to dwell on Serena. She was a handy but temporary distraction. Paloma knew that her psychiatrist father would think so, anyway. "An avoidance technique," he'd probably say, "stopping you from dealing with what you are supposed to work through."

She covered her head with the pillow again, hoping to fall into a dreamless sleep. But her back tensed. Without thinking, she pushed the pillow aside, edged off the bed, and peeked out the side of the window. Serena hadn't left. She stood on the sidewalk below and twitched, as if she were suffering from some slight but continuous electrocution, while her one blue eye and one opaque green eye stared straight up at Paloma.

Prickling with alarm, Paloma raced to the bathroom. She knew she was being ridiculous, but Serena's unwavering glare made her want to bolt. And if she had to endure one more song burst, she might lose it herself. She slammed the bathroom door, curled up on the clamshell-shaped rug, and breathed through the aftershock cramps kicking inside her gut. She had to focus on something else. A sense of calm distracted her from the pain as she replayed one of her favorite memories of her mother, Esther. On the morning of Paloma's fifth birthday, Esther had held both her hands. Her eyes shone as she whispered about a secret library that held books and books full of stories she'd share with Paloma when the time was right. Although Paloma guessed that her mother was making it up, she still asked where this secret library was. Her mother bent down and kissed her gently on the middle of her forehead. "When you are old enough, my sweet Paloma, I will read them all to you." She pulled Paloma close and held her tight. "Just know that no matter how long things take, I will always love you, will always be there." As Paloma now smiled to herself in the dimly lit bathroom, she recalled how her mother's love warmed her like a glowing bonfire, no matter the expanding darkness.

Chapter Three

After waking up on the bathroom rug, Paloma emerged from her hole to call in sick to work. She still felt uncomfortable telling Reed over the phone, even though she knew that he'd want her to share their loss as soon as possible. Instead, she decided to wait until he came home that night; after all, why not give him another day of ignorant bliss? Finally, though, she did call Justine back—who, of course, talked her into coming over. Justine had been adamant about wanting to be there for her, and if Paloma had said no, she would have showed up at her door anyway. Paloma had learned long ago that it wasn't worth delaying the inevitable. But once there, she wished for a way out. It was too soon after this latest miscarriage. Also, tiny electrical signals were sparking her skin, a weird sensation that always occurred before a vision was going to strike. So, there she was, perched on the edge of an immense sectional in her friend's chic living room, trying to ignore the pins-and-needles warning.

"You must be devastated," Justine said as she leaned over to pat her three-year-old son Harrison's head while he nibbled a snickerdoodle on a plush throw rug by her feet. Justine then straightened her back and reached for Paloma's hand, squeezing it with just a tad too much force. "I'm so sorry."

"I know." Paloma's shoulders tensed, preparing for the onslaught of kindness, an aggressive form of helpfulness that oftentimes left Paloma feeling more drained than understood. "But I'll get through this—"

"Do you think you can finally talk Reed into adopting?"

Paloma leaned back into the couch's sea of throw pillows. "I hope so."

"Or maybe you guys could look into finding a surrogate?"

"I don't..." Paloma watched Harrison as he solemnly ate his cookie. He looked at her with the innocent yet intense gaze of a young child. "I don't want to use a surrogate."

"Why not?"

"I know it seems like a solution, but it doesn't feel right."

"It doesn't feel right?" Justine undid the band holding up her yellow-blond hair, only to resecure it into an even-more-severe ponytail.

"I can't explain—"

Justine held up a hand. "Okay, so you don't want to use a surrogate. But no matter what you decide, you have to stop blaming yourself—you didn't ask for these miscarriages."

Paloma looked down at her bare feet, her sandals having been abandoned by Justine's front door. She wished she could erase the heartbreaking memories of her mother, the ones when the paranoia took over and her mother's gentle voice was replaced by pleas of innocence and harsh whispers that sometimes turned into outright screams. "I know it doesn't make sense, but I can't help but blame myself." Even as Paloma fought to separate herself from the fallout of her mother's schizophrenia, Esther had still managed to pass down a sad and unknowable guilt.

"You have to know that it's not your fault—you didn't *decide* for the miscarriages to happen. Besides, maybe there's something wrong with Reed's sperm." Justine crossed her legs and pressed her hands into a prayer-like gesture. "Maybe it's time to see an expert."

"Justine…"

"What?"

"I can't deal with the possibility of a fourth miscarriage."

Nodding slowly, Justine sighed. "I understand, but…"

Paloma inhaled Justine's citrusy perfume, a consoling balm of the familiar.

"But just remember," Justine said, "that you have to stop feeling guilty about things you have no control over…and that all your childhood losses had to have some kind of effect on you."

Paloma nodded, knowing Justine was right on that account—even as the self-condemnation continued to gnaw at her. Yet if she put up a good front—especially to herself—maybe she wouldn't become entrenched in it like the other two times, when all she could manage to get down for weeks at a time was lukewarm broth and vanilla wafers while becoming so sleep deprived, she couldn't sort her dreams from reality. "No matter what, I'll get over it—like I have before." She gave Justine a weak smile, hoping her friend didn't notice the wobble in her voice. "You don't need to worry."

Justine narrowed her amber eyes as she studied Paloma with a discomforting mix of care and conviction. "But I do worry about you."

Paloma drew in a breath. "Everything will work itself out." It was a phrase Reed often used and Paloma didn't necessarily believe, but it was a handy comeback. "Besides, I'm hoping that Reed *will* consider adoption now."

"But you have to—"

"I know you mean well, Justine. But sometimes even the best advice in the world can't change things." Paloma smoothed her fingers against her forehead, even though she knew it wouldn't ease the bristly feeling spreading across her brow. She thought about cutting the visit short, but trying to explain her way out of there would be more exhausting than staying. And, yes, Justine was overbearing, but her sole remaining friend from childhood also knew Paloma better than anyone else. There was a comfort in that even when it was uncomfortable.

"I wish you'd let your wall down." Justine looked at her with a combination of wide-eyed sympathy and set-jawed determination.

Paloma crossed her arms, trying to ward off Justine's pity. "I'll be fine."

"But you've been through so much." Justine's gaunt face tightened in what Paloma knew was frustration at not being able to *do something.* "You need help."

Paloma wiped the sweat from the back of her neck. She reached for the right words, but could only stare mutely out the window. Shards of summer sunlight bounced off Justine's perfectly clean pool. Paloma took in the odor of chlorinated water, the sterile scent that epitomized Justine's spotless, well-kept life. A life, Paloma understood, that Justine had built in order to combat the messy neglect of her childhood. "I'm sure Reed and I will find an answer."

Then her insides shuddered. She wished she could stop the upcoming vision. But whenever the tingling turned to trembling, whatever vision she was trying to stave off could not be avoided. Hoping this time would be different, Paloma watched Harrison grab a kid's tablet from his mother. He hugged it to his chest, waddled over to the other side of the coffee table, and plopped down. Within seconds, Harrison zoned out, looking like an angelic addict with his wide, unblinking eyes illuminated by the screen.

"You're all pale and sweaty," Justine said. "You're not about to get one of your visions?"

Paloma put on a distracted smile and waved the question off. "I'm okay." She knew it was best to make a joke of it. "It's just my body adjusting to the caffeine I'm now allowed to pour into it again." Maybe the vision would be a mere couple of seconds; maybe she'd be able to move through it without Justine knowing.

"You don't," Justine's voice rose with concern, "look anywhere close to okay."

"I'm just hot." Paloma tried to focus on the contrast of cream-colored rug against the gleam of walnut wood floor.

But the vision came crashing in. She was swimming in the ocean, the taste of saltwater in her mouth. Her Aunt Ruby—whom she hadn't seen since childhood—was frantically beckoning from shore, but she ignored the open-mouthed yelling, muted by distance, wind, and the shoreline's pounding waves. Instead, Paloma was drawn to a rowboat that was just ahead of her and pitched so violently it looked as if it were trying to launch itself into the air. The boat appeared empty, but Paloma sensed someone scrunched at the bottom of it, someone paralyzed with fear. The faster she swam toward it, though, the farther the boat lurched away.

Like a nightmare, Paloma had no control over where the vision was heading. Although she heard Justine ask her repeatedly to say something, and if she was okay, Paloma remained a hostage of her own mind. She watched the boat capsize as it heaved a mournful groan while whoever was inside disappeared without a sound. Paloma's heart twisted. She inhaled as much air as she could and dove, hoping to find the hapless soul. When her lungs were about to explode, she kicked herself back to the surface and jerked her head out of the water. Now the overturned boat was only feet away. Desperate to save whoever was thrown into the sea beneath it, she tried to reach the hull, but a wall of water swallowed her, a sudden, swirling realm of no escape. Then an invisible being clasped her around the waist and yanked her down. Yet Paloma wasn't scared. Somehow knowing that it was the person in the boat, Paloma didn't fight the desperate grip. With eyes wide open, she succumbed to the blue-green world below.

Then just as quickly as it had struck, the vision retreated. Paloma squinted like an alien who had just landed in the lemon-oiled world of Justine's polished living room.

"I know what just happened," Justine said. "You had a vision. Before you try to get Reed on board about adopting again, you need to figure out a way to block them."

"Justine, I know you want the best for me, but you have to remember that I've been trying to get rid of them since I was a kid. If there was a way to block them, I would have figured it out by now." With an unintended sigh, Paloma struggled from the cushy depth of the down-feather sectional, wondering why her long-lost aunt had showed up in her vision—and, come to think of it, where was her beloved Auntie Ruby now?

Justine broke into her thoughts. "Maybe there's something you haven't thought of yet—"

"You know how much your friendship means to me, but no one has all the answers—even you." Paloma stood on shaky legs, planning her retreat, but exhaustion knocked her off kilter. She sank her heavy body back onto the couch.

"I'm just trying…" Justine frowned. "To help."

"I know you are." What Paloma had never shared with Justine was that even though her premonitions were stressful, they did provide a sense of meaning. If she could sometimes see a sliver or more of prediction, then maybe life wasn't as pointless as it appeared. "Besides, they're not always so bad."

"But remember Scott Bentley?"

"Of course." How could she forget? "Why are you bringing *that* up?"

Justine cocked her head in her curious, finchlike way. "I was just thinking…"

"What?"

"If you learned how to take better control over your own mind, then—"

"Then what?" A bitter taste crept up from the bottom of Paloma's throat. The memory of a long-ago vision she had in high school of Scott Bentley's broken body flashed in her mind, and how later that afternoon, a truck had plowed into the passenger side of his cousin's Fiat. From that day forward, she wasn't quite sure if her visions were merely premonitions of what could be—or did her mind somehow *cause* the actual events?

"If you learn how to make them disappear," Justine said, "then you could move forward."

"I don't know what you're talking about." And then Paloma felt it—a familiar bolt of fear surged through her: Would she ever feel as if she had any real control over her own life?

"You look even worse than before." Worry creased Justine's brow. "We should take Harrison to a matinee; it'll help you stop dwelling on whatever vision you just had."

"I have to get home." Where she really wanted to go was to her job at the florist shop—a place where she could lose herself in the beauty of color and the fragrance of hope—but didn't dare say that. Justine, who brought in a substantial income as a real estate developer, didn't understand why Paloma continued on as a floral designer. In fact, she often preached about how Paloma had to start thinking about a way to bring in "a serious revenue." According to Justine, Paloma would never make enough as florist, and Reed would never rope in enough income as an insurance salesman, for them to be able to afford a *real house* and a *nice car*. What Justine never seemed to grasp was that Paloma didn't share her fear of not having enough—and how Paloma didn't care about those things, anyway. She was content with the fact that she'd never acquire the riches Justine had accumulated because, more than anything, she loved working with her hands, loved knowing that at the end of the day she had brought a bit of beauty into the world, no matter how brief.

Justine tapped her shoulder. "Please let me help you."

"I..." There was no way Justine would ever understand how much the visions drained her. "I'll be fine...I promise." Paloma smiled as she nudged Justine's arm—their special code since junior high that said to drop whatever they were talking about before the one who did the nudging became too annoyed. She hoped this would finally set Justine's busy mind at ease.

Justine gave her a raised-eyebrow look of disbelief. Paloma nudged her again, this time with more force. "Please know I'm stronger than you think." It was true. Through it all, she *was* stronger than what her capable friend—and even pragmatic husband—thought her to be.

Harrison looked up from the tablet, his gaze ping-ponging between his mother and Paloma. He stood and toddled to Paloma, the morning light crowning his whisper-blond hair. "Wanna a cookie, Loma?" He reached into a pocket of his oversized shorts and offered his half-eaten snickerdoodle. Paloma glanced at the crumbly cookie resting on his palm.

"Thank you, Harrison, that's very nice of you." She leaned over, picked it up and took a nibble, then handed it back. "Let's share. You have the rest."

"No, you eat." Harrison pushed the cookie at her again.

She made herself take another small bite and then closed her hand around it, discreetly hiding it in the side pocket of her purse, not wanting to hurt Harrison's feelings.

Harrison wrapped his arms around her neck. "I love you, Loma."

"I love you, too." Paloma's eyes watered. Justine reached over and patted her arm.

"Everything *will* work out," Justine said, her face softening.

All Paloma could do was shake her head, recalling the vision of the capsized boat.

"Let me drive you home." Justine stared her down. "You can get your car later."

"Thanks, but I can drive myself." Paloma plastered on the best smile she could, knowing that she was going to head to the safest place she knew: work.

"Are you sure?" Justine shot up and raced across the room to grab her purse and keys before Paloma could answer.

Paloma stood and waited for Justine to turn around and face her. "I'm sure." She saw the hurt in her friend's eyes. "But thank you for being here for me."

Justine trudged back and abruptly embraced her. Surprised by the unusual display of affection, Paloma hugged her sharp-boned friend.

Chapter Four

"Who" hat're you doing here?" Anca stood behind the wooden counter, a knife-scarred workstation that very well could have been an original fixture of the 1928 florist shop she'd inherited from her mother. Gripping her floral knife, Anca clucked her tongue in her maternal way, which made Paloma's jaw clench with irritation—but at the same time, spread appreciative warmth across her chest.

Anca deftly cut through a mass of rubber bands binding a bundle of lemon leaf. "You should be home getting better, not dragging yourself to work." Anca's steely-eyed glare seemed to pierce Paloma, and it wasn't the first time Paloma felt that Anca could see right into her. "Besides, I'm not expecting too many orders this week." She wagged a finger at Paloma.

The overflowing orders of baby's breath, lemon leaf, and leather fern as well as the abundant carnations, roses, gladiolus, and various other flowers resting in black-coned containers behind the frosty glass of the walk-in cooler told Paloma otherwise. She inhaled the rose-spiced perfume of intermingled petals and tried to swallow the lump in her throat. "Anca, I called in sick because…"

Anca set the waxy leaves on the counter and held two thorn-embedded fingertips under Paloma's chin. "What is it?" A substantial woman, Anca's full face combined with her sturdy body always reminded Paloma of a mother-goddess statue Paloma had seen in one of her father's art books.

"I had another miscarriage." She wanted to collapse in the security of Anca's arms but caught herself. Anca wasn't her real mother.

But Anca reached to embrace her and caressed her back with such sincerity that Paloma could not stop herself from crying. Still, she held herself back from full-blown sobbing.

"It's okay," Anca crooned. "You let it out now; it's better to let it all out."

Paloma wished that were possible. But even with the well-intentioned Anca, she worried that the raw brutality of her sorrow would repulse her cherished friend and boss and make her turn away forever.

Anca tightened her embrace and then stood back and studied Paloma. "Don't dare blame yourself again." Pursing her lips, Anca reached for her coffee cup. She gingerly sipped it and then set it next to her floral knife. "You didn't miscarry just because you were worried or got stressed out. If that were the case, *no one* would be able to have children."

Paloma shook her head, knowing how impossible it would be to ignore all the self-loathing reasons—with the worse ones being that her body rejected all three of her babies because deep down she knew she wouldn't be able to handle motherhood. Or, worse yet, maybe the fear that she'd inherit her mother's schizophrenia had somehow caused them. She knew, though, that these "reasons" were illogical. If a mother's mere psychological state could induce a miscarriage, why would millions of other women with way worse histories and horrendous life circumstances still be able to have babies? She looked straight into Anca's eyes while she tried to hide her trepidation. "I know it's not the end of the world," she said. "But I don't want to try anymore. It's not going to work...and I don't have it in me."

Anca nodded. "Of course you don't."

Surprised by Anca's response—and at the same time grateful for her empathy, Paloma looked down at her hands, hands that would carry on despite the emptiness.

"I'm not saying you're weak, dove."

Paloma managed to smile at Anca's term of endearment that she often used when talking to her own offspring as well as to Paloma.

"I just mean that it's a good time to accept this and move on to other answers," Anca said, nodding with assurance.

"Yes, other answers," said Paloma. "I hope to talk Reed into adopting. Maybe this time he'll be more open."

Anca nodded again, her eyes half-closing in that way they did when she was working out a problem in her head. "No matter what, you'll find happiness."

The jingle of the door's welcome bell announced Tatiana's arrival. Anca raised her eyebrow at her young daughter and pointed to the clock. With a shake of her head, she turned her attention back to Paloma. "See, I have my help. You don't need to work this week. Spend some time at the beach—or just relaxing at home."

Dressed in purple jeans and a red-and-black-striped T-shirt, Tatiana mumbled a hello to her mother and then smiled at Paloma. Her round, open face made the harsh words that often shot out of her mouth that much more biting. Still, Paloma was fond of the girl. She had a boldness that Paloma admired—and the optimism of youth she applauded. Paloma saw Tatiana as a self-possessed mountain lion who proudly strutted through town. While Tatiana swished her long black hair and stared down all the boys, her huge eyes often flashed a brazen, sarcastic look that seemed to dare anyone to cross her. Thick-muscled and sure of herself, seventeen-year-old Tatiana had her mother's solid body and her father, Leonardo's, down-to-earth personality.

Her big sister, Serena, had inherited Leonardo's sinewy physique, light olive skin, and at least one of her eye colors was the same shade of his blue. The odd green eye, according to hazel-eyed Anca, ran generations back in her family. What Serena didn't inherit was either of her parents' personalities. She was definitely her own person: wild, loud, free. Though she'd never been formally diagnosed, Paloma's father had mentioned once that Serena probably had a delusional disorder. Paloma could see why he thought that—yet whatever the label, she also sensed that Serena's fantastical imaginings were her way of dealing with an illogical world. And even though Anca seemed to ignore Serena's mental health condition and could be too judgmental toward Tatiana, she clearly loved her daughters. She often talked about how much she cherished them both, how very grateful she was to have had them, explaining how hard it had been to conceive each daughter and that the large age gap between siblings was due to "hormonal difficulties." Paloma had once asked Anca about what those difficulties were, but Anca merely waved her hand in the air, explaining that it was all water under the bridge and what was important was that they had made it into the world.

"Hey, Paloma." Tatiana swooshed by, but then turned around. "You okay?" Her eyebrows scrunched downward in suspicion.

"I'm fine," Paloma answered, wondering if she looked as battle fatigued as she felt. "Why do you ask?"

"You seem weird," Tatiana answered. "Like you're hiding something."

Anca frowned. "Tatiana, she looks fine—"

"I seem like I'm hiding something?" Paloma straightened her back.

Tatiana glanced at her mother and then tilted her chin up rebelliously. She studied Paloma's face with the disconcerting gaze of a teenager who felt she knew more than the exhausted women hovering around the edges of her life. "What's going on?"

"Not much…"

Tatiana smirked. "Yeah, right."

Paloma's stomach cramped. She didn't respond, knowing that Tatiana saw through her bravado.

"Get your apron on, dove." Anca placed a hand on Tatiana's shoulder. "I have some arrangements I need to get done before Kenny makes his last delivery."

"Relax, Mom." Tatiana grinned at them both. "I got it handled."

Paloma watched Tatiana strut toward the back room, her mane shining under the fluorescent light.

"I worry about that one." Anca shook her head. "She's getting ahead of herself."

"What do you mean?"

Anca clamped her lips into a straight line. "A mother can sense these things."

"But what do you mean by *getting ahead of herself*?"

"She acts like the world is her playground." Anca exhaled loudly. "But the world is a difficult place, and she's too confident that nothing bad will ever happen."

"Isn't that normal at her age?"

Anca glanced at the back room. "She's got a lot of talent," she whispered. "But also, too much ambition."

Paloma stepped back and looked Anca in the eye. "What do you mean?"

"It's a cruel life trying to be an artist. I just want her to be happy without having to 'make it.'"

"If anyone can make a go of it, it'll be Tatiana." After the words left Paloma's mouth, she realized the implication. Since Serena was also an artist—but was too anxious to attend her own art openings—Paloma hoped Anca hadn't taken it the wrong way.

Anca's eyebrows shot up as if she was considering this, but Paloma couldn't tell if her remark had upset or relieved her. "Still, that daughter of mine needs to know how disappointing an artist's life can be."

"But since Serena's paintings have been in local galleries, and Tatiana has just as much talent as her big sister…" Paloma didn't dare bring up that Tatiana had recently shared how she was about to apply to several out-of-state art schools.

"You know it's different," Anca said. "Serena is above us all. She doesn't care about money or fame. But Tatiana wants it all."

"Maybe that's just who Tatiana is. Maybe it'll help push her forward in life."

Anca shot Paloma a harsh, narrow-eyed look. "Even a seventeen-year-old should realize that life holds many sacrifices."

"You're too serious, Mom." Tying her apron around her waist, Tatiana emerged from the back room. "Life can be easy if you let it."

"You cannot always trust the world. You must protect yourself." The deep indents of Anca's worry lines between her eyes creased into what looked like fissures in a parched earth.

Tatiana lifted one of her cherry-red Doc Martens boots. She stomped on the putty-green linoleum and then slid her boot against the floor, scraping a clod of dirt off the bottom. "Lighten up, Mom."

Anca huffed out an exasperated breath. "I'm your mother, Tatiana. You need to respect the fact that I know many things you do not yet."

Before Tatiana could answer, Paloma chimed in, "Anca, I see you've got a pile of work orders. Maybe I could fill some of them?" Even though her body sagged with fatigue, the satisfying process of cutting water-soaked floral foam—its consistency somewhere between pound cake and pumice stone—into a size that would fit the liner of a basket, and then focusing on an arrangement itself, felt like the only thing she could do to take her mind off things.

Anca shook her head. "No, you need to go home and rest. After what you've been through, I want you to take another week off before you come in again."

"What do you mean what she's been though?" Instead of looking at her mother, though, Tatiana stared at Paloma.

"Tatiana, I've—"

"No, Tatiana, sometimes people aren't ready to talk about things," Anca said. "You don't need to know everything right when it's happening."

"It's okay, Anca. I don't mind telling her." Paloma knew that she was overstepping Anca's authority, but it was *her* story. And after what Tatiana had said about her hiding something, the girl deserved an explanation. Paloma met Tatiana's scrutiny. "I miscarried...again." She watched the mixture of sympathy and disgust cross the teenager's face. She felt powerless—and, yes, even repulsive. She glanced at Anca, wishing that she had let her tell Tatiana when she wasn't around. "But really, I'm fine, Tatiana. You don't need to worry about me."

Tatiana's face flushed. "I'm sorry," she mumbled, and then hesitantly reached for a work order.

Paloma couldn't be sure, but it looked like Tatiana had been thrown off balance. "You okay?" Paloma asked, never having seen Tatiana flustered before.

Without looking up, Tatiana snatched her personalized floral knife from the counter, its handle wrapped in skull-and-crossbones-patterned tape. She pulled a block of floral foam out of a bucket of water and sliced it cleanly in half. "I'm *always* okay." Tatiana nodded with a smirk. "My mom's right. You should go home. I can deal with everything here."

Paloma glanced at the top work order. It was for a birthday arrangement, Anca's neat handwriting adding that the customer requested the most fragrant flowers. "I want to fill at least one order."

Tatiana shrugged. "If it means that much to you."

"It does." Paloma ambled to the cooler and returned with sterling silver roses and stalks of tuberoses, relieved at the chance to create something as easy and certain as a floral arrangement—something that would be delivered safe and sound to whomever it was meant for.

Chapter Five

Paloma's stomach tensed at the click of Reed's key in the lock. Once the door creaked open, remorse flooded her body: *He should* have been the first to know. How was he was going to react to not just the sad news, but why had she waited all day to tell him? What was wrong with her? Curled up on the blue-green twill of the couch, she waited as his quick whistle and the clip of leather wingtips reverberated down the hall.

Reed strolled into the living room, his body still bristling with workday energy. He tilted his head and drew his eyebrows together. "Were you napping?" His insurance-salesman tone carried over from his day of statistics, meetings, and phone calls. He carried his office smell home with him, too, an efficient blend of toner and hand sanitizer.

Paloma shifted from her fetal position on the sofa, her body heavy with defeat. Although the bleeding had stopped, she suddenly realized that she should have made a doctor's appointment—but would have to deal with that tomorrow. "Reed, I need to tell you…" She stabbed her fingers through the thicket of her unwashed hair, a snarl of frizzy confusion.

He remained stuck on the year-old laminate floor, its fake wood veneer already peeling back in places. "You look beat." He checked his cell and then flashed a boyish grin. "Work okay?"

She felt sorry for him, knowing that even though she hadn't told him yet, a part of him had to know. All he had to do was look at her hollow-eyed, shriveled-up self. This wasn't about being tired or having a hectic day at work. It was sorrow. Just plain, raw, ugly sorrow. She smoothed her hand over her shirt and looked at him evenly. "I lost the baby."

He stared at her in openmouthed shock. She wished she could say something that could make it okay, something reassuring that they'd both believe. But the only sound was the cry of a gull. Paloma pictured the bird gliding over waves, free from the drama unfolding inside the condo. She looked at Reed's disbelieving face as she silently dared him to acknowledge her words.

"Are you sure?" He jammed his cell back in his pocket and crossed the floor. His jaw was set in sharp-edged determination, but his mouth crumbled.

"I'm sure." She grabbed a pillow and held it against her stomach. "This is my third miscarriage. I know what happened."

Reed lowered himself onto the sofa's edge, knees cracking. "Why didn't you call me?"

She caught the hurt in his voice. "I wanted to, but—"

"Didn't you see that I had called you earlier?"

He looked out the window with such stern concentration that Paloma wondered what he was staring at. But when she followed his gaze, she could only see a brazen sky, too bright for the end of the day, even if it was the height of summer.

She forced herself to sit up, wanting to melt into his arms but at the same time wanting to remain autonomous. "I'm so sorry, Reed. I don't blame you for being hurt."

"But I would have come right home to be with you." Reed's shoulders caved in and he looked smaller—vulnerable, even.

"I should have." She leaned into him. "But I didn't want to break down over the phone—plus Justine wanted to see me, and then I decided to go into work for a couple of hours." These were feeble excuses, she knew—and not the normal behavior of a loving wife or someone who had just experienced her third miscarriage. But how could she explain the terror of what would happen if she shared the full depth of her pain with him? She couldn't even articulate to herself all the whys and what-ifs behind this fear.

He looked at her without a word, but a sorrowful shake of his head said it all.

"I am sorry." She gazed down at her ragged fingernails. "I know I should have told you before anyone else."

"I wish," he said, "that you had."

Paloma nodded. If only he knew how much she longed to unbutton her despair in front of him, how much she craved for him to do the same for her. Yet if she let it out, she might not be able to rein it in again. Loss hovered over them in the compact rectangle of their living room while the gleeful shrieks of kids racing out to play on a neighbor's trampoline trailed through the window.

"You did see the doctor, didn't you?" Reed grazed her shoulder with tentative fingertips but quickly withdrew his hand.

He seemed afraid to touch her as if physical contact would make the loss more real. Paloma hitched her feet on the edge of the couch and clasped her arms around her knees. "Not yet." She pictured the obstetrician probing inside her, informing her that he'd have to do an ultrasound to make sure that *everything was out.*

"Maybe you just lost tissue." Reed's words strained with forced optimism. "Or maybe the doctor somehow missed a twin, another baby—"

"No, Reed." His clawing grasp for hope set her insides on fire. "I thought the same at first, but it happened exactly as it did the other two times." She turned away and lay back down. Scrunching her body into a tight ball, she inhaled the dusty smell of the back cushion. "I've lost another baby, and nothing can change that." She had no choice but to voice the very thing he didn't want to accept: "We'll never be able to have children."

"Don't say that." He caressed her back with a touch that was both hesitant and demanding. "You have to stay hopeful. Everything will work itself out." He paused, the silence as taut as tightrope. "But you need to start believing it."

How she wanted to tell him that she loved him, no matter their losses. But apprehension silenced her; the visions were encroaching more than ever. She wasn't sure what it meant but didn't like how they burst through with a poignancy that oftentimes felt more authentic than reality. And even though she had endured them since childhood, could their escalating intensity mean that she had, indeed, inherited her mother's schizophrenia? Perhaps this was just the first symptom worming into her brain through the most familiar path it could find. She drew in a breath, reminding herself how grief could twist one's thoughts. Finally, she turned around and sat back up. "Maybe our future will be different than the one we had planned." She wasn't sure what she meant by her own words, but somehow knew there was a bigger truth to them than either of them could realize in that moment.

He eyed her cautiously. She felt like a caged beast, restless, angry, ready to bite.

"You do remember the doctor saying that a lot more women miscarry than you'd know," he said. "It's a very natural thing." With a confident nod, he continued on, but then his measured tone cracked midsentence. "After the doctor says it's okay—"

"I can't do this anymore." Her throat constricted with the strain of wanting him to understand. Although she knew not to say it, she wholeheartedly believed that each miscarriage was not only a sign but also a warning that they had to stop trying.

"What are you talking about?"

"I'm not getting pregnant again. I'm done." The injured look on his broad face, and somehow even the cowlick escaping from his dark brown hair with its premature flecks of gray, made the guilt in her chest grow even tighter.

"I can understand why you feel this way now," he said. "But…"

Paloma watched him rub his brow in a frantic back-and-forth motion. She caught his hand and gently held it in hers, a heaviness sinking into her joints. "But what, Reed?"

"I don't know...I guess I'm tired, too." He squeezed her hand. "But it'll be okay. Things will change."

Paloma pulled her hand from Reed's grip and clenched her fists against her sides. "That's what you said after the last miscarriage. I wanted to believe it then, but now I know not to."

"But you can't know for sure...." Reed fidgeted next to her.

Her heart raced so fast that she imagined bolting out the door, away from their life and far away from their barren future. "I know how much you want this to happen, but it's not going to," she said, trying to keep her tone level. "I wish I could make it work. I really do."

Reed hung his head. "I'm here for you, Paloma. Please remember that...."

How could she explain that she knew she wasn't meant to get pregnant again? How could he understand that the thought of turning to the technology that helped so many other couples achieve their "biological baby" dreams only made her certain that they would step into a world with false hope and ultimate loss? She knew this would anger him; any whiff of her intuition—let alone her full-blown visions—made him recoil in disbelief. And just like Justine, he felt it wasn't healthy for her to focus on her gifts. If only he understood that not everything in the world could be explained—and get over his own fear of what she knew to be her power, however perplexing it was. "It's just not meant to be," she whispered.

"We'll find an expert; we'll do some tests—and then you'll have our baby in your arms sooner than you can imagine." He looked at her, his determination vibrating in the air between them. "Then all your sadness will be behind you."

"But…" she said, trying to keep her anger at bay. "My sadness started when I was just a kid myself—and, besides, that's not a good reason to have a baby."

Reed exhaled so loudly that Paloma imagined he was wishing his breath could blow away the dark, dispirited part of her. He opened his mouth to say something but abruptly stopped.

"I'd love nothing better," Paloma said, "than to create the carefree childhood I never had—and I know how much you want kids, how you want to recreate all the great memories you have growing up with your brother and sister." Reed nodded, and she reached for his hand. "I'd love for it to happen, Reed. I really would." Paloma squared her shoulders. "But parenthood is not meant to be a fix—and it shouldn't be based on nostalgia, either."

"I just don't understand why you won't agree to see another doctor. It won't hurt and can only help—"

"And I don't understand why you won't consider adoption."

Reed shook his head. "Can we at least agree to see another doctor who could give us more answers? Understand all our options before going down that path?"

She knew his request sounded reasonable—but agreeing would only make it that much worse, would only get his hopes up when she flat-out knew she was done. "I can't." Her throat grew hoarse with frustration. "You have to believe me." Part of her wanted to fly right out the window, but another part of her wished they would stop all the arguing and simply hold each other.

Reed crossed his arms without saying a word and Paloma looked away. Suddenly, Serena's warbling drifted through the evening air, giving voice to Paloma's frustration—yet, at the same time, transporting a lightness through her body that made it seem as though anything were possible. Why this sudden hope had materialized Paloma didn't know—yet she remembered that this was a periodic reaction to Serena's crooning throughout the years, especially when she felt the most stuck. Reed cleared his throat, a habit that Paloma noticed he had developed in response to Serena's strange serenades.

He stood and walked over to the sliding glass door of their balcony. Paloma knew Serena was swaying on the sidewalk below. "You've just suffered another loss," he said. "Give yourself time."

The long-simmering anger flared inside her. She wasn't sure if it had to do with Reed himself or their situation, but guessed that it was a combination of the two. "I'm not going to change my mind." She wished it were possible for them to find an answer they could both wrap their hearts around. Although she knew he truly wanted to have babies with her, she also sensed that his objection to them adopting was due to the inevitable rejection of the idea by his mother, Patsy, an abrupt woman who threw out other's opinions before they were halfway out of their mouths. She also knew that Reed and his siblings protected their mother with a ferocity that was beyond over-the-top. In fact, just last month, his brother had given Paloma the cold shoulder during a family visit after Patsy had gotten so drunk that she narrowed her eyes accusingly, calling Paloma that "shadowy little flower girl." It was beyond Paloma why he reacted this way. Did he really think that Paloma was at fault and his mother the injured party? But right after the scornful words had leaked out of Patsy's mouth, he gently patted his mother's shoulder and then refilled her drink—like that would help matters. Reed had been in the other room, but when Paloma had told him how angry his mom had looked and pissed off she sounded (plus what the hell did Patsy mean by *shadowy little flower girl* anyway?), Reed merely shrugged, saying she shouldn't take Patsy's drunken tirades seriously. Still, Paloma knew she'd never measure up.

"Hey," Reed said, "where are you?"

Paloma knew they'd only fight if she brought up his mother. But on the other hand, maybe he needed to take a look at how much he was being affected by her. "I was just thinking that—"

"Please know that I love you." Reed turned toward her.

Paloma held back sudden tears. "I love you, too."

He walked back to the couch and sat with her again. "Don't give up, Paloma."

"I'm not." Paloma stared at him. "Adoption is the *opposite* of giving up."

Reed didn't answer. Paloma shivered. His disappointment enveloped her like fog—a cold, dense sensation that was only going to expand the space between them. She forced herself off the couch and went into the kitchen for a glass of rice milk, Reed's behavior a too-close mirror of his mother's.

Pouring the milk, she remembered how Patsy's hostility toward her had intensified after the first miscarriage. Previously, her mother-in-law would at least present a show of gap-toothed greeting whenever they all got together, engage in *some* friendly small talk, and even if a dig slipped from her orange-lipsticked mouth, Patsy always made sure to flap her hand in the air as if to say she were only kidding. Yet even her new, more-overt resentment was still dismissed by Reed, always the deferential son.

The blame oozed out in a number of ways, including the hasty turning away to check on something when Paloma was in midsentence or, worse yet, the zealous compliments bestowed upon the established mothers in her brood. At least, though, she still texted Paloma (even sending a smiley emoji once in a while) and did recently remark how beautiful Paloma's floral arrangements were, which she always made sure to order for all her friends' birthdays. Yet in light of Reed's older brother's crew of two sons and two daughters, alongside his little sister's trio of tow-headed boys, Paloma couldn't stop herself from thinking that she was a failure in Patsy's eyes. Gulping her milk, Paloma wished she could neutralize Patsy's influence on Reed—and their marriage.

Somehow, though, she still liked Patsy. Even though her mother-in-law could be clannish and mean—especially when she'd had one too many drinks—she could also be unpretentiously smart, unknowingly funny, and unsentimentally generous (especially with her time volunteering at the dog shelter). Also, there was something fragile beneath the tough-beaked exterior, something that Paloma knew she could relate to, if given the chance.

When she stepped back into the living room, Paloma cleared her throat. She had to try again. "There are so many parents raising kids who aren't their biological children—and they love them just the same."

Reed's nostrils flared with defiance. "I know that," he said. "But I can't help the way I feel."

She shook her head. Where was the affable, open-minded guy whose whole world was his friend? "I know what we're going through is just as disappointing for you as it is for me," she said, "but it's my body that's been put through hell with every miscarriage—not yours."

"I get that—"

"Then you can at least take some time to *think* about adoption."

"You have to understand…" he bowed his head. "…how much this means to me."

"But the world is growing more volatile every day. God knows what's going to happen with the next pandemic and how much climate change will continue to wreak havoc on the earth. It doesn't seem right to force another life into it when we can adopt."

"I hear what you're saying…but maybe our baby would help make the world a better place."

"And who is to say that a child who happened to be adopted wouldn't as well?"

"I'm just concerned.…"

"About what?" She guessed that he was thinking about his coworker Ramon's two-year-old newly adopted son from Russia, who wasn't throwing the normal temper tantrums, but instead was so shut down that Ramon *wished* the kid would kick and scream instead of gloomily staring into space. "If you're thinking about Ramon's son, he's still going through an adjustment period."

"I understand." Reed shook his head. "And I think Ramon and his husband are amazing for adopting an orphan. But I'm afraid I wouldn't be able to handle whatever could come up if we did."

"Reed, no one knows what'll happen—whether you adopt or give birth."

"Besides," he said, "I want to honor my father."

"But your brother and sister already have kids—" Paloma wondered at the complex ways people dealt with a parent's death, especially when it had shattered one's childhood.

"I know it's hard to understand," Reed said. "I can't even explain it myself. But I really want us to try again."

His tone was so adamant—and yet so fearful—that Paloma looked away, and instead of countering with the argument about how many unwanted babies were being born at that very moment, she lay down and turned her back to him. She thought about her long-lost mother, as she always did in times of loss. But the fear that she'd end up dealing with the same fate only made things seem that much worse. She gripped her pillow, remembering how her stomach had jumped into her seven-year-old heart the day she vowed that she'd never suffer like her mom, who was the most kindhearted lady she knew, but got so scared sometimes that her eyes couldn't see what was right in front of her. No, she could never end up like her mother.

Chapter Six

Although Paloma wanted to distract herself with work the next day, she heeded Anca's advice and took the day off. Tired yet antsy, she headed to the beach. Against the glare of another yellow-hot day, she hid her blotchy face under a straw hat and swollen eyes behind oversized sunglasses. Dressed in baggy shorts and an old T-shirt of Reed's, she walked along the shore, grateful for the breeze, however slight, that swept in from the Pacific. The tide skimmed over her bare feet, a small, cool blessing that sent much-appreciated tingles up her spine. The beach was empty except for a few surfers out at sea, bobbing in their shiny, black wetsuits as they waited for the next set. Paloma breathed in the scent of saltwater. Although she had just miscarried the day before, her grief loosened.

Then she caught sight of Serena charging into the ocean, her wiry back muscles tensed, miniature wings bracing for underwater flight into the oncoming surf. Paloma stopped in her tracks and watched. Part of her wanted to run right after Serena into the glistening water, but the other part—the careful one—kept her feet in the sand. Serena dived under a wave and then rose to the surface on the other side. How graceful and at home Serena looked as she continued to glide through the water. Paloma stepped toward the waiting ocean. But a memory of Esther intruded, one of the dreaded times when the paranoia overtook her usual gentle demeanor.

On a bright-blue Sunday, her mother had sat with elbows glued to the kitchen table, her long, glamorous fingers caressing both sides of her bewildered face. Morning light spilled in from the window, illuminating her tan skin and long, copper-colored hair. Without notice, she began to laugh, and then started babbling about how the bottom of the ocean was where she was meant to be. Eight-year-old Paloma and her father continued eating his special cinnamon-and-raisin oatmeal. Paloma wanted to put her hands over her ears to block out the nonsensical laughter but knew this would upset her mother. In fact, the only time Paloma had dared cover her ears around her mother, Esther stared at her, fear crackling off her body like the red-hot sparks from a fire. Her mother then sprinted into the bathroom and slammed the door so hard that Paloma imagined the whole house was going to fall inside itself. But then there was only closed-door silence, a dark lack of sound that scared Paloma so much she felt like her belly was full of rocks and lava. So, this time Paloma continued to eat her oatmeal, continued acting as the peaceful girl who pretended all was okay. Even so, her mother suddenly smacked a hand on the table and then dropped her head, sobbing, into folded arms. Paloma's father scooted his chair next to his distraught wife and wrapped his arm around her heaving shoulders, his face a mask of calm. Paloma stood, not knowing what to do next. His saggy eyes looked up at her, and he whispered that she should go into her room and color. All she could remember from there was the stab of longing, the wish that her mother's ongoing promise that they'd have a "lovely" swim together in the "safety of the sea" would one day come true.

Trying to release the suffocating memory into the atmosphere, Paloma squinted at the sky. But the scene lodged even deeper into her core, another unhappy memory that couldn't be erased. She slogged away from the upcoming tide and made her way to the wide stretch of sand. She lay face up, the back of her legs burning against the blistering-hot grains. But she didn't move. She merely closed her eyes and listened to the soft crumble of surf. With a sigh, she reminded herself that her past was not her present—nor need it be her future.

She woke about half an hour later, groggy from heartbreak and heat. She pressed her hand against her chest, which felt even more heartsore from her lonely four-in-the-morning crying session. She had tiptoed into the closet so that she wouldn't wake Reed and then sobbed uncontrollably into a bunched-up shirt. Now, even under the blazing sunlight, sorrow returned. She wiped her eyes, remembering how her mother would furiously write in a red-leather journal after her own crying stints. Were her mother's tears due to ongoing grief as well?

Ten-year-old Paloma had secretly searched for the journal after her mother had died. After checking to make sure that her father was still at work in his office, she rummaged through her parents' bedroom, inside the closets and storage boxes throughout the house and garage, even under the couch and its heavy cushions. But she never found it—and she never asked her father about it, as she knew that he'd only shake his head and tell her that it couldn't be found. Shaking her own head, Paloma wondered if her father had kept any of her mother's belongings—besides the threadbare denim shirt Paloma had later asked for. She'd always assumed that in his grief, he'd given everything else away, as she never found a stitch more of her mother's clothes, any of her many books, or even the black-and-white shots of the beach she'd been so proud of taking with her old Nikon camera.

Paloma made herself sit up and looked out to sea. Past the surfers and beyond the kelp beds was a lone swimmer, arms arching in and out of the shine of blue ahead, feet kicking a small cloud of water behind. Paloma guessed that it was Serena and continued to watch until the swimmer grew so distant that it was difficult to distinguish the human disruption of the ocean's surface from the splash of diving seabirds. Finally, Paloma stood, reminding herself that she had to call her father.

Once she got home, she closed her front door and pressed her back against the wall. All she wanted to do in that moment was melt onto the floor and fall asleep again. With a sigh of resignation, she walked into her bedroom and flipped off her shoes. Breathing in the gluey, chemical aroma of her bedroom carpet, she burrowed her feet into its warmth and phoned her father.

After their hellos, she paused and then drew in a breath. "Dad, I want to let you know…" She heard Serena start in with some shanty about a sinking ship and stopped. The quick-footed Serena must have raced out of the ocean and headed straight over when she saw Paloma amble off the beach. Was there anywhere she could find peace? Yet, the ragged voice below the window pulled her away. Paloma felt like she was caught in a riptide, swimming with a false sense of control but in actuality being sucked out to sea. For some reason, the loud, punctuated verses sailing up from the sidewalk made telling her father about the recent miscarriage even harder. Why, she didn't know. But she couldn't tell him just yet.

"Sorry about that, Dad. Serena's singing distracted me." Because her father knew about Serena's ongoing enchantment with Paloma, his silence was expected. Paloma wondered why she had even mentioned it. "How are you?"

The low voice of her psychiatrist father, Abel Rodriguez, finally emanated from the phone. "I'm well enough," he said. "And you? How are you feeling today?"

Paloma dared to look out the window, her gaze falling to where Serena stood below. Serena abruptly stopped singing. "I'm...okay." Serena stared straight up at Paloma with a challenging hands-on-hips stance, yet her eyes also widened with concern. The hairs on the back of Paloma's neck bristled and she backed away. "Serena seems even more agitated than usual. Isn't there anything you can do for her? Anyone you can refer her to?"

Silence greeted her from the other end. Her father's way of pausing too long before responding was a habit, she knew, that came from his work. Even so, she clenched her jaw so tightly that she felt the muscle tension travel all the way to her temples. She let out a breath, thinking how the sides of her forehead were probably pulsating in the same green-veined way that she remembered her mother's used to whenever she ran out of her Benson & Hedges.

Her father finally answered. "We've been through this before. The Nicholson family refuses help. Serena refuses help. And you know as well as I do that if she's not a danger to herself or others, there's nothing I can do."

This time it was Paloma who paused. Images of her mother flashed in her mind once again. The wretchedly beautiful woman with the sculptured face and long neck was vivid in Paloma's memory, and she was instantly transported back in time, an uncertain girl visiting her unpredictable mother. She could see Esther's tobacco-stained but beautifully lithe fingers tapping the sides of the wicker chair as she sat on the side porch of Haven House, merrily laughing at something another client said and then, for no known reason, looking downward in soundless despair.

Then, Paloma saw Esther smiling grandly at her. Paloma handed her a bouquet of wildflowers that she had picked that morning, knowing how much her mother loved the unassuming beauty of seaside daisies and purple statice with its intermittent burst of miniature white flowers. Esther held the bouquet against her chest. "Thank you, my darling girl." Her sky-blue eyes looked like they could see into another dimension, but then she looked straight at Paloma. "I love you more than you can ever know."

Abel broke through the memory. "Are you sure you're okay, *mija*?"

"I'm…" Paloma knew he was worried when he used the term *mija*. She slumped on her bed.

"What is it?

"Why did you marry Mom?"

"Why did I marry your mother?" Her father responded in an opaque-sounding tone that reminded Paloma of the cooler's frosted glass inside the florist shop.

Paloma thought about how Abel's own father, Carlos, had fallen in love with Abel's mother, Miriam who, just like Esther, had shied away from her Jewish heritage, died young—and had also suffered from severe schizophrenia. Family history often repeated itself in ways that even a psychiatrist couldn't fathom, especially when it had to do with one's own family of origin.

Paloma was only a baby when the tragedy happened; she never knew what her mother had been like before the schizophrenia had set in. Soon after that, Abel placed Esther in Haven House, a psychiatric facility on the outskirts of Sunflower Beach. A grand Victorian refurbished as an in-home care and counseling refuge for mentally ill adults, Haven House was a ten-minute drive from home.

When Paloma was about four years old, she asked her father why her mother didn't live with them. She never forgot how his hands trembled when he tried to explain it to her, telling her that her mother had an illness that wasn't her fault, wasn't anyone's fault. In his measured way, he said, "Your mother lives in a caring place that is also very close to us." It became his mantra whenever Paloma asked if her mother was ever going to come home for longer than a day. Later she'd find out that after a year or so there, Esther could have lived with them and gone to outpatient counseling, but she chose to stay at Haven House as an inpatient because life was "too poisonous on the outside." No one ever explained to Paloma, though, why her mother would say this, since she sometimes ran away for weeks at a time to a place where no one could find her, tossing her medications into the ocean along the way.

"It's simple," Abel finally answered. "I loved her."

"But what was she like when you first knew her?" Wishing she could have known her mother before the schizophrenia had invaded, Paloma studied the cowry-shell brown of her forearm, thinking how she had inherited her mother's blue eyes and bright auburn hair but thankfully—so far at least—not her mental illness. If Esther hadn't died of pneumonia at the young age of thirty-two—the same age Paloma was now—would her mother have ever been able to find peace?

"*Mija*, I hear your stress. Are you worried about something?"

"It's just that…" She stared at the rise and fall of her still-swollen stomach bulging under her T-shirt. When was she going to tell him about the miscarriage? Besides Reed, her father should have been one of the first people to know. Paloma lugged her body off the bed and shuffled into the living room. She stopped in front of the hutch, studying the one photo she had of her mother amongst the scads of family pictures from Reed's side of the family. She peered at the stunning beauty of the tanned, light-eyed Esther sitting on a white beach towel, legs demurely curved. Esther stared from the long-ago shot taken by Abel, the backdrop of an ocean wave caught in eternal descent.

"*Mija*…"

"What is it, Dad?"

"Honey, you do remember that the anniversary of your sister's kidnapping is coming up next month?"

Paloma paced from hutch to couch and back again. She had only been a baby at the time, but she knew the story. As soon as she had been old enough to understand, her father had explained that when her mother was walking her two-year-old sister, Annie, to the beach, something very bad had happened. While Abel stayed home with the napping Paloma—who was only one year younger than her big sister—a bald man blocked her mother's path and pushed a gun into her gut. He forced her into a van as she screamed. But no one was around. After prying the shrieking Annie from her arms, the bald man banged Annie's head against the inside of the van and then pushed Esther out. The other kidnapper, who sported a scraggly, gray ponytail, was at the wheel. This "mute monster," as her mother described him, then peeled away. Esther ran as fast as she could after them until she collapsed in the middle of the road. And then Annie disappeared forever.

Police later located the abandoned van in another small beach town near the border. They found strands of Annie and Esther's hair—but no Annie. The kidnappers had presumably fled to Mexico, and although there had been some suspected sightings in Ensenada of the man with the gray ponytail over the years, neither of them had ever been captured.

After that, Paloma's mother became catatonic for a short time—a dead-silent woman with arms and limbs frozen in odd angles of trapped anguish. When Esther finally emerged from her state, she was never the same. The schizophrenia that had been lurking below broke through the surface, the trauma of Annie's kidnapping most likely having been the culprit in releasing it. Or perhaps it'd already been seeping through before the kidnapping, and Esther concealed her symptoms so well that no one could detect it—not even Abel.

Of course, Paloma didn't remember this from her babyhood, but her father gave her the full details when she was old enough to grasp it, wanting her to understand the why of her mother's illness. Paloma knew it was his attempt to help her cope—by laying it all out, he hoped that she wouldn't blame herself, as children so often do when their parents can no longer keep it together.

"I know," said Abel, "that even after all these years, we're both greatly affected by it."

"You're right, Dad." Paloma's legs grew numb, an odd sensation that crept back whenever they discussed the tragedy. She pushed down the irrational anger that ever since she could remember boiled up, an unwarranted reaction that her patient father did not deserve. What had happened wasn't his fault, but she guessed her agitation had to land somewhere safe, even if it was unfair. And worse yet, she also could tell that his unrelenting grief for both Esther and Annie remained locked inside him, never to subside. The summer day smothered her with its humidity as she told herself that now was the time. "There's something I need to tell you, Dad."

"So, I hope all is well with you," Abel said.

Paloma wished he'd consider a hearing aid. As much as she didn't want to, she spoke in the loud, punctuated way that would hopefully get through to him. "It's been hard—"

"I've been having to contend with a growing health concern," he continued.

"What is it?" she asked, hoping that whatever ailment he was currently obsessing about wasn't serious. Her father often battled symptoms, but the maladies were only sometimes diagnosable. Although she knew that his friends jokingly labeled him a hypochondriac, Paloma guessed that her father suffered from extremely sensitive pain receptors. She also wondered if he possibly shared her over-the-top empathy response, which often translated other people's emotions into her own physical symptoms. He still hadn't responded. "Dad? Did you hear me?"

"I did," he said, not answering the question.

"Well, what is your health concern?" She slowly walked back to her room.

"After telling my new doctor how fast my heart sometimes beats, she wanted me to do an EKG."

"Did you get the results yet?"

"I will soon."

That was another of his confusing traits: the more serious the potential illness, the longer he took to share what was really going on. "You promise to tell me as soon as you know?" She swallowed.

"Yes, I promise." He sighed. "But how are you? I trust everything is going along swimmingly this time."

She clenched her cell's pearl-green case. "Dad…I miscarried again."

From the sidewalk below, Serena wailed. "My Bonnie lies over the ocean, my Bonnie lies over the sea…"

"Hold on, Dad." Paloma slammed the window shut, frustration pumping through her veins. With everything else wrong with her life, why did she also have to contend with Serena's relentless invasion? "Sorry about that." Her father didn't answer. "Did you hear what I said?" From her end she could only make out a muffled pause that sounded like the swooshing of tide. "Dad, you there?"

She heard his breath catch. "I'm so very sorry."

"I know you are." She understood his heartbreak. They had both endured too much loss. "You know that I'd really like to adopt."

"That would be lovely, Paloma. Just lovely. So many children need homes."

Paloma collapsed onto her bed, trying to ignore Serena's warbling, which continued to creep through the closed window. "The problem is that Reed is still dead set against it," she said. "And I'm not sure he'll ever change his mind."

"Is it because he wants to beget his own biological children so badly, he doesn't see that parents and their adopted children have just as big as a bond—or because he knows how his mother would react?"

Paloma smiled. This was one of the many things she adored about her father: the I'm-always-in-your-camp-in-this-crazy-world paternalism she could always count on. "I think it's both. Sometimes I wonder if it's because his dad died when he was so young. I think he feels this *duty* to carry on his father's bloodline. And then, as you know, Patsy *is* obsessed about the Leary clan having to pop out babies like there's no tomorrow."

"If you want, I could try to talk some sense into that *terco* mother-in-law of yours."

"That's sweet of you. But I don't think she's ever going to change—or that Reed wants to give up on his dream of us trying again, anyway."

Her father paused for so long that Paloma was sure he hadn't heard. But then he sighed so loudly that she pictured him with his knotty fingers clasped against his liver-marked forehead as he shook his head. "Honey," he said, "you have to be prepared that he may never change."

"I know, Dad." She held back tears as the melancholic sound of Serena's muted song floated through her window like forgotten dreams that surface without notice.

"You stay right there. I'm taking you out to lunch," he said. "And I'm not taking any kind of no for an answer."

⌣

Paloma's father showed up at her door with a rumpled smile that showed just how very sad he was. Although he still had a full head of black hair, he looked at least a decade older than his seventy-two years, but even when Paloma was a little girl, he'd always seemed like a senior citizen to her—probably because he was nearly twenty years older than Esther. And, with time, his wrinkles, deeply carved canyons of sorrow and worry, made him not only appear more worn down, but continually dejected as well. "Let's get on our way," he said, with a chivalrous extension of his arm. "I made reservations at Yolanda's."

Paloma nodded and took his forearm. Ever since she could remember, her father treated her to meals at Yolanda's— whether it was to celebrate an A-plus on an English test, a comfort dinner after Danny Shelton dumped her for popular Janis Whitley on Paloma's seventeenth birthday, or just the ordinary lunches and dinners when father and daughter wanted to flee the memories darkening their motherless, lost-forever-sister house.

They shuffled down the condo's stairs, Abel holding onto the handrail while Paloma kept her hand steady on his other arm. Finally, they emerged, blinking like moles unexpectedly struck with sunlight. They slowly walked to the car. The sweltering day was coated with what Paloma imagined to be an oppressive, solidifying amber that deadened both movement and thought.

Before they reached Abel's Camry, the hairs on Paloma's arms stood. She turned around. Sure enough, Serena was right behind them. Had she been skulking on their heels since they had stepped onto the sidewalk? Or had she just appeared? Regardless, how had Paloma not seen her?

Serena flashed a disconcerting grin at Paloma and curtsied.

"Hi, Serena," Paloma said, hoping to normalize things. "How's it going?"

Serena squinted at Paloma. "Here you are with the blind man—the blind man, the blind man," Serena sang. "Oh, is he ever the blind man."

Abel winced. "Come on, Paloma, now…" His voice shook with uncustomary alarm. "Let's not be late."

"Tsk, tsk, old blind man." Serena spat on the sidewalk, her body twitching like oil sputtering in a heated pan. "Are you ever going to open your eyes? Are you? Are you?"

Even though Serena was now staring at the usually responsive and calm Abel, he ignored her. He pressed a shaking hand against the small of Paloma's back with a nervous energy that prickled through her cotton T-shirt. Without meaning to, Paloma pulled away.

"Paloma, Paloma, Paloma, want to go swimming with me in the glittering sea?" Serena sang the words in a nursery-rhyme lilt. "The glittering sea. Just you and me?"

All at once, Paloma did feel like swimming. Maybe it was because of the heat. Maybe it was because she was still in shock from the miscarriage. Or maybe it was because Serena was hypnotizing her with those luminous eyes. But whatever it was, Paloma found herself blurting out the words that she really hadn't meant to say: "Yes, Serena, I do want to go swimming with you."

Abel coughed so violently that Paloma forgot about Serena and turned to pat his back. "You okay, Dad?" He stooped over, hacking into his cupped hands, looking so frail and defeated that Paloma's frustration at him evaporated.

He gasped for air. Paloma could only wait.

"Look at that poor, poor soul," Serena cooed. "He's just as lost as lost could be."

Slowly, Abel unfolded himself and stood without saying a word.

"Dad, you okay?" Paloma asked again.

He waved his hand in the air as though swatting away a fly. "Let's get to lunch, Paloma."

Even though his eyes were stern, his mouth trembled. Paloma steered him away from his car and walked him toward her metallic blue Kia. She opened the passenger door and he settled in with the air of an exhausted child who had already gotten in too much trouble for the day.

She slammed her door and before driving off, checked the review mirror. In the middle of the street, Serena danced in a jerky up-and-down rhythm, a desperate sea creature flapping on the deck of a boat, wishing to return to sea.

Chapter Seven

With their stomachs full of chicken mole and rajas con queso, Paloma drove them back in bloated silence. Abel scrunched uncomfortably forward, his particular body odor, which smelled like a combination of moldy sourdough bread and eucalyptus, made Paloma roll down her window even though the air conditioning was running full blast.

"Anything you want to tell me, Dad?" At Yolanda's they had faced each other in the vinyl booth, their conversation like a cool brook gliding past the jagged rocks of her mother and the miscarriage. Now Paloma wanted more than the inconsequential chitchat of past meals and weather.

"I'm very sorry about your miscarriage," Abel said. "I know how disheartening this must be for you."

"Thanks, Dad." She thought about how sad the word disheartening sounded. She pictured an actual heart shriveled up in a corner where some defeated person had discarded it, a burden too heavy to keep lugging around. Paloma let her fingers dangle out the window as she noted a peculiar change in the air that made her think of the rare Southern California thunderstorm. She'd heard on the radio that morning that a tropical storm was hitting Mexico, the forecast predicting that it'd reach Sunflower Beach in the next couple of days. But when she peered up at the sky through the baked dirt on her windshield, only sunshine glared down through a blank atmosphere.

In her peripheral vision she could see Abel staring at her. "What is it?"

"Do you ever think of your sister?"

How could she answer? Ever since she'd been a kid, she had wondered what happened to the sister she'd been too young to know. Yet she had also experienced an early vision that showed young Annie lying on her stomach in the sand with chin propped up in her chubby, little-girl palms. Like a long-lost friend, a sea lion barked a hello to Annie as it waddled out of the ocean to sun itself on the beach. Annie's face lit up as if she, too, were about to reunite with an old chum. This vision comforted Paloma for a while—yet as she grew older, she knew that after so much time had gone by, Annie had most certainly died. And by the time she was a teen, she realized that her long-ago vision was merely colored by wishful thinking. Still, it continued to provide a tiny grain of make-believe peace. Paloma, though, had never shared this with her father.

"I do think of Annie," she said. "Probably not as much as you do, but more than you can guess."

He nodded.

"But why do you ask?"

"I merely wanted to..." He coughed into his hand, never finishing the sentence.

They came to a red light and Paloma stared at his profile. She could tell by his far-off gaze that he was lost in the past, so she didn't push it. They continued on, their separate thoughts thick in their heads under the indifferent heat of the day.

⁓

She parked in front of her condo, the tarry smell of asphalt assaulting her lungs. She looked for Serena and saw that she was busy staring at a mother who had just moved into the neighborhood and was now strolling by with her baby in a sling and daughter by the hand. When Serena wasn't painting, swimming, or following Paloma, she often stalked young families. Most long-term residents had long since learned the avoidance tactics that made Serena a mere nuisance who easily slipped out of sight and mind. Newcomers and tourists, though, weren't experienced at spotting the gristly thin woman from afar and stepping briefly into open shops until she passed or recognizing her loud warbling careening around corners and crossing the street with eyes averted until she moved on.

At first the parents would try to ignore her when she came too close. Then they would nervously smile when she stepped in front of them, as her mismatched eyes stared hungrily at their babies. When Serena continued to follow them, they'd race-walk to the safety of their sedans and SUVs. Then Serena would stand in the middle of the street and moan at the finality of slammed car doors and hurried engines. They didn't know her like Paloma did. They did not know the Serena who had pulled her up when she'd tripped on the way home from the market and then tenderly wiped the gravel from her knees before quietly walking on.

They did now know the young Serena who had spat into bigoted Tommy Whitmore's face when he had called Paloma a "dirty, burrito-bagel bitch" after finding out that her father was originally from Mexico and her mom had been Jewish. They did not know the real Serena.

From inside her car, Paloma and Abel continued to watch Serena follow on the heels of the young mother and her children. Much to Paloma's surprise, the mother turned to face Serena—but didn't look concerned. Instead, she nodded. Then she said something—probably a benign greeting—that made Serena pause. The mother waited for Serena's answer, which, from the looks of it, never came. After caressing the top of her baby's head, the mother turned to go. Serena stood as still as a heron until the little girl looked back at her and waved. With a mournful downturn of mouth, Serena lifted a hesitant arm and waved back. The little girl laughed and then abruptly turned her head. Without a backward glance, she marched ahead with her mother. Serena slowly trudged off in the opposite direction.

Abel shook his head. Neither Paloma nor he mentioned what they had just witnessed, yet Paloma's chest ached at the sorrow in Serena's eyes. Abel cleared his throat, breaking the silence. "It was good to have lunch together." He looked at her with an empty expression that Paloma couldn't read. Then he climbed out of the passenger seat and grimaced as he stood next to the car, his chest caving in.

Feeling a sudden pang in her heart, Paloma quickly got out and faced her father. "Dad, I know you said you're waiting for the results of your EKG, but I have a feeling you already got them. What's going on."

He looked down. "I'm embarrassed to tell you that the doctor thinks it's just anxiety." He smiled sheepishly as the tips of his ears turned red.

"I'm glad it's not your heart, but how bad is the anxiety?"

"I just have to heed my own advice and not worry over everything, maybe even start meditating." He sighed. "I'll be okay, don't you worry. Now, get yourself out of this heat and try to rest."

Paloma wrapped her arm around his shoulder. "Please know you can always talk to me." She tried to swallow the lump expanding in the back of her throat. "I'm sorry if I've been short with you today." She held out her hand. Shuffling him along, she apologized again.

"You've just experienced yet another loss." His hand shook as he fitted the key into his car door. "I understand."

"I know you do." For some reason, the memory of her mother with back hunched and fingers clenched around her ballpoint pen as she wrestled words onto the pages of her journal suddenly emerged again. She grasped her father's arm. "I need to ask you a favor…." She didn't want to stress him out, but it was time. Time to understand her mother. Time to understand herself. "I'd like to see Mom's journal."

He pinched the sides of his nose. "Your mother's journal?"

"I know you remember it. She wrote in it all the time. It had a red leather cover—"

"It's lost."

"Please. I'd like to read it for myself."

"Paloma, I never found it." He stared down the road, watching Serena's retreat. "Your mom must have thrown it away before she died."

"But she cherished it."

He paused, nervously tapping his fingertips together.

"What, Dad?"

"I'm sorry," he said, "but I searched through every single thing she owned."

Paloma gritted her teeth. Maybe he hadn't looked hard enough? Maybe her mother had hidden it where she knew it couldn't be found? Paloma wanted to question him more but saw a sad haze forming in his eyes. "I understand," she said, planning to find it without his help.

"I really did try." He held a hand over his chest and now looked in the direction of the ocean, even though it was blocks away and could only be seen in tiny, ice-blue slices between the motley structures of apartment buildings, condos, and overbuilt remodels. After several moments, he finally broke out of his reverie and gave her a hug. He then slowly lowered himself into his car, a beaten-down man drained of hope.

She leaned into his open window. "Dad…"

"What is it?"

"I just want you to know how much I love you."

"That means the world to me, *mija*," he said. "The world."

Chapter Eight

Not at all sure of what the outcome would be, Paloma found herself walking to the beach in search of Serena. Because Serena had actually asked if she would swim with her, maybe the two of them would connect beyond Serena's typical serenades, which always ended when she slunk away in ultimate withdrawal. Paloma walked closer to the ocean's edge, searching. Within minutes, she caught sight of her. Serena gazed at her from a poised position on the largest rock jutting into the water of upcoming tide. A secretive smile played on her lips, a knowing glint in her eyes. Paloma stopped in wonder. After all these years, Serena's ethereal looks struck her. For once, the usually jittery woman looked at ease in the world, and Paloma could see that beyond the unkempt hair, sun-ravaged skin, and gritty teeth was an extraordinary face of chiseled cheekbones, full mouth, a long, elegant nose—as well as her unusual eyes, one shining blue and the other an otherworldly green.

Paloma couldn't stop herself from staring. With the afternoon light reflected off Serena's gaze and her black hair knotted like tangled seaweed, she looked like a beautifully composed mermaid. Perhaps, Paloma thought, just like the one she insisted was her real mother "who never got lost," which Serena oftentimes wailed on about when she followed on Paloma's heels. Entranced, Paloma continued toward her as she visualized the most striking painting from Serena's last art show: On a storm-shattered sea, a boat struggled against what looked like gale-force winds. It was one of the most emotional works of art Paloma had ever seen. And now that she thought about it, the painting could very well have influenced the vision she had at Justine's house of the capsized boat.

Serena extended a sinewy arm and with her thin fingers beckoned Paloma closer. Before she knew it, Paloma stood within a few feet of her. The tide, frothy and cold, swept up Paloma's ankles. But she didn't mind. A tourist couple capped with matching neon-yellow visors passed by, gawking. Paloma ignored them and smiled at Serena. Serena's expectant gaze made Paloma feel like this was the only place in the world she was meant to be. She briefly closed her eyes and breathed in the curious scent of beached seaweed combined with the gardenia perfume that Serena doused herself with daily.

"Hot sky, cool sea," Serena said. "You've come to swim with me." She glided her arm through the air in a dreamy fashion that made Paloma think of a kelp forest swaying underwater. "Now down with your long hair of copper curls. It is time to let it down. Let it down, I tell you."

Without thinking, Paloma undid her bun and stared at Serena. She knew it was just her imagination, but she swore that the shape of Serena's side-bent legs beneath the folds of her skirt looked like the contours of a mermaid's tail—if such a thing really existed.

"You…" Serena shifted her body into a squat. With feet planted against the rock's rough surface and chicken-bone knees jutting out from her now hiked-up skirt, Serena pointed at her. "You are staring at me. Staring at me like I am not me."

Before Paloma could answer, a faint growl of thunder rumbled through the afternoon sky. Both Paloma and Serena turned their attention south. With hand over brow, Paloma saw miles-away storm clouds like fat, gray mountains painted on the horizon. Though she knew the storm front must have blown up earlier than predicted, it still surprised her to see it accumulate so quickly on the fringe of this sun-drenched day.

Serena turned her gaze back to Paloma. "Things can go willy-nilly on a whim of the wind," Serena said. She neither smiled nor frowned, but somehow her tilted expression made it look as though she was in on the biggest cosmic joke of them all.

"I guess you're right," Paloma answered. "Things can change fast."

Another far-off rumble vibrated through the sky. Even though there was still no sign of lightning, Paloma knew that thunder could seldom be heard beyond a ten-mile radius. Although some people thought the opposite, her father had taught her that lightning always came before thunder, whether you could see it or not. Even if it was shrouded in a distant cloud, it didn't mean danger couldn't eventually strike.

"See, Paloma?" Serena jumped off the rock and danced a jig as she held her skirt up, her brown feet splashing water arcs. "See what's out there for you?" she said, her words strung tight with excitement.

"What is out there for me, Serena?"

Serena wiggled out of her skirt, whipped off her shirt, and tossed them on the rock. She stood in a turquoise swimsuit, poised like an athlete ready to train. "Everything is out there for you, Paloma." She grabbed Paloma's hand. "Everything, everything, everything."

Then before Paloma knew what was happening, they were charging into the ocean. Serena's grasp was so sure, there was no other choice. Ignoring her fear of lightning, Paloma let herself be swept into the waves. Even in her shorts and T-shirt—and with her belly still full from lunch—the ocean continued to push her forward. The humid air also made the water that much more refreshing. As they dove under the first wave, though, Paloma realized that it probably wasn't a good idea for her to swim in the ocean so soon after a miscarriage. Yet when she popped her head up after pushing past the pull of undertow, she saw how clear the water was and decided that she'd risk a possible infection. It was worth it to stay in this bracingly cool world alongside this unrestrained woman who, in her inexplicable way, made Paloma feel saner than anyone else could. How strange that the person she'd felt the most trepidation about was now the person she felt the safest with.

Paloma thought she heard yet another vague roar of thunder but still saw no trace of lightning. So she let herself continue on beside the grinning Serena. They barely made it over the crest of the next wave. Then without a word, they swam past the breakers and beyond the kelp beds until the shore was so far away the tourist couple no longer looked real.

What was it about being in the ocean that made everything on land seem farther away than usual and somewhat surreal?

Treading water next to Paloma, Serena sang. "Creatures of the deep, deep sea swim up and see me. See me. See me. See me. I want to see you. See you. See you. See you."

Just as Serena took in a breath to sing her next refrain, a white-blue artery of lightning flashed through the sky all the way to the horizon. Fearful, Paloma tapped her on the shoulder. "We better swim back now."

"No, no, no," Serena sang. "I want you to see the mermaids. The mermaids have to be seen. They have to be."

Before Paloma could answer, a boom of thunder hit, the blow of a wrathful god pounding his fist against a planet-sized drum. Paloma's breath grew tight. It seemed that she was drowning on the very air she was trying to gasp. "Really, Serena..." Paloma inhaled, trying to coax more oxygen into her lungs. "We have to go back."

"Wait," Serena shouted, even though they were right next to each other. "Wait, wait, wait." Her gaze even more intense than usual, she continued to yell, "You need to wait."

Paloma debated whether she should swim back by herself, but she couldn't leave Serena. What if Serena drowned or—improbable as it was—got hit by lightning? She'd rather die herself than live with the guilt. It was such an overpowering emotion that Paloma almost cried. "One more minute, Serena," Paloma sputtered, trying to channel the blind, brave part of herself that assumed nothing catastrophic would happen. "Then we need to go."

Serena shook her head. "Wait." This time she didn't shout, but her words held just as much force. "I need to see my mermaid sisters. We both need to. We both need to see. To see. To see."

Paloma continued treading water, wishing she could pull Serena back to shore and yet, at the same time, feeling a crazy anticipation that made her want to stay. Within a minute, the sky dimmed, and rain fell, the drops pinpricking Paloma's skin. Perfect circles formed on the ocean's pearl-blue face.

"Look!" Serena shouted. "Look over there."

Paloma fastened her gaze where Serena was pointing. Less than twenty feet away, a pod of dolphins ripped through the ocean. Sleek bodies that dove in and out of the water headed toward them. In awe of their strength and at the same time fearful of it, Paloma watched.

"I told you. I told you!" Serena sang. "Our mermaid sisters have come to take us home. Homeward they'll take us. I tell you, homeward."

"Dolphins are amazing," Paloma whispered, gently willing Serena from her delusional world. But Serena merely clenched her mouth shut. With fins slicing through the surface, the dolphins then passed by, oblivious to both Serena's fantasies and Paloma's hopes. As Paloma watched their retreat, she thought she saw a flash of green. It appeared to be a huge translucent-green tail, which looked so out of place in the middle of the feasting throng that Paloma guessed she had imagined it. No fish off Southern California's coast could be that big. The shiny fan of feathery green was nothing like the sturdy dolphins' gray, rubbery flukes. This anomaly vanished as fast as it appeared. It was probably just some fish that had changed its route due to a shift in temperature. Or had the fleeting hallucinations she had experienced from time to time in her childhood—the ones that were just as vivid as her visions and that her father affectionately labeled as her overactive imagination—come back?

"That's what happens when you don't believe in mermaids, dear Paloma. They just move on and on and on." Serena's tone had lost its singsong quality. Now it sounded as sad and tired as an old woman who'd been betrayed. "You don't believe. You don't. You don't."

Paloma wanted to reach out to her, to tell her how very sorry she was, but the horizon lit up again, a dramatic, upside-down tree of lightning that made everything seem to stop, even the flow of ocean current. "We have to get to shore now," Paloma said. This time, she didn't wait for Serena's protests, or for the boom of thunder, but simply swam to the beach, hoping that Serena would follow.

Chapter Nine

The next morning, drowsy-gray clouds covered the sun. Though rivulets of sweat were already running down her back as she trekked through the muggy air, Paloma was grateful for the continued break from the summer's glare. She had decided to take a hike through town to the gated community of Ocean Hills, where Justine was waiting in her mini mansion.

As she made her way up Sunflower Beach's main artery, Paloma walked by Pacific Street's storefronts with their green awnings and faded flower boxes. A woman in full workout gear strode toward her pushing a sporty stroller with a cushion-enshrined baby. Instinctively, Paloma smiled at the little one, who couldn't have been more than a year old. She was rewarded with a toothless grin. Paloma had to duck her head as abrupt tears of loss blurred her vision. The mother pushed on, though, distracted by the chirp of her cell.

Knowing she was about to lose it, Paloma slipped into a nearby alley and continued into the shadows until she hit a dead end graced with cigarette butts, a torn-in-half Reader's Digest, and a stuffed animal that looked to be a cross between a doleful-eyed wolf and a mistreated coyote. Next to the pile stood an overloaded dumpster, its reek of rancid grease and moldy bread wafting over her. She held a hand over her nose and averted her gaze. Hoping no one could see her, she inched away, and then pressed her back against the building's stucco wall. Shutting her eyes, she hugged herself. After several minutes, she finally let go and sobbed without a sound, her body heaving, dispelling layers of grief. Then, without meaning to, she let a stark, needy cry emanate from the bottom of her throat and force itself into the alley's rank air, both startling and somehow soothing her. Then she quietly swallowed down the rest of her tears, listening to a slow, dank drip that came from somewhere overhead and landed in some undefined space by the dumpster. She pushed herself off the wall and wiped her eyes. If she didn't hurry, she'd be late— and she didn't want to anger Justine, who abhorred any form of tardiness. Before she turned back into the world, though, she paused, studying the stuffed animal. Its mournful eyes stared back. Without thinking, she stepped toward it. She bent down and picked it up. She patted its bedraggled head and hummed a long-ago lullaby that her mother used to sing to her. Then, with a sigh, Paloma set the stuffed animal back down and slowly returned to the sidewalk.

She walked a pace and then stopped. Something was out of place. And then she realized: Serena wasn't following her. She looked up and down the sidewalk and watched early morning patrons milling in and out of cafés, specialty stores, and various boutiques. But there was no sign of Serena. Although she was anything but cold, Paloma shivered. Was Serena still angry with her for not believing in mermaids?

Paloma trudged forward as she recalled the crestfallen set of Serena's face after they had emerged from the ocean. After that, Serena had stalked off, and when Paloma called after her, she turned with such a furrowed look of betrayal that Paloma could only stand mute under the increasingly fat raindrops.

With outrage sparking like fire from her eyes, Serena shouted, "You had your chance to meet your mermaid sisters, and you wouldn't see. So now I'll go and let you be. Let you be." Arms wrapped around her soaked body while the rain continued to beat against her skin, Paloma watched Serena trail up the beach. A sudden, unnamed fear snaked all the way to the pit of her stomach. Paralyzed with emotion, Paloma's feet sank into the wet sand until the very last glimpse of the far-off Serena blurred.

Now guilt coiled inside her as she glanced at a homeless man scrunched beneath the window of Beach House Café. "Help me," he whispered.

Paloma dug into her pockets, hoping she had a dollar or two, but couldn't produce anything more than a couple of quarters. "Sorry, that's all I have," she said.

He shoved the coins in the front pouch of his backpack. Uncrossing his feet, which gave off a sea-rot stench of dead seal, the man's gaze fell. "Got to get." Then he started shouting full force, "The darkest horse is trampling me." He cowered with arms over his head and leaned into the building. "It's here. It's here."

At first, Paloma reached for him, but that only made him cower more. Slowly, she backed off, giving him space but then stopped. She knew Reed would tell her to walk away, that she wouldn't be able to do anything anyway, but something kept her feet cemented to the sidewalk. The young man continued to shriek about the dark horse until Beach House Café's restaurant manager, with her spiky black hair and hot-pink streaks, stormed out.

"James, this is the second time in a week." The woman's brows furrowed with both concern and frustration. "I'll have to call the cops unless you quiet down." But James continued to yell, and then scraped the side of his face against the brick exterior. Paloma winced.

The manager leaned over and lightly tapped one of his hands. "James, it's Pauline." With a sigh, she straightened up. "Please look at me."

"Don't you go about demanding the devil to see you face to face." James gaped at some invisible demon, his eyes wide with horror.

Pauline pulled her cell out and phoned the police. After repeating the café's address and her name, Pauline turned from him, hunching her back. "James is having another one of his psychotic breaks. I think he might really hurt himself this time." She shook her head and clicked off her cell. For a moment, James stopped yelling, and in the sudden stillness, Pauline gazed up at the heavy dome of cloud cover, her eyes scanning the answerless sky.

Then James moaned so loudly that Paloma's stomach cramped in empathy. She stared at the side of his face, a smear of blood mixed with street grit and patchy facial hair that could not yet be called a beard. Paloma realized that he was a lot younger than he had first appeared to her. James squeezed his eyes shut, oblivious to all around him. Paloma turned to Pauline. "Will they be able to help him?"

"I doubt it, unless he says he's either going to kill himself or hurt someone else. I'm hoping they can at least get here soon, so they can see I'm not exaggerating." Pauline pulled her fingers through the uppermost spikes of her hair. "I really want them to get him into a shelter that'll give him long-term care. But every time I call, he shuts down before they get here." She bent her thick legs and peered at James. He looked right through her, stuck in his inner world that must have seemed as real to him as the dove-gray morning light reflecting off the café window and the manager's clunky black clogs were to Paloma.

"James, honey, it's okay," Pauline said.

Paloma watched, thinking about Pauline's conflicted sentiments of wanting the cops to witness how much James needed professional help and at the same time wishing he'd calm down.

James grew so still that Paloma was afraid he had fainted. Yet in the next moment, he shrieked so violently that even Pauline backed away. Paloma wondered what kind of world it was where a manager at a breakfast joint had to act as a social worker—and beyond that, why so many people had to deal with such unsurmountable pain.

Finally, James quieted down. He then fell into an abrupt sleep, curled like a puppy around his backpack. Amazingly, his face became so composed, with wet eyelashes closed to the world and mouth ever so slightly curled up, that he appeared at peace. At one point, not so long ago, this man had been someone's child. Where were his parents now? It'd be easy to blame these unknown people, but maybe what happened to their son was out of their control, maybe they had been searching for him for so long, they thought he was dead. Paloma swallowed, wondering at the heartbreak so many mothers and fathers had to endure. Would she be able to carry on if she couldn't find her own child? But, of course, that *did* happen to her own mother and father with Annie's disappearance.

Pauline touched her shoulder. "You okay?"

"Sorry...I was just thinking." Paloma looked down at the sleeping James. Then, she said goodbye to Pauline, who nodded back with a what-else-could-we-do? shrug. Paloma slinked off. With a catch in her throat and tears in her eyes, she continued onward to the gated community that encircled Justine's world.

⤳

Justine shook her head. "You walked here?" Her nose crinkled and her lips puckered as if something curdled had passed through them, the exact face she used to make when she was a teenage girl disgusted with everyone and everything around her. "It's so muggy out today. You're all sweaty"

"I don't work out at a private, air-conditioned gym like you do." Paloma caught herself. How quickly their conversations turned into the petty quibbles of hostile siblings. Paloma crossed over the entranceway, wondering if they had become friends for the simple reason of growing up within a block of each other and another more complicated one having to do with Paloma's mother's schizophrenia, while Justine's dad had such intense bipolar disorder that before he'd been diagnosed, he had wrecked two cars in one year by first flying over an embankment and then, months later, plowing into a storefront window. But no matter what the reasons why, they became and continued to be friends, and Justine's intent was always good, even as her words often stung.

"That came out so wrong, Paloma. I'm sorry." Justine raised her eyebrows in apology. "I was just thinking how devastating it is for you to suffer through another miscarriage. And typical me, the more nervous I get, the bitchier I sound."

"It's okay. I know." Paloma also knew that Justine felt an unwarranted guilt about having Harrison when all Paloma had were losses. But what Justine didn't seem to grasp was that Paloma was genuinely happy for her—and that she considered Harrison a light in both of their lives.

Justine strode to the kitchen and Paloma followed. They entered the immense room. The stench of rotting peaches wafted from a crystal bowl. Paloma wondered why Justine would buy too many for her family to consume before most of the thin-skinned fruits would go bad. "I'm glad you forgive me…" Justine smiled over her shoulder. "Because I booked us side-by-side pedicures today."

"What about Harrison?"

"The babysitter took him to his playgroup."

Paloma didn't know what to say. She hated the thought of being stuck in the acetone stink of a nail bar while some underpaid stranger polished her toenails. But Justine was only trying to help.

Justine motioned for her to sit. "I picked up some of those croissants from La Playa Bakery you love so much."

They settled on bar stools surrounding a large granite island. Justine shoved La Playa's blue-and-white-striped box filled with croissants and bran muffins toward Paloma and then plunked a napkin in front of her.

Paloma lifted a croissant, peeled the outer layer, and popped a piece of tender middle in her mouth. She closed her eyes, savoring the buttery, white-flour decadence. "Thank you. This is the best tasting thing I've had all week." She noticed a stack of tile samples by Justine's sink. "You going to redo your kitchen again?" Justine remodeled her home every couple of years.

Justine flashed a smile. "I know you think I'm wasteful, Paloma. But I can't help myself. I love the whole renewal process."

"I get it." On one hand, Paloma *did* get it; it would be nice to update stuff when she wanted to and live in a place that was so clean and organized. Still, she wished that Justine would wait at least every ten years or so and donate the money she would have spent to charity.

"I know that furrowed-forehead face." Justine wagged a finger at her. "But look at it this way: I help our local contractors—and all their workers—stay in business. Hell, I've probably even bankrolled some of their kids' tuitions."

Paloma took another bite of her croissant, thinking. Who was she to judge what made others feel sane? She looked at the gleaming kitchen, remembering the dirt and mess of food-encrusted dishes, the soured neglect of unwashed clothes, and the black-mold bathroom of Justine's childhood home. Then there were the parties Justine's mother threw. In the mornings, ashen-faced people were strewn like rag dolls across couches and rugs as the skunky odor of pot smoke continued to stink up the house. "You know what, Justine? You deserve to do your thing."

"You said it, sister." Justine grinned. "So…I have something I want to ask you." She clicked her mauve-painted fingernails against the slick granite, her smile quickly fading. "But you need to keep an open mind."

Paloma dropped the rest of her croissant on the waiting napkin. "What?"

"My friend Lisa told me how she saw this amazing healer who specializes in fertility issues."

"Please don't tell me it was Daphne Hollow." This was so Justine, lecturing her about how she should learn how to push away her visions—and then going on about some supposed healer.

"It is! Lisa swears by her. She says she had two miscarriages, and after Daphne worked with her, she gave birth to a healthy baby girl."

Paloma held up a hand. "Justine, I also saw Daphne after my second miscarriage."

"You did? I don't remember you telling me."

"I didn't bother because it was such a bad experience."

"What happened?" Justine cut a quarter piece from one of the bran muffins, picking at it and rapidly chewing each tiny bite, reminding Paloma of Harrison's pet hamster, nibbling a thousand miles per second on the bits of sweet potatoes that Harrison gleefully plopped into its cage.

Paloma didn't want to share what Daphne had said, worried that Justine might agree. "Let me put it this way," Paloma said. "She wasn't helpful."

"She certainly helped Lisa. Daphne told her that she had a deep-seated fear of motherhood. Lisa didn't believe her at first, but after she started chanting Daphne's specialized mantras, everything fell into place."

"This is ridiculous." Paloma swallowed. "Lisa would have had that baby without having to see Daphne."

"How can you be so sure?"

"For $125 a session, Daphne Hollow said the same thing to me. She's a rip-off artist. She preys on people's need for hope—and I bought it until I realized what a phony she was."

For a moment, doubt crossed Justine's face, but then she arranged her expression back to its sure, assertive cover. "That doesn't mean she's a fake. It wouldn't be that weird if two women had similar issues."

"She's not the real thing."

"Just because it didn't work for you," Justine said, "doesn't mean she's a scam artist."

Paloma gritted her teeth. Daphne Hollow was the last thing she wanted to talk about.

"But what *if* fear is affecting you...?" Justine murmured.

"Please don't psychoanalyze me, Justine."

"But what about your visions?"

"What about them?"

"Did any of them foretell your miscarriages?"

"That," Paloma said, studying Justine's face, "makes no difference." Had her friend guessed her ongoing fear that her visions weren't just previews of the future but could somehow *make* things happen?

"We're all afraid, Paloma." Justine gave her a sad smile and then glided over to her stainless-steel monster of a fridge. "Feel like a Diet Coke?" she asked, sweeping her earlier words away.

But Paloma wouldn't let her. "This is not about me being afraid." She stared at her friend's sharp shoulder blades.

Rummaging in the fridge for a Coke, Justine did not respond.

"Come on, Justine."

Her head still in the fridge, Justine finally answered, "Maybe she picked up on something."

"There was nothing to pick up on." Paloma's stomach tightened, anticipating another emotional punch to the gut. She had never shared her fear about inheriting her mother's schizophrenia, although Justine must have guessed. Odd she didn't question her about it but then again, maybe even Justine had the finesse to know when she was hitting too close to home.

Justine abruptly stood and slammed the refrigerator door. She looked at Paloma without saying a word, the side of her mouth spasming in an angry twitch. Yet Paloma felt Justine's sadness pass through her, a heartsore sorrow that made Paloma's chest hurt.

"You okay?" Paloma asked.

"Why are you acting so close minded about this when you yourself have visions?"

"I'm not close minded. I believe there are true healers, but I also think there're people like Daphne, who are either complete con artists or who talk themselves into believing that they're gifted but are as receptive as a loaf of bread."

"But she helped Lisa," Justine said. "I hoped that she could help you, too."

Paloma took in a deep breath. Sometimes, the only way to confront Justine's stubbornness was to try and tap into her empathy. "You have to step back and realize that if you were in my shoes, you'd be questioning her so-called 'specialized' mantras too." Paloma slid off the stool and stood before Justine.

Justine looked away. Emboldened by her friend's silence, Paloma forged on. "I know you mean well, but you can't take this personally." Justine possessed such a need for others to follow her advice—solicited or not—that it bordered on the obsessive.

Justine shot up an eyebrow. "Take it personally?"

"Yes," Paloma said, bracing herself. "This is not about you."

The color drained from Justine's face. "Oh my God," Justine said, staring at the rotting peaches.

"What?" Had Justine just noticed the decaying fruit? Or was she gathering up more ammunition?

"I've been a total bitch, again, haven't I?"

Paloma sighed. "Maybe not a *total* bitch."

"I'm so sorry." Justine bowed her head. "I was just talking about this with my therapist yesterday."

"What do you mean?"

"I have to work on my control issues."

Paloma nodded. She understood how Justine's history had most likely affected her—how her father left when Justine was twelve years old to pursue an acting career and never looked back, how Justine's zoned-out mother, who would leave young Justine for weeks at a time to follow some guru with an unpronounceable name, blamed her husband's departure on Justine's feisty nature—and continued to do so.

"You do know," Justine said, "that you're my only friend who understands."

Without a word, Paloma got up and hugged her.

Justine let her hold her for a moment and then pulled back, laughing. "Those peaches smell awful, don't they?"

"They really do." Paloma wondered how long the true Justine would last before she wrapped herself in her shiny exterior again.

Then, sure enough, Justine went right into how they had to make their pedicure appointment and actually stomped her foot when Paloma told her she wasn't up for it. Even though she hadn't been there that long, Paloma couldn't take another moment of her friend's unrelenting prattle. Claiming a pounding headache (which actually was the truth), Paloma extricated herself from the gleaming interior of Justine's house. Justine gave her a pout before slowly closing her front door. Feeling like a stray cat who wasn't sure which way to dart, Paloma froze. But when she inhaled the hopeful scent of fresh-mowed lawn, her chest expanded and she knew that even if there weren't any clear-cut answers, everything would work out—eventually.

Chapter Ten

Paloma plopped onto her bed. She listened for Serena, but the only sounds that drifted through her window were the coo of doves from the oak across the street and a jet ripping through the sky. She hugged her pillow and wished Reed could be home with her now. He had kissed her on the bridge of her nose that morning before going to work and though it was a split-second gesture, it had stayed with her all day.

For a moment she let herself wonder what it would be like to look into the eyes of their baby and understood Reed's desire for her to get pregnant again. And even though she would never share this with him, she actually did wish she could go through the birthing process—no matter how painful it would be. She imagined growing big and round and then bringing life into the world; it seemed like the ultimate magic. She thought about how Reed would be by her side, his eyes shiny with joyful tears she'd never seen him shed before. About how she'd nurse the tiny new life that would forever be a part of them both. About how they would leave their childhood sorrows behind as they watched their own children thrive.

But it wasn't good to fantasize about something that could never happen.

She picked up her cell, hoping to distract herself with some inane news story. But her skin became electrified. Bracing herself for an upcoming vision, she closed her eyes and waited. First the pins and needles traveled all the way from her head down to her limbs, and then it intensified to the point where her whole body trembled. Paloma breathed through it. Within minutes, the vision came through. She was at the florist shop. Beams of afternoon light flooded through the storefront window. Surrounded by dozens of wedding centerpieces, she was at work with Anca and Tatiana. A sense of peace came over her as she breathed in the scent of eucalyptus combined with the fragrance of English roses. Serena strolled into the shop. Surprised that she was there, Paloma's stomach fluttered. Serena looked from Tatiana to Paloma and smiled. Then she whispered, "…it will be a name that no one will be able to toss to sea." Everything around Paloma became blurred. She was brought to tears but didn't know why.

The vision quickly vanished. Wondering what it could mean, Paloma blinked away her real-life tears. Although it was a peaceful vision, it still left her depleted. But she had to carry on, had to take care of the here and now; it was time to shower off the day and start preparing the coleslaw she was going to bring to Patsy's later. She made herself get up. Hoping to clear her head, Paloma took a moment to gaze out the window. She didn't expect to see anything much, just a car driving by or perhaps a skateboarder cruising to the beach. Yet she peered at the empty street.

Within a minute, Ramiro Summers strolled down the sidewalk, and in top-notch clarity whistled "Singing in the Rain," even though there wasn't a cloud in sight. A bow-legged tree-trunk of an old man, Ramiro always made her smile. He owned a small hardware store in town that locals liked to frequent not only because the people who worked there actually cared, but for a chance to chat with Ramiro himself. Customers would often stop by in hope that he'd be there, and if he wasn't, they'd find some excuse to come back within a couple of days to buy some small thing, like an extra roll of duct tape or another pack of thumbtacks. Paloma knew this because she realized she did it herself.

For where else could you go to find an outrageously funny and generous store owner who would spontaneously treat you to lunch at his favorite restaurant just because you wore a polka-dotted shirt that day? Even his tattoos were endearing. With classic anchors, nautical stars, swallows, and shark tattoos on every visible body part except his face (even his knuckles were inked, each finger graced with the individual letters of the phrase "Hold Fast"), he looked like a sailor from a 1950s comic strip. Ramiro enjoyed doling out his sage advice to whomever needed it. And with a mischievous grin, he also relished spouting out risqué jokes but never offended anyone because his humor was never mean-spirited, and besides that, his outlandishly large ears wiggled at every punch line.

Paloma watched Ramiro walk his dog, Petunia, a jaunty little pug and pit bull mix. Petunia stopped to sniff a jasmine vine growing on a neighbor's fence, and as Ramiro patted her, his words rose through Paloma's window: "Who is the most beautiful girl in all of the land?" Paloma smiled as she watched Petunia wag her whole self at his words, her mini bodybuilder frame, exaggerated short-legged stance, and extreme underbite made her a perfect match with her stout owner and his charmingly waggish face. As Petunia looked up at him, Paloma could see the uncomplicated love in her protruding eyes. Ramiro patted her again, and then grinned at the day. He resumed his whistling as they continued on.

Paloma turned from the window. If an old, single—and childless—man could be happy, why couldn't she?

Chapter Eleven

As much as she would have rather stayed home with Reed that night, they had to go to his brother Pete's thirty-eighth birthday party. It didn't matter how old her offspring were, Patsy Leary always insisted on a family celebration for each of her children's birthdays, and unless you were dying or, better yet, already dead, there wasn't any acceptable excuse for a no-show.

At least Reed had listened to Paloma and hadn't shared their latest pregnancy with anyone in his family. Now they didn't have to share the latest loss. Paloma smoothed a hand over her long, billowy dress, hoping that she'd be able to compartmentalize her grief for the evening. For a half-second, she had fantasized about telling Reed to go by himself, trying to think up an acceptable lie that the rest of his family might buy, even if Patsy wouldn't. Would her mother-in-law really hold a grudge if she were told that Paloma wasn't feeling well? But one of Reed's family members might have been driving up Pacific Street and seen her walking through town earlier. Anyway, it wasn't fair to put Reed in that position. She knew how much he appreciated her being part of his family and how letdown he felt when, as he put it, *she shut herself out.*

Even though they were only ten minutes late, everyone was already there. With the Leary clan's chatter bouncing off Patsy's living room walls, the party sounded three times the size it really was. Paloma sought out her favorite relative, Kitty, Reed's thirty-year-old sister and the baby of the family. With her strawberry-blond hair in a messy bob, Kitty resembled a frizzy-haired Peter Pan, but her personality was wonderfully down-to-earth. She was busy trying to wipe a gob of onion dip from her three-year-old son, Brett's, nest of blond curls. From what Paloma could gather from Kitty's rush of reprimands, Brett's six-year-old brother, Brody, had smeared it in, while the middle boy of the family, four-year-old Braden, goaded him on. Both Brody and Braden shrieked with laughter, no doubt reveling at the genius of their prank.

Paloma watched the three round-faced boys as she held back her own laughter. Kitty, of course, was too annoyed with her eldest sons to find any humor in their antics. Paloma smiled at the squirmy Brett, knowing that if she ever got to experience the messy domesticity of day-to-day parenting, she would be just like the frenzied Kitty, who took pride in how overwhelming—and yet, wonderfully lively—her life had become.

After she went to get a wet washcloth to assist Kitty in the smudgy clean-up of Brett's onion-dip smeared locks, Paloma grabbed the dish she had brought and ventured into Patsy's kitchen. Although Paloma knew Patsy would rather get everything organized herself and expected everyone to wait in the living room while she did, she wanted to make sure Patsy knew that she had contributed to the meal. Last time Paloma forgot her potato salad and was chided several times for the missing side dish.

Dressed in white slacks and a yellow-checked shirt, Patsy fussed over her beef stew. How Patsy, who loved her daiquiris and ever-present bag of cheese puffs, managed to stay so slim and energetic was a mystery to Paloma.

"Here's the coleslaw I made," Paloma said, hoping to be heard over the increasingly loud chit-chat of already tipsy adults and clamor of her seven nieces and nephews invading into Patsy's kitchen.

Patsy nodded without looking at her. "Put it in the fridge till I'm ready to get all the food on the table."

"Sure," Paloma said. But when she opened the refrigerator, she found no room. "I'm not sure how to fit this in there."

With irritation furrowing her drawn-on eyebrows, Patsy sighed. "I'm sure you can find a way."

Frustrated, Paloma began to take out a bowl of red Jell-O embedded with mini marshmallows and bits of pineapple, but Patsy held up a hand. "Not that. What's wrong with you?"

Patsy was even edgier than usual. Instead of trying to defend herself, Paloma thought about how Ramiro Summers would react. She pictured how he'd widen his crinkly set eyes and say something nonsensical, as she'd seen him do when he had to deal with the rare grouch of a customer. As best she could, she channeled his self-deprecating humor. "How could I have been so ridiculous?"

Patsy's mouth flew open and she stared at her as if she had just stabbed Mrs. Sweetie Pie, Patsy's nip-happy Yorkshire terrier, who was anything but sweet.

Patsy examined Paloma with the curiosity of a clinician trying to come up with a diagnosis. "You know I suffered four miscarriages myself." Patsy held up a hand, extending her fingers as she went. "Two before I had Pete, one before I had Reed, and then one a year after I had Kitty."

"What?" Paloma wasn't prepared for Patsy's abrupt disclosure.

"I'm sorry," Patsy said. "But I want you to know I understand what you're going through."

Stunned, it was now Paloma's turn to stare gap-mouthed. If the woman had endured four miscarriages, why had she acted so hostile toward Paloma after she had gone through hers? "I'm so sorry, Patsy." She thought about patting Patsy's puckered arm or even gently pressing her palm into the mosaic-freckled skin of Patsy's hand. But Patsy was not the sort of woman who appreciated sympathetic gestures.

"We need to have a heart-to-heart," Patsy said.

"Okay." Paloma wondered how and if her mother-in-law could tell she had recently miscarried, or was what Patsy had said merely a drunken, loose-worded reference to Paloma's past miscarriages?

"You need to be strong." Patsy held her gaze. "You need to be strong and make it happen. If I could have four miscarriages and three healthy pregnancies, then you can have babies, too."

"Or Reed and I could adopt." There, she finally said it to Patsy's face.

At the word, "adopt," Patsy winced. "You're young and healthy." A sudden sorrow seeped into Patsy's eyes, making her appear much less formidable than usual. "You and Reed can try again."

"Just because you were able to have children doesn't mean it will happen for me."

"But Reed wants to have kids with you. You can't ignore that."

Just then, little Brett, who still had wisps of onion dip decorating the ends of his curls, flew into the kitchen. "I want you to make hot dogs, Gamma Patsy, I want hot dogs!" He made sure to skirt around Mrs. Sweetie-Pie before he hugged Patsy's legs.

"Hot dogs?" Patsy scowled, her customary in-charge persona erasing the fleeting sadness. "Those are for ball games and picnics. We're having my special beef stew."

Brett looked up at her. "My mommy said I could have one."

"You go on and tell little Miss Kitty that we're all having beef stew for dinner." Patsy clasped her hands on her hips and stood firmly in her no-nonsense sneakers, cementing herself onto the worn squares of her parquet floor.

Paloma watched Brett's defeated slope of shoulders as he slumped away. It was a hopeless battle arguing with Patsy Leary; even a three-year-old boy knew that.

Patsy turned her attention back to Paloma. "Listen, Paloma. I know I'm not the warmest mother-in-law in the world, but you have to know I care about you."

"I don't know how to explain this…" Paloma's nose stung, but she couldn't let herself cry in front of Patsy. "I just know it's not going to work for me."

"Maybe we can change that." Patsy smiled and raised one of her eyebrows. "You know what?"

"What?" Paloma swallowed.

"There's more than one psychic in this family."

"What do you mean by that?" Paloma's heart raced.

Patsy tapped her index finger on the middle of her own forehead. "For a boozy old broad, I can still pick up a lot. I have dreams like you'd never believe."

"What are you talking about?" Paloma glanced at Patsy's drink. Could her mother-in-law be so drunk that she was making things up now?

Patsy stirred the stew, a satisfied smile playing on her lips. "Just what I said. We both have gifts. You have visions—"

"How do you know about my visions?"

"That's not important. What I was going to say before you cut me off is that I have dreams."

"You have dreams?"

"And my dreams are every bit as telling as your visions."

"What do you mean?"

"My dreams have been known to show—" Patsy interrupted herself and then fussed over the stew again. "I stopped talking about them a long time ago."

"Why?"

Patsy frowned. "Why what?"

"Why did you stop talking about them?"

Patsy paused. Then, she put on a tight smile. A tight, phony smile, Paloma noticed. "It's no big deal," said Patsy. "I just don't like going on about things that make people look at me like I suddenly have two heads." Her smile disappeared. "I bet you don't much like blabbering about your premonitions either."

"How do you know about them, anyway?" Paloma wished she could have hidden the scrunched-up look of worry that she knew crossed her brow, but saw by Patsy's grimace, that her mother-in-law had noticed.

"Reed's told me about them. It's not the end of the world." Patsy gulped the waiting daiquiri, her lips suctioned on the edge of the glass in a thirsty pucker.

"Reed told you about them?" Paloma's throat went dry. She had begged him not to share her "gift" with the Leary clan for fear that they'd turn it into a big family joke. "When did he tell you?"

"I can't remember exactly." Patsy shrugged.

Paloma stared her down. "What do you know about my visions?"

"Oh, girly, don't get mad at Reed." Patsy set her glass down and reached for her bag of Cheetos, crunching down on an especially long cheese puff. "He certainly didn't volunteer the information—and tried not to even say anything. But you know me." Patsy winked. "I quizzed him about it until he finally coughed up what I already knew."

"What you already knew?"

"You see." Patsy gave her a conspiratorial smile. "I had actually heard about them before you two were even an item."

"How?" Paloma averted her gaze, the same heated childhood shame about being "different" melded with the embarrassment over her own strange premonitions.

Patsy laughed, making her silver starfish-shaped earrings swing against her crinkled neck. "Really, Paloma, there's no need to be paranoid. We do live in Sunflower Beach." She dipped a cheese puff into her stew, crunched it down in one bite, and then nodded. "Years back, I overhead some woman at the bank go on about how you had envisioned Scott Bentley's horrific death hours before it happened."

"What you heard was an exaggeration." Paloma wished what happened in the past would stay there. After all these years, it was still hard to believe that the gossip passed on from a few classmates Justine had blabbered to about Paloma's premonition of Scott's death had multiplied into such a huge thing that it had become part of Sunflower Beach lore. Since then, she kept her visions to herself, with the exception of the once-in-a-blue-moon share with Reed and the now-adult Justine, who Paloma was sure had kept her promise of confidentiality. "My visions are symbolic, like dreams. They don't usually amount to anything—and when they do, it's probably just coincidence." She wasn't sure why, but didn't want Patsy to think she took her own premonitions seriously.

Patsy shook her head. "Did you ever stop to think your visions serve a purpose?"

"Really, Patsy…it's nice of you to say, but I'm coming to the conclusion that the only thing they amount to is trouble." Paloma had never heard Patsy talk about anything else besides her "best little gremlins of grandkids," her work at the dog shelter, and the often-repeated—yet completely understandable—refrain of how she had to become a single, hardworking mother of three after her husband, Richard, was killed in a freak car accident. So this sudden interest in Paloma's visions was unexpected—and somewhat suspicious.

Paloma watched Patsy swig her daiquiri. Paloma guessed it was *not* her first of the evening.

"Don't they give you some sense of meaning, even though it can also make life that much more confusing?" Patsy tilted her head in the same way that Mrs. Sweetie Pie did when she heard an unfamiliar noise.

"I guess so." No one had ever got that close to understanding what it had been like for her. "Do your dreams make you feel that way?"

"Never mind about my dreams." Patsy waved the question away. "But I have to say, I know how different it can make you feel, how it can make you question everything so much that you start to think you're a freak."

Paloma nodded, flabbergasted that Patsy seemed to—in her own way, at least—get it.

"But you know, most of what's around us is unseen," Patsy said.

"Unseen?"

"You know. Things like atoms and molecules, even those black holes that scientists like to go on about. You can't see them. And if you can't see what science has already proven, who's to say what other unseen stuff is real or not?"

Paloma stared at the sleeping Mrs. Sweetie Pie, wishing the snarky little dog could answer her questions. Had Patsy started a new medicine? Or had she drunk even more than usual? In all the years Paloma had known her, there had never been the slightest indication that her mother-in-law believed in anything more than what was standing right in front of her.

"This is a whole new side of you," Paloma said, smiling. Then something about the way Patsy averted her eyes hit her. Her mother-in-law was holding something back. "Patsy, is there something you want to tell me? Something about one of your dreams?"

Patsy bent over to pet Mrs. Sweetie Pie, who lay on a raised dog bed near Patsy's feet. The terrier rolled over in her sleep, making a growly happy sound as her teeth clenched into a gum-less grin. Paloma imagined that she was dreaming about sinking her miniature crocodile teeth into Paloma's ankles. She then studied Patsy's unreadable face, debating whether she should repeat herself, as Patsy still hadn't answered her.

But as soon as Mrs. Sweetie Pie fell back into her regular muffled snore, Patsy's mood shifted. With her hands-on-hips and tennis-shoes-splayed-firmly-on-the-ground stance, she grinned. "You have to let go some. I've learned that in life. More often than not, we have a choice." She shrugged. "But then some things just happen. You have to realize that sometimes it just amounts to plain, stupid luck. Just damn-straight, stupid-ass luck that we have to make the best of."

"Patsy?"

"Yeah?"

"Could you fix me a daiquiri?"

Patsy's eyes lit up. "Finally, she's letting go." Patsy reached for her metal shaker. "I'm going to do you right." She proceeded to pour a good portion of rum, squeezed a half-cut lime, threw in a splash of sugar syrup, tossed in some ice cubes, then shook it while she did a quick marimba step. Without straining it—Patsy never strained her daiquiris because, she said, she liked biting down on the pulp of the lime—she handed it to Paloma and grinned.

Paloma tasted the sweet-sour potion and then peered at her mother-in-law. "Why now, Patsy?"

"What do you mean 'why now'?"

"Ever since I've been with Reed—and especially since my miscarriages—you haven't been the nicest. Why are you being so kind now?"

Patsy lowered the flame under her stew and exhaled so loudly that for a moment, Paloma was sorry she had asked. Then Patsy faced her. "You think I'm a testy old bitch, don't you?"

"I was just—"

"Well, I know I am," Patsy said. "I just know I'm usually right and don't care if someone feels accepted by me or not—and I don't go about liking people just because my kids married them."

Paloma gulped her daiquiri, the tang of lime and the sweetness of rum and sugar making her want more—much more than what was in the glass. "What is it that makes you not like me?"

Patsy pursed her lips, a wizened woman sporting tangerine lipstick and blue eye shadow. "Don't you go on thinking you're special now, Paloma," she said. "For the longest time, I didn't especially like Kitty's husband." She rolled her eyes. "And Pete's little wifey, Susan, still drives me up the wall and back down again."

Completely flummoxed, Paloma was at a loss for words.

"It just takes me a while, that's why." Patsy turned to the fridge and started taking out the side dishes that other family members had managed to stuff in there before Paloma and Reed had arrived.

"No, Patsy. This is too abrupt—even for you. What happened?"

Patsy paused in mid unwrap of a black bean and corn salad, grimacing. "Susan managed to throw in way too many onions again."

Tapping her foot against the floor, Paloma hoped to break into Patsy's eagle-eyed scrutiny of the food. "You still haven't answered me, you know."

"Answered you? What are you talking about?"

"Patsy, you know very well what I'm talking about."

Patsy sighed and then proceeded to pick out the onions with her fire-orange fingernails, flicking them into the sink with vengeance.

"Well?"

Clearly irritated, Patsy threw an onion chunk so hard that it ricocheted off the faucet onto her blouse. She picked it off and eyed it, then proceeded to flick it down the drain. "I told you I have dreams," she said, her usually robust volume lowering into a dry whisper. "And I've learned not to share them anymore." She cleared her throat. "But I should tell you this one."

"Why?"

"Because last night I dreamt about you."

"About me? What was it about?"

"You won't shake your head at me like I'm a nutzo, will you?"

"As long as you promise not to shake your head at me."

"Fine," said Patsy. "It's just that you have to remember that most dreams are the stuff of undigested pot roast and whatever random thoughts that had congealed in our brains during the day. But other dreams mean something. The first kind is all gauzy. The second kind is like a slap in the face."

"What did you dream about me?"

"You won't tell Reed?"

"Why wouldn't you want me to tell Reed?"

"I don't want to upset him."

"Upset him?"

"Just…" Patsy said, "just make sure that if you do have a burning desire to share it with him that you let him know I'm well aware that this is just information. Nothing else."

"I can tell this is making you nervous." She quickly patted Patsy's arm. "So, I do appreciate you sharing this with me." She had to know more. After all, how strange was it that Patsy, of all people, also experienced her own kind of premonitions.

"He is my son and I've known him a lot longer than you have."

"Patsy, I don't want you to stress out—"

"No, I want to share this with you. You need to know."

Paloma looked Patsy in the eye. "What is it?"

"I dreamt that you were very sad," Patsy said with a hushed tone. "You came to me crying, telling me that you had lost your baby girl."

"I lost a baby girl?"

Patsy averted her gaze. "When I woke up, I realized you must have miscarried again."

Paloma's whole body grew hot. "Reed didn't tell you, did he?"

"No, he didn't." Patsy pursed her lips and rewrapped the bean salad. "You probably don't believe me."

"I do believe you, Patsy." Paloma's mouth went dry. "I just had to make sure—"

"I'm used to people not believing me." Patsy heaved out a loud exhale. "But I guess you're used to that, too."

"I guess so." What Paloma didn't tell her was that it wasn't so much about others not believing her, but that she herself sometimes questioned her own visions. Even though a number of them came to pass, it was a lot safer to label the most horrific ones as unconscious fears rather than burden herself—and others—with the enormity of a message that may or may not be wholly accurate. Still, deep down, she knew this was an excuse, an excuse that one day she'd have to overcome.

Her mother-in-law clicked her fingernails against the counter, pulling Paloma back in. "I knew with the kind of certainty…" Patsy said, "…that makes your heart stop that it wasn't just your unborn baby you lost, but another soul trying to get back to you."

"Another soul?"

Patsy's eyes misted over and her face softened. "I can't really explain it…" Patsy looked upward. "Just know that you're not alone."

Paloma suddenly pictured Esther's lopsided smile and faraway eyes. "Was it…" Paloma shivered. "Was it my mom?"

"I believe…" Patsy reached for her hand and held it tightly in hers. "Yes, I believe it was."

"Thank you," Paloma whispered. She exhaled, but it didn't ease the sadness clogging her lungs.

"You do know that I love you," Patsy said.

Paloma blinked back tears. "I love you, too." She leaned into Patsy's rum and lime scented breath and hugged her. Without a word more, they held each other under the kitchen's fluorescent light.

Chapter Twelve

On their way home, Reed made a detour and parked on a side street near the beach. He turned to Paloma. "I think I just saw Chance."

"Really?"

"I could have sworn he ran in front of the car and then darted over here."

Paloma rolled down her window to look for their neighborhood cat, a stray whom Reed fed whenever he saw him lurking on their street, even picking him up and cradling him like a baby—whenever the scraggly feline allowed it. "I didn't think he'd go this far," she said.

"I hope he's okay." Reed peered out the window.

"I've only seen him roam around our block. Besides, you know he's a survivor." Chance had been named by a neighbor, because no matter how many whisker-close calls the tabby had with moving vehicles, he'd never been hit. The tomcat yowled up to their condo intermittently, probably on those nights when he hadn't caught anything, or hadn't been able to sneak food from outdoor pet bowls. He always seemed to be aiming his mournful calls to Reed. But it wasn't until after the first miscarriage that Reed had started to feed Chance, keeping a rolled-up bag of dried cat food inside his trunk. It broke Paloma's heart that the condo association didn't allow pets. Reed would have loved to have taken Chance in—and she would have loved watching him baby the scrappy feline.

Reed sighed. "I guess you're right. He's probably curled up next to the laundry room as we speak."

"You feeling okay?" Paloma asked, the downcast look in his eyes making her throat ache.

"I'm fine." He put the key back into the ignition.

Paloma held her hand over his. "Let's not go just yet." The thought of entering the stagnant air of their condo made her wish they could flee to some place where past and future could be transformed. Because, in spite of all their problems, she really did love her husband. And in spite of his hemmed-in ways, Reed really was a good guy. "Let's take a walk on the beach."

"But it's ten thirty on a Thursday night." Reed shook his head.

She leaned her head out the window and inhaled the night air. "I have to tell you that mixing daiquiris and German chocolate cake is making me woozy." Did her words sound as slurred to Reed's ears as they were to hers?

"You had a daiquiri tonight? That's my mom's drink."

"It sure is," she said, wondering if she should tell Reed about Patsy's dream. "I can see why she likes them."

Reed gave her a peculiar look. "Let's go for that walk."

When they got down to the beach, Paloma tightened her grip on Reed's arm. "Hold on to me," she said.

They slipped off their shoes and ventured into the mist of the nighttime shore. A slice of moon sneaked through a cloud, casting a dreamlike lighting that seemed to swath sand and sea in navy-blue gauze. Otherwise, there wasn't any other light to speak of, yet Paloma could still make out the white crash of shore breakers, silhouettes of rocks, and, of course, Reed's tall presence next to her.

Smelling the briny odor of sea and then the underlying scent of gardenia, Paloma squeezed Reed's arm and stopped. "Do you smell that?"

"What?" Reed took her hand and pulled her forward. "I only smell ocean."

She inhaled as deeply as she could. "Gardenia. I definitely smell it."

"Nope. Just smells like typical beach to me—saltwater and seaweed, nothing more."

Paloma shook her head. Could Serena be nearby? She turned around but saw only the night's vague, grainy-looking moisture.

"You sure you're up for a walk?" Reed asked.

His words sounded as though they were traveling away from her, like the tide going back out to sea. She was definitely drunk, having had knocked down another one of Patsy's monster daiquiris after the first. "It'd make me feel better." She heard a loud bark of a seal and remembered how Serena had insisted that the passing dolphins were mermaids. She wondered if it were at all possible that such a thing existed. If humans evolved from apes on land, was it feasible that mermaids evolved from dolphins in the sea? The fleeting image of the green tail she saw among the pod of dolphins suggested a possibility that she couldn't fathom before.

Reed broke through her reverie. "You sure you're okay? Maybe we should find a place to sit down for a while."

They walked toward the lull of waves smoothing themselves against the shore, and then sat on a sandbank, their legs dangling over the edge.

"Reed?"

"What is it?"

"Did your mom ever tell you about her dreams?"

Only the reverberation of a tumbling wave answered. "Well?" she said, wondering what the jab of panic, which seemed to bolt directly from his stomach to hers, was about. Was this a trigger for him? And if he did know about his mother's dreams, why hadn't he shared them before?

"Yeah," he said, his tone a notch lower than usual, a secretive tone that didn't normally belong to him. "Believe me, I know all about her dreams."

"Why haven't you ever mentioned them?"

"Because like your premonitions, they're the stuff of magical thinking—and mere coincidences." He threw a nearby rock into the upcoming tide, a dull, sinking thud marking its descent.

Paloma edged away, feeling the grit of sand beneath her dress. "Don't you think it's possible that there's such a thing as an inner knowing we can't explain?"

"Random coincidences might make it seem that way. If you run into someone you've just thought about, you might conclude that you'd had a premonition, but statistically things like that are bound to happen."

Too exhausted to argue the point with examples that defied his pragmatism, Paloma thought about how his down-to-earth mentality was what first attracted her to him, what had made her feel safe. And she remembered, now, how much she wanted to believe him when he had explained away the visions as being a combination of her acute observational skills and plain old reasoning. According to Reed, even her high school premonition of Scott Bentley's demise was because she had probably known that his cousin was a lousy driver who took too many risks. Perhaps her brain had even registered the scent of pot wafting from his cousin's clothes without her consciously knowing. She had countered back that it still didn't explain the truck plowing into them. Reed only crossed his arms, insisting that the cousin's slow reactions probably contributed to the deadly collision.

But now his refusal to entertain even the remotest possibility of anything beyond physical fact made her feel more frustrated than soothed. She looked at the outline of his back, a curve of hunched-over worry. Not so long ago, his body had radiated upright optimism. Hoping he'd find it again, she swallowed. "We may all be more connected than you think."

"What I think is that if you live your life as honestly as you can and you're good to others, then you don't need to look further into whatever metaphysical stuff you think gives your life meaning."

"So, you don't think that it's at all possible—"

"Don't get mad, but that whole 'everybody is connected' thing isn't based on real science."

"I know it seems out there, Reed, but..." She debated whether or not she should tell him how his mother had dreamt about the latest miscarriage but thought better of it.

Reed grabbed another rock, but this time, he tossed it up in the air, caught it, and then held it fast inside his fist. "And even if premonitions could be real, what good do they do?"

"What good do they do?" Paloma gritted her teeth. Why was she so upset? Even she questioned whether or not her visions could help anyone—and hadn't they only caused her dread and shame as well?

"Look," Reed said, "this way of thinking causes a lot of unnecessary pain."

Paloma stared at the gleam of water sliding toward the sand bank. "What do you mean?"

Reed let out an irritated exhale, ignoring the question. The dank, underground odor of his sweat hit Paloma. Something was definitely upsetting him. The only other time his smell of fear had managed to seep through the sharp scent of soap and antiperspirant was when he happened to be home during her first miscarriage.

"You feeling okay?" she asked.

"I'm fine," Reed said, his tone sounding anything but.

"Don't you think it's weird that your mom and I could both be considered clairvoyant?"

"I don't think that you could exactly," he said, "call it that—"

"What's making you so scared?"

Reed shook his head. "I'm not scared. I just want us to live a normal life...to be happy."

Reed was hiding something, and it wouldn't do either of them any good if she let it pass. "What is it about your mom's dreams that makes you so defensive?"

Even in the inky lighting, she could see a sadness settle over him. She sensed his pain, too, an old sorrow that choked him, which sent a wheezy feeling into her own lungs. She tried to exhale the discomfort away as she edged closer to his side. "Tell me." She wrapped an arm around his back.

"It's so long ago…."

"What happened?"

"It has nothing to do with anything—"

"I'm your wife, Reed. Just tell me."

"It won't make a difference." Reed's body became rigid.

For a moment, neither of them said a word. Then, the call of a night heron pierced the evening air, and Paloma felt Reed's body shift.

"My mom's dreams were always bad," he whispered cautiously.

Paloma sensed that he didn't want to say it too loudly, fearful that it would wake up memories he wanted to keep asleep. "You mean she had nightmares?"

"Nightmares she couldn't control." Reed rubbed his hands together. "Nightmares that made her feel guilty, that told her she could never love again." He stood. "Come on," he said, "we should get home now."

Paloma let herself be pulled up. Before she could fully stand, she thought about how Reed's father, Richard, died. She sucked in her breath.

"What is it?" Reed asked.

"Nothing. I'm just dizzy. I need to wait here for a second." Wishing she could have known Richard, Paloma pictured how much the big-grinned man emanated warmth in the family photos displayed throughout Patsy's house.

Reed held her hand. "Take a deep breath," he told her. "It'll be okay."

"Tell me more about your mom's nightmares."

"Please don't dwell on this." Reed sighed. "It won't help." He turned and walked toward the car.

As fast as she could, she followed the dimming retreat of his light-blue shirt and finally caught up. "Reed, I want to know what happened."

"Listen," he said, "with our recent loss, it's a bad time to talk about it."

"Why?" Paloma grabbed his wrist. "Help me understand."

"I want us to put our energy into moving forward. I'm busting my ass at work so I can help us get ahead. I want both of us to start putting our focus on how we're going to have a family and real, concrete things, like how we're going to save up for the future. Getting stuck in the past won't help us get any closer to our goals. In fact, I think it'll make them that much harder to reach."

"I want those same things, too," she said. "But we may have to get there in a different way than we had envisioned."

"We can't let ourselves get defeated." He paused for a moment, clenching his jaw. "There is hope—we just have to find it."

She stared at the glints of moonshine on sea, thinking how odd it was that they looked much like sunshine reflecting off broken glass.

Reed touched her shoulder. "And," he said, "please know how much I love you."

"I love you, too, Reed." She remembered how they had once made love on this very stretch of sand under a moonless night, how tight they held each other afterwards, how she felt she was afloat on a life raft with the only person in the world who truly understood.

"We can do it." He wrapped his arm around her shoulder. "We just need to be strong."

She wanted to shout back that if he wanted to be strong, good for him. And if she wanted to fall apart and be "weak," it was her own business—and how acting brave and tough wouldn't change things anyway. But she made herself take a deep breath and tried as hard as she could to keep a rational tone. "Your mother said I should be strong, too. But that won't stop any future miscarriages."

"That doesn't..." He shook his head. "We should head home now."

Without a word more, they walked toward the black stretch of unlit street. Then, right before they were about to step off the sand, she had a sudden revelation. It slammed so hard into her brain she knew it had to be true. "Was the nightmare your mom had about your dad? Was it about his death?"

Reed stopped in his tracks.

"What is it, Reed?"

"She wouldn't have..." his voice faltered, "told you about that."

"She didn't." Paloma reached for him, but he crossed his arms. "I just guessed."

Reed leaned back, his eyes peering up at the night mist. "Listen, Paloma, we're both tired—"

"Did she feel guilty that she couldn't stop the accident—is that what you meant by her nightmares making her think that she could never love again?"

"If you really want to understand, you have to realize…" Reed bowed his head. "You wouldn't have recognized my mom before my dad died. She was a different person back then."

"A different person?"

"She was a soft-spoken, nice-to-everyone lady who never rocked the boat. It wasn't until after my dad died that she became the tough-minded woman you know."

In the murky light, Paloma looked at his downturned face. "Why haven't you ever told me this before?"

"I don't know." Reed sighed. "I just don't like to think about it."

"But it's important."

"I'm sorry." Panic sliced through Reed's words. "But you have to swear to never mention this to her."

"I won't." Paloma's neck stiffened. What the hell was so awful that it couldn't be talked about with thick-skinned Patsy?

"I didn't tell you this before because I believe it's better to leave the past where it belongs."

Paloma waited. How many times had she asked about what his dad was like only to hear him quickly change the subject after a bare-bones anecdote? How many times had she started to share details of her mother's life only to hear him say that she needed to focus on the here and now?

When he finally spoke again, his words erupted, compressed emotions that had been buried underground for so long that the only way they could emerge was to explode. "She was destroyed after my dad died. It wasn't the normal grief of losing her husband and father of her children. It was all tied into the power of her dreams—that my father, in his ignorant, bighearted way, had actually believed."

"His ignorant, bighearted way?"

"My dad was always distracted with work. If he wasn't at the office, then he was talking about it. But no matter how irrational she was about her dreams predicting the future, he believed her." Reed shook his head. "It was foolish. Very foolish."

Hoping he'd tell her everything, Paloma tried to think of the best way to keep him talking. "What do you remember?"

"Whenever she brought up the subject about how her dreams predicted the future, he'd drop everything and hang on her every word. I have to admit that she was pretty convincing in making it seem like there were some real connections there."

"Did she ever share the content of her dreams before she heard about what happened to the people she had dreamt about?"

"I think so...." Reed trailed off. But when he continued, his words grew as clear as glass. "She must have, or why else would my father have believed everything she claimed?"

Paloma scrunched her feet into the sand, the granules that had taken thousands of years to transform from rocks and shells to a fine beach carpet pressed against her soles, a reminder that no matter what had happened, it was a long time ago. But no matter how accurate Patsy's dream predictions were—or were not—the history of her dreams was still affecting Reed. For someone who thought that dwelling on the past made the present worse, maybe he pushed it down with so much force, it had scraped him raw, becoming a secret wound that couldn't stop bleeding.

"The day she told him..." Reed said, breaking off in midsentence. He took in a long, quivery breath. "When she told him that she had dreamt about his death, my dad took her so-called premonition to heart." Reed turned his face toward the ocean. "And that's what killed him."

"What are you talking about?"

A stone of silence, Reed stood stock still. Not sure if he had heard her or not, Paloma caressed his forearm. "What killed him?"

"My father was supposed to fly to Boston to go to his father's funeral." A ragged, holding-back sound emanated from the back of Reed's throat and Paloma knew that he was doing all he could not to cry. He managed to take in a breath and continued. "But my mother begged him not to go because she had a nightmare he would die there. She said it was clear as day to her that he'd perish in a gruesome car accident if he went."

Paloma felt a whole new layer of camaraderie with Patsy. "It sounded like she was really afraid for him."

"She was screaming and crying for him not to go. My father was torn because his family was expecting him—and of course he wanted to be at his father's funeral—but he put more stock in my mother's prophecies than his obligations."

Paloma paused. She knew that his father had died in a car accident while on a quick Saturday errand to pick up treats for Reed and his siblings, an ongoing tradition in which he treated them to a box of donuts after they finished their chores. On one of the rare occasions Reed shared anything about Richard, he had explained his death. It'd been a head-on collision with another driver who went the wrong way on the freeway, the oncoming traffic managing to dodge the drunk's errant truck—until the grossly inebriated man crashed his pickup right into Richard's green Plymouth. "Reed," she said, finally guessing what happened, "did your dad die the same day he was supposed to go to Boston?"

That was when Reed finally cried. She held him longer than she ever had before.

When they finally stepped off the sand, the scent of gardenia followed them all the way home.

Chapter Thirteen

A listless couple of weeks followed, during which she and Reed only talked on the surface, covering such benign subjects as whether they should hire a plumber for the leaky bathroom faucet or what movie they should watch. The miscarriage, his father's death, and anything concerning dreams and premonitions were unspoken land mines. With ever-so-wary footing, they managed to tiptoe above the most traumatic stories beneath their lives.

At the same time, communication with her father only led to evasive conversations, an inane game in which they had to jump over any squares marked relevant or emotional. And when she tried to talk to her mother-in-law, all Patsy did was apologize for having acted so overemotional and blame too many daiquiris for her "silly sentimentality." And when Paloma pushed her further about the dream concerning her last miscarriage, Patsy merely chuckled, and in her flippant, self-deprecating way scolded Paloma for taking any stock in the "drunken ramblings of a salty old broad." Paloma didn't know what to say. In the past, Patsy had always denied being affected by alcohol.

Through all this, Paloma considered phoning Justine, but every time she clicked on Justine's name, she hesitated. Since Justine hadn't made any attempt to contact her, Paloma guessed that they were going through another one of their breaks, where everything would be forgotten when they talked again. Maybe it was best not to stir things up again—and besides, she knew that Justine often got so caught up in the whirlwind of work, renovations, and parenting, that she wasn't purposely ignoring her. But, still, Paloma missed her, even if Justine's bossy, know-it-all attitude often set her teeth on edge.

The thing that hit the hardest, though, was how Serena had slipped from her life. Ever since she had stalked away after their swim, there were no longer any song bursts, beach sightings, or even a glimpse of her frantic body racing down the sidewalk. Much to Paloma's surprise, this abrupt absence not only saddened her but also stirred a strange longing. Though Serena had a strong constitution, maybe she had succumbed to the summer flu that had been making the rounds through town. Maybe that's all her absence meant.

Paloma wanted to ask Anca, who had insisted that she take even more time off work, but she knew her boss would only evade the question, as she always did whenever people asked about her elder daughter. Besides, Paloma guessed that it wasn't about Serena being ill. She was still probably angry with her for not being able to see the hallucinatory mermaids, who, in Serena's mind, were so clearly real. Paloma knew Serena well enough to wager that she thought Paloma had insulted them and so blamed Paloma for their retreat.

Uninspired, Paloma spent much of her free time plodding along the beach, hoping to run into Serena. But more often than not, she simply napped, curled up inside her muted dreams. Oftentimes she'd eat nothing but buttered noodles, tomato soup, and vanilla wafers, the comfort food from childhood and the only sustenance she could summon an appetite for. By late afternoon, she'd text Reed that if he wanted dinner, he'd have to pick up take-out, or cook something himself. Depression seemed to descend into her very marrow. She wished she could feel something more than exhaustion—even if it was as disconcerting as the fear that had coiled up inside her after Serena's withdrawal.

Paloma wrote off her malaise as an aftereffect of the miscarriage. And now she had to face the fact that she and Reed might never crawl out of their mucky standoff. Perhaps they would never become parents. Reed would never be the affectionate, fun-loving dad that he remembered his own father to be. She would never be the calm, happy mom that she'd so wished her own mother could have been. That unresolved future was much scarier than swimming with Serena under thunderous skies—yet still not as confusing as her absence. What didn't make sense, though, was why she missed Serena so much. Just a short time ago she'd been complaining about the relentless stalking and asking her father if he could help. Now she actually craved knowing that Serena would be following close behind and then hearing the sea shanties sweep through her window.

Then one morning, she woke up with a prevision tingle racing down her spine. Before she had a chance to roll out of bed, it hit. Her heart pounded as she fell under its spell. She was walking on the beach with her mother. A sharp wind blew through their hair as it whipped up whitecaps across the ocean's agitated face. Esther put her arm around her shoulder, laughing. "We both love how the wind blows all our sorrows away, don't we?" Paloma nodded. Then her mother turned to face her. "I want you to find it now." She grasped Paloma's hand so tight that it hurt, but then quickly let go. "It's time you understood." Paloma reached for her, but she suddenly flew up into the sky, her colorful blouse fluttering like a kaleidoscope of butterflies as she sailed over the sand and then out to sea.

As soon as the vision floated away, Paloma jumped out of bed and called her father. But just like before, he denied ever finding her mother's journal. She knew without a doubt, though, that even if she never found it, she'd uncover something that would bring her closer to the truth. Paloma raced to her childhood home, and when her father opened the door, he gave her a hangdog look that hovered between empathy and exacerbation.

"Dad, I don't want to stress you out, but I really want to see Mom's journal."

"You have to believe me…I never found it." He led her into the house, the very air saturating her with its years of sorrow.

"But where is everything else, all of her things? They couldn't have just disappeared." After all these years, she finally had to know—even if it would make her father's face crumble with grief.

Standing in the living room with its dark antique furniture and overbearing bookcases housing rows of heavy, out-of-date resource books and hardback classics, her father cleared his throat. Paloma waited as the wall clock's tick punctuated the silence.

Finally, he spoke. "You have to understand…" He frowned and a strange, unfocused look in his eyes made Paloma's throat ache. "It was painful—but, no, I did not give *any* of your mother's things away," he said. "I packed them in a storage facility."

"Why have you never told me this before?"

"I'm sorry. I wanted to…but I was worried…."

"I don't understand." Paloma breathed in the weary odor of the worn-out drapes and threadbare rug. "What were you worried about?"

Her father shook his head. "I don't know…."

"But her stuff can't still be in storage after all of these years."

He motioned for her to follow. Once they crossed into his study, he paused. "*Mija*, please remember how much she loved you."

"I know she did," Paloma said. "But what does that have to do with me trying to find her journal?"

Abel slowly lowered himself into his desk chair. "I just want you to remember that no matter what you do or don't remember about her, she loved you and your sister with all her heart." He pulled open a bottom drawer and rummaged around for several moments.

"Has it been in there this whole time?" Paloma leaned over to look at the contents but could only see a rubber-banded bundle of pens, a closed jar of grimy, old coins, and some faded thank you cards.

He grimaced as he grasped something in the very back. "Here it is." He held up a small key. "This will open the lock at the storage container." He stared at his hand, hesitating.

"I don't want you to be disappointed. Please know you're not going to find it. As I already told you, I had combed through it all."

She reached for the key and stowed it safely in her purse. "I know you did," she said, hoping that he had somehow missed it. Maybe it was sandwiched inside a box of clothes or even stuck between stacks of books. Regardless, it was a start. "But I want to look for myself."

⌒

She drove to the northernmost exit of Sunflower Beach and turned right, which led her straight to the storage facility. Abel had called the office ahead of time to let them know she was coming, and when she presented her license to the lone security guy at the front desk, he merely grunted. She wondered how often her father visited—if ever. Regardless, she understood why he continued to pay the fees after all these years; it must have been unbearable for him to pack all of Esther's possessions in the first place, and now it was too much of a heartbreak to hold the memories and hopes of a past that could not be changed, let alone throw any of its mementos away. Paloma walked slowly to the small garage door and stared at the lock. Her hands shook as she inserted the key. Amazingly, it clicked open right away. Wondering if her father kept the lock oiled or had actually replaced it every couple of years—which she could picture him doing—she held her breath and pulled up the door. Inside the walk-in-closet sized space, plastic boxes with dark blue lids sat neatly on top of each other.

With the nearby freeway noise, a rushing river of rubber and metal, rumbling in her ears, Paloma opened the first container. Inside was a jumbled mess of her mother's clothes: worn-out shirts, frayed bras, knee-length dresses in floral prints, and a pair of black, kitten-heeled shoes. Paloma held a pink T-shirt up to her nose and inhaled. Even through the mildew, she could smell the cigarette smoke and rose perfume of her mother. Each box was packed in the same urgent manner (which was the opposite of her father's typical, well-ordered style). There was a haphazard mound of paper containing her mother's sketches of boats and gulls; her moody, black-and-white photos of the beach; a few of Paloma's old crayon drawings; stacks of frayed paperback books and faded women's magazines. One box held a jumbled mess of mascara tubes and eyeliner pens, caked rouge, several half-used lipsticks in shades of deep red and dark burgundy, and even a plastic bag containing two ancient pieces of her and her mother's favorite candy: red licorice. But none of the boxes held the journal.

Yet there was one thing that delivered both a memory and a message. Under a pile of electronic junk was Paloma's favorite picture book. Sitting on the concrete floor, she held it to her chest and closed her eyes. Nestled on the living room couch during a spring rain when Paloma was five, Esther had read to her from this very book. At the end, Paloma burrowed even closer to her mother, staring at the picture of a bird and her new baby cocooned inside their nest. Paloma remembered how her mother carefully closed the book, how she wrapped her arm around her, just like the mother bird had draped her wing over her baby, love and protection swathing them both. For what seemed like a very long time after that, they watched the rain until it finally stopped. Then, without a word, Paloma curled herself inside her mother's arms, and they napped together in the afternoon light.

Paloma wiped her eyes. Slowly, she leafed through the book, remembering how much she'd beg her mother—and only her mother—to read it to her. Then, at the very last page, she found a folded-up piece of notebook paper. Telling herself that it was probably just some random doodle, she opened it. Scribbled in her mother's tiny but firm handwriting were the words: "Tell Tillie and…that I'm innocent." After the word "and" was another word, most likely another name, that had been violently scratched out.

Paloma's hand flew to her chest. What in the world could her mother have meant by that? And who in the world was Tillie—and why was the other name scribbled out? Paloma refolded the note and tucked it away in her wallet. In a cold sweat, she shoved all the containers back into their allotted spaces. She pulled the door shut and locked it, shaking her head. What the hell was she supposed to do with such an unnerving message? As she drove away, though, she told herself that there was nothing she should—or could—do with it, as it was merely an artifact of Esther's paranoia.

Chapter Fourteen

~

Minutes after Paloma arrived home, someone pounded on the door. She ducked into the kitchen, hoping that whoever it was would leave. But then the doorbell rang with an urgency that was hard to ignore. Yet she stood stock still as it rang several more times. When it finally stopped, her cell dinged. It was Tatiana. Paloma picked up, sure that Tatiana was wanting to trade an upcoming shift with her.

"I'm at your door." Tatiana's voice caught, and Paloma could tell that she was holding back from crying. "You home?"

"Sorry, I didn't know it was you." Tatiana had shown up at her doorstep a number of times in the past, always due to yet another battle with Anca about some overblown rule or restriction. Paloma went to the door and let Tatiana in without either of them saying a word. Taking a deep breath, Paloma prepared to walk the balance between understanding and neutrality. Even though Tatiana could be rebellious, Anca was way too strict. So strict, in fact, that her seventeen-year-old daughter wasn't even allowed to date yet.

Tatiana headed straight for the living room and collapsed on the sofa. She grabbed a pillow and held it against her stomach.

"I take it you and your mom had another fight?" Paloma settled on a nearby chair, thinking about her own mother and wondering what their relationship would have been like if Esther had lived long enough to see her through her teenage years.

"We did, but that's not why I need to talk." Tatiana picked at her pinky finger's cuticle, drawing a thin line of blood. "I don't know what to do."

"What is it?"

"I took a pregnancy test today." Tatiana's eyes watered as she gripped the pillow. "It's positive."

"What?" Paloma couldn't have heard right.

Tatiana stared at the floor. "I'm pregnant."

Paloma rushed over and sat next to her. She held Tatiana's hand, honored that the young teen trusted her with this delicate news. "Are you sure?"

"I'm sure."

"How far along?" Paloma studied Tatiana's face, still not quite believing.

"Far enough to know that the test is right."

"What does your mom think?"

Tatiana yanked her hand back. "Why are you asking me what my mom thinks? It's my body. I'm the one who has to live with whatever happens."

"You're right, Tatiana. It is up to you." Paloma's chest ached. "Just give yourself some time to think...."

Tatiana hunched over, hiding her face in her hands. "The thing is, I know I want to be a mom someday."

"I understand how hard this must be."

"But I want to go to art school. I want to live my own life. "If I have a baby..." Tatiana shuddered. "I'll be stuck forever."

"You won't be stuck…but your life will change." Paloma took in a painful, achy breath. "No matter what, you can make it work…."

"Easy for you to say." Tatiana stood. She stared at Paloma, her face reddening as she cracked her knuckles. "Bet you never had to make this kind of choice."

Paloma's heart clenched, but she told herself how fearful and out-of-control Tatiana must be feeling, that no matter how insensitive her words had been, Paloma couldn't take them personally. "No, I haven't had that choice." Paloma sighed. "But I do know life is full of compromises—and beauty, too, if you let it in." She got up and embraced Tatiana, who leaned her head against her shoulder, even though her back remained rigid. "Just remember…" Paloma whispered, "It may feel like the end of your world—but it could be a whole new beginning."

⌒

The next day, Paloma stepped into the florist shop. She rubbed the back of her neck, bracing herself for Anca's reaction. Thankful, though, to be enveloped in the cool, fragrant air of her workplace, Paloma tied her apron around her waist, wrangled her hair up in a bun, and strode up to the workstation to check orders. As soon as she saw her boss, she stopped in her tracks. Anca's eyes were tight and glittery, and her lips set in a thin line of anger. Paloma understood right away that no matter what Tatiana decided, Anca would take it upon herself to "make things right." Not sure what Tatiana had told Anca—and if Anca had been informed that Paloma already knew—she merely asked: "What is it?"

"My Tatiana has gotten herself into big trouble." Anca flung a bunch of mini carnations on the worktable and then vigorously cut the cotton twine holding them together.

Paloma patted Anca's arm, trying to soothe her frayed emotions. "Whatever it is—"

"It is something that should never have happened." Anca shook her head. She stared at the worktable and whispered, "The girl is pregnant."

"You must be in shock, Anca, but—"

"She wasn't even allowed to date…I just don't understand how she could have been so reckless." Anca bowed her head in her hands, crying.

"It'll be okay." Worried that Anca might have shamed Tatiana, Paloma wished she could step in without alienating mother or daughter.

"I know she is a girl with her own mind, but I didn't think she would have allowed this to happen."

Paloma wondered how honest Tatiana had been with her mother. "What does she want to do?"

"She wants to make a bad choice—a very bad choice." A now tearless Anca looked at Paloma, her stony face resolute. "And I cannot let her."

The room seemed to tilt sideways, and Paloma realized she needed to breathe. "What do you mean?"

"She wants to have it."

Utterly surprised, Paloma was sure she had heard wrong. Just yesterday, the teen had no idea what to do—and, besides, a "bad choice" in Anca's eyes would surely have meant the opposite. "She wants to have the baby?"

Anca's clippers fell from her hand and thudded to the floor. She slowly bent down to pick them up, and when she stood, tears welled up in her eyes again. "She's only seventeen. She doesn't know what will happen to her. I cannot…" Anca gripped the clippers so tight that her knuckles turned white. "…I cannot allow her to go through with this."

For a moment, Paloma let herself imagine what it would be like if she and Reed adopted Tatiana's baby. But then her stomach plummeted. What Anca was thinking was more immediate. "What do you mean?"

"She needs her art, Paloma."

Paloma frowned. Had Anca forgotten that she only recently complained about how Tatiana didn't understand how difficult an artist's life would be? But she didn't dare bring that up now. "What about the father?" It was a question that had woken her up in the middle of the night and one she kicked herself for not asking Tatiana herself.

"He's just a young boy from school who's probably just as confused as she is. She needs to see a doctor. She needs to listen to her options."

"Yes, she is very young…." Paloma hoped that Tatiana would open up to her again. "How is Leonardo taking this?"

"Leonardo?" Anca shook her head. "Tatiana is his baby girl. He doesn't need to know."

"But—"

"He'd be devastated." With that, Anca blew her nose and then angrily snipped several inches from the bottom of a clenched handful of gypsophila.

Paloma was unable to move. She stared at the cheerful yellow-and white-arrangement Anca was working on. As her thoughts ranged from the early tragedies of her kidnapped sister and mentally ill mother to the three miscarriages within the last three years, Paloma drew in a sharp breath. "If she's adamant about having the baby, what about adoption?"

"That would be too hard on her."

Paloma wondered if Anca meant that it would be too hard for herself as well. It had to be heartbreaking to think about her daughter's infant being whisked away into the arms and hearts of another family. But what about Tatiana's feelings? "If she wants to have her baby, what can you do?"

"No one is talking about force, Paloma." Anca gave her a cut-glass look that made Paloma wish she could still be hibernating on her couch, deaf to the world and all the complicated people in it. "I am her mother, and no one knows her better than I do. I can make her understand what is best for her."

"But I—" The floor vibrated beneath Paloma's feet. She grabbed Anca's arm. "Are we having an earthquake?"

Anca's eyes went wide. "No…" Anca waited another moment. "I didn't feel anything." She stared at Paloma. "You look like you're going to be sick." Anca touched Paloma's forehead with motherly concern.

"I'm okay, I think…." Paloma's heart raced. She held her hand to a fierce, scorching heat radiating from her chest. A violent buzzing hissed inside her head. Then without any warning, she was whisked outside her own body, a sudden flight that separated her mind from her physical being. Terrified, she tried to make sense of what was going on. This had never happened before. She had to be hallucinating. That's what it was. Exhaustion and stress had created a crazy, momentary reaction. But when she looked down at her collapsed form lying on the floor, she grew even more fearful. What was happening?

Anca crouched next to Paloma's body, and then looked up. Could Anca somehow see her hovering up there? But Anca quickly turned her attention back to Paloma's limp form sprawled on the work floor. Desperate to reunite with her body, Paloma struggled without any effect. Horrified, Paloma wondered if she was, indeed, going crazy. She had heard of out-of-body episodes, but this was too sudden, too real. It certainly wasn't anything like the meditative state she'd read about. Then, before another thought could enter her head, she flew straight out the ceiling, feeling as if her body had somehow shot through a layer of wet floral foam. She continued her flight over the building and with a dizzying speed, found herself above the ocean.

For an astonishing moment, absolute bliss blew through her. A pure calm, it showed her that everything in this insane world was heading to a place of serenity, a place that made sense once you got to the end. Floating in the clearest of skies, she wished Reed could experience this with her. But even if that were possible, he'd still explain it away until all that was left was doubt.

Then something made her look down. A swimmer was maneuvering through the ocean's rough surface. When Paloma willed herself closer, she saw it was Serena. At least a half-mile offshore, shiny, brown-skinned Serena was swimming farther out to sea with the determined stroke of someone who knew where she was going. With a brisk wind whipping through her hair, Paloma again willed herself toward Serena. As Serena continued to forge her way through the choppy Pacific, she remained seemingly unaware of Paloma's presence.

Yet the second after Paloma thought this, Serena stopped mid stroke and looked up. "I see you, Paloma." Treading water, Serena kept staring. "You think I can't. You think you're invisible, but I can see you. I can—" A gust of wind interrupted her. She took an audible breath. "You miss me so much you want to cry," Serena screamed, both rage and sadness piercing every syllable. "Well, my dear, so do I. So do I."

Such a weighted sorrow filled Paloma that she was afraid she was going to drop right out of the sky and drown under the very sea that had always buoyed her. She had no idea why Serena's words hit so hard. But then again, why should anything make sense to a woman floating in the air? Worried that she *really* had metamorphized into an ethereal form, Paloma checked herself over. She sighed with relief when she saw that her arms and hands and legs appeared as normal and solid as ever—even if her physical body was still waiting inside Anca's shop. She even noticed the same loose thread hanging from the end of her sleeve she had meant to snip off that morning. Yet this couldn't be real. She squeezed her eyes shut but when she opened them, she was still a woman lighter than air.

"That's right, my dear Paloma. You're up in the sky. Up in the sky, you will be by and by." Serena's shouting, now shrill as the shriek of a gull, made Paloma wonder if she could somehow prove to herself that this was really happening.

Then an abrupt charge in the air jolted her back into her solid form. She awakened with her head cradled in Anca's hands. With the cool linoleum against her back, Paloma stared mutely at Anca's face.

"Are you okay?" Her eyes wide with concern, Anca peered at her. "You fell to the floor, but I caught you before you hit your head."

It took Paloma a moment to find her words, her thoughts blurry and out of reach. "Did I faint?"

"Perhaps that is all it was," Anca whispered, her face still etched with worry. "Let me look into your eyes."

Paloma nodded and allowed Anca to check her pupils.

"They are the same size; that is good." Anca shook her head, though. "But you need to see a doctor."

"How long…" Paloma scrambled for the right words, "… was I out?"

"Only moments." Anca's eyebrows furrowed. "But to me, it felt like hours."

"Moments?" There was no way all that had happened in such a short time. "Did I say anything? Do anything?"

Anca pursed her lips. "No. You did not."

"You can tell me the truth—"

"I said no and I meant it, dove." Anca's face softened. "You don't need to worry."

Paloma wasn't sure what to believe, but knew it wasn't worth pushing Anca into a corner. Besides, Anca had never lied to her before, so why would she now? Then she realized that she hadn't even acknowledged Anca's help. "Thank you for catching me."

"Of course." Anca nodded.

Paloma gave her a weak smile. Then she pictured Serena's matter-of-fact response to Paloma's out-of-body form. Was it possible it really happened? "Do you know where Serena is right now?"

Anca smoothed back the wisps of Paloma's hair that had escaped from her bun. "Come now, let me help you up." She gently laid Paloma's head on the floor and then, with a grimace, stood.

"I'm fine," Paloma said, although she felt as limp and defenseless as a rag doll.

"No, I need to help you. It is not right for you to get up by yourself after something like that."

Paloma trembled. Anca offered her hand, an open palm filled with intricate lines like the veins on the underside of a leaf.

Not at all surprised by Anca's strength, Paloma let herself be pulled up. But when she stood, she realized that her body had not quite settled in itself. She grabbed the edge of the workstation, unable to move. Then it came to her. What if this was a sign of complete mental descent? What if she *had* inherited her mother's schizophrenia?

"Do you really think that I just fainted?"

"Don't worry, Paloma. You'll be fine," Anca said. "Just fine." Anca patted her shoulder. "But you're not ready to go back to work yet. You need to go home and rest more." She muttered something under her breath.

"What did you say?"

Fear darkened the worry lines between Anca's brows. "Nothing. You must see your doctor and take more time off work."

Dizzy and exhausted, Paloma swallowed. "What about Tatiana?" Without thinking, she yanked off the loose thread dangling from her sleeve and eyed it before letting go. She watched its slow descent and waited for Anca's reply.

Anca shook her head. "Do not concern yourself with Tatiana right now."

"But I am concerned, Anca." She pushed her shoulders back. "I can't help but be."

"You must remember that you are not her mother." Anca faced her, jaw set and eyes so shielded that all Paloma could do was walk away.

Chapter Fifteen

Paloma sank into the couch. Maybe if she fell asleep, she could forget everything that had just happened. But as soon as she burrowed under a pillow, fear knuckled down on her. She slowly got up, trying to stave off the anxiety. She paced the living room. Was she losing her mind? Her ongoing visions where one thing. But now she was flying out of her body. It was all too bizarre. Had this same thing happened to her mother before she lost it? Paloma clenched her hands against her sides. Perfectly sane people sometimes experienced insanely strange phenomena.

She opened the sliding door, stepped onto the deck, and closed her eyes against the afternoon's heat. She stood waiting for something that she could not name. For a moment, everything around her went still. Then the scent of gardenia drifted through the air. Though she could hear nothing but the rustle of nearby palm fronds, she knew Serena was close. But she wasn't quite ready to open her eyes, the memory of unexpected bliss during her out-of-body experience whispered against her skin like a feather of hope. Finally, she allowed herself to look down at the sidewalk.

"Mermaids are only part women," Serena sang up to her. "The other half is of the sea. Of the sea." A fierce challenge in Serena's eyes made her gaze appear more otherworldly than usual. "But you and I already know this is part of who we were, who we are…and who we'll be. Who we will be."

"Serena!" A rush of relief made Paloma's heart jump. "Don't go anywhere. I'll be right down."

Paloma bolted out her condo and raced onto the sidewalk, relieved to see the very person whom she had wanted to push away such a short time ago. For a moment neither of them said a word, Serena, no doubt, in shock from Paloma's unusual display of excitement in seeing her. She hoped Serena had forgiven her for not believing in mermaids. "I'm glad to see you."

Serena stared at her. "You are as alone and as deserted inside as I am," she sang. "As alone and deserted as me. But you need to be. You need to be." She paused, holding her arms up in the air, emphasizing her point with a triumphant shake of fists. "But my little Tatiana is not alone. She is not alone, not alone at all."

Paloma held her hand over her stomach. Did Serena know that Tatiana was pregnant—and that Paloma had miscarried? Uncannily perceptive, Serena had seemed to guess at many of Paloma's thoughts throughout the years. "Why do you say that, Serena?"

"You know why," Serena said. "But you know many things that others do not. You know you do. You know."

Then Paloma remembered how Serena had acknowledged her during her out-of-body flight. "Were you swimming in the ocean earlier today?" She studied Serena's hair, but the dark, tangled curls always looked as if she had just emerged from the ocean.

"Of course I was. I swim and I swim and I swim. I swim so far that you wouldn't believe where I've been. Or what I've seen. What I've seen, seen, seen." Serena gave her a sly smile.

"But did you see me, Serena? You acted like…" She watched Serena's eyes widen. *Was* it possible?

Serena threw her head back and laughed, exposing the dark grit between her teeth. Then, too abruptly, she stopped. She peered at Paloma with a fixed stare, her eyes glistening with anger. "You would not believe in mermaids with me. You would not believe."

"I'm sorry." An overwhelming urge to hug Serena came over Paloma, but she was sure Serena would jerk away. She splayed her hands out in apology. "I wanted to wait with you when we were out swimming, but the lightning made it too dangerous."

"Waiting and believing are very, very, very different things." Serena spat on the sidewalk. "Waiting just says you don't know what's going to happen. Believing is knowing that it will. That it will."

Paloma clasped her hands and watched Serena's face darken. What could she say to keep Serena from bolting again? Serena stood now with her arms straight at her sides. Her usual shirt had been replaced with a tank top sporting a surfboard company's logo of a curled wave. The latest item of clothing, Paloma was sure, that Serena had nabbed off someone's beach towel, thinking it was the newest gift from her mermaid mother. "Please know how very sorry I am," Paloma said as she watched Serena's body quiver.

"I don't know if I should forgive you." Serena crossed her arms.

"I didn't mean to make you mad," Paloma said. "I mean…" She paused. A pair of crows passed overhead, their flight as determined-looking as Serena's gaze. "I want to believe in mermaids with you." Paloma hoped Serena would trust her apology. In a way, she really did want to believe in mermaids. It'd be nice—liberating, even—to believe in something so magical. To trust that there was different life right below the surface.

"I don't know if I should bother. Should I? I think not. I think not, not, not."

"Please do. Please forgive me," Paloma pleaded. She locked eyes with her elderly neighbor, Virginia. The eighty-plus-year-old woman stared at her in panic. Virginia was particularly fearful of Serena, always shambling out of her way as fast as her arthritic body could move in order to avoid any contact, while covering her mouth and nose as though Serena's mental condition were an airborne infection that could be caught. Virginia froze on her walkway and gaped at them.

Virginia's head shook as she yelled at Serena. "You get on home, now. Go on, get."

Paloma glared at Virginia. Even though she had defended Serena in the past when others had been less than kind, she'd never felt such overpowering anger at the offender. The old woman's demeanor reminded her too much of the ignorant remarks she'd had to endure about her mother's mental illness—especially the times when people gossiped about the possibility of her mother's guilt regarding Annie's disappearance. "Don't you dare talk to her like that!" Paloma continued to stare at Virginia. "She's a person. You need to respect her."

Virginia froze. "I..." she sputtered.

Serena winked at Paloma. "You see, she's a scared little rat. You see, she's the kind that never wants to believe. She only wants to see what's in her TV. That is all she can see, see, see."

With bugged-out eyes and an open-mouthed gasp, Virginia looked so horrified that Paloma was afraid she was going to keel over in her nearby cactus garden. Just as Paloma was wondering if she should try to assist Virginia back to her decrepit little hovel (that is, if the terrified old woman would let her), Virginia managed to get ahold of herself, hobbling away as fast as she could.

"You do not want to be that kind of dead woman living in a dead world." The singsong quality had flowed back into Serena's voice. "You need to believe. You need to be free to believe. And then believe again."

Paloma watched Virginia make her way toward her front door. No, she didn't want to become a bitter old woman who never believed in what could be.

Cocking her head, Serena studied Paloma. "My sister's going to have a little one," she sang, her tone sweeter than anything Paloma had ever heard warbling from her mouth. "This little lass will be of the sea just like you and me. You'll see. You'll see."

Serena *did* know her little sister was pregnant. "Did Tatiana tell you she's going to have a baby?" For some odd reason, hearing Serena say it made it that much more real.

Serena merely winked again.

"Serena, listen to me." Paloma tried to make eye contact, but Serena kept her gaze on the sidewalk. "How do you know that your sister is having a baby?" If Tatiana went so far as to tell Serena, then the girl *was* dead set on keeping her baby. Tatiana had always pushed Serena as far away from her life as she could, remaining civil yet aloof, never indulging in the usual sibling banter or sisterly teasing. Paloma was sure, too, that Tatiana never shared anything close to a secret with her big sister.

"I just know." Serena then went into electrocution mode, her body jerking in such an alarming way that anyone who didn't know her would guess she was having a seizure. Paloma knew better than to try and intervene, but still reassured her that all was going to be okay.

As Serena continued to twitch about, Paloma clasped her hands together. After a few strangled moments, it was finally over. With a shuddery breath, Serena held up her head, and Paloma saw tears in her eyes. "Please let me help you," Paloma said, venturing a quick graze of her hand on Serena's wrist.

Serena jerked away and turned with such a look of sadness weighing on her ragged form that Paloma's eyes stung. She watched Serena walk away as the day's heat rose off the sidewalk, the same heat that had to have been burning through the calluses on Serena's bare feet.

Chapter Sixteen

Not sure what to do or where to go next, Paloma inhaled the humid air. Finally she decided to head to the beach. It seemed the only place she'd be able to keep her head above the incoming wave of depression.

Once on the sand, she took off her sandals and strode past where surfers and sunbathers gathered. She ambled down the coast until she reached her spot. A small cove strewn with the smoothest of rocks and pebbles, it remained an isolated inlet which she had often run off to when she was a child. She smiled at the clumps of sunflowers growing at the base of the cliff. When she was a little girl, a massive storm saturated the field above, causing the edge of a sunflower farm to tumble down the bluff. Ever since then, beach sunflowers reseeded at the bottom of the cliff every year, their bright-yellow petals a contrast against the gray rocks. Paloma crossed sunbaked stones to the nearest bunch of flowers and touched her nose to one of their faces. It smelled of earth and honey.

She turned her back on the flowers and sat on the largest rock she could find. Warmth permeated the cotton folds of her skirt as she watched the ocean. Would she ever be able to share this place with her own child? But what about Tatiana's future? Paloma wondered how the teen had reacted to her mother's pleas to end her pregnancy. Any way about it, it was going to be rough. If Tatiana listened to her mother, would regret follow her the rest of her life? If she had the child, would she yearn for freedom? And if she let her baby be adopted, could that lead to regret—and yearning as well?

But if they could agree upon an open adoption from the beginning, it could work out for everyone. The child could grow up knowing that Tatiana was her birth mother, who made a tough but loving decision. Tatiana could visit the child whenever she wanted, Anca and Leonardo could act as grandparents—along with Patsy and, of course, Abel. And then there'd be the wonderful gaggle of aunts, uncles, and cousins from Reed's side of the family. In fact, this baby could enjoy a future in which she would not only grow up but also thrive in a childhood filled with the love and attention of a big, extended family.

Maybe Anca would realize that it'd be okay if Tatiana decided to go through with her pregnancy, that everything would work out in the end. With hope expanding her lungs, Paloma noticed a pod of dolphins playing offshore. Flipping in and out of the water, they appeared as joyful as her fantasized future.

Yet her body became rigid. If she stayed a moment longer, she might jinx everything. She stood like a sentinel on the rock she'd been sitting on. This was the fear-based thinking that often seized her happiness. The grief counselor she had seen after her mother died referred to it as magical thinking. It was after she shared how she had made a habit of blinking her eyes exactly eight times before grabbing her backpack to go to school for fear that if she didn't, something horrible would happen. Paloma knew at the time that it didn't make sense—and she knew enough not to share it with Justine—but this one simple act gave her a sense of control. Eventually, with the therapist's help, her ten-year-old self learned to replace her obsessive actions with positive thoughts.

Paloma's stomach tightened. But was magical thinking really such a bad thing to succumb to sometimes? Didn't most people want to hold some sort of talisman in their emotional pocket? And it was a hard thing to ignore—especially when it struck as hard as it sometimes did for her. She stepped from the rock onto to the sand. When an unexpected spray from the crash of a shore breaker splattered her skirt, she looked toward the ocean again.

Though it was irrational, she couldn't shake the dread. If she left right now, then she might be able to evade it. But this type of magical thinking was unhealthy. She squinted against the glare. The sleek creatures cut in and out of the surface between air and sea. Then she saw it again. The same translucent-green tail appeared for a split second, just like it had when she had been in the ocean with Serena.

Fear surged through her. She swallowed. It had to have been her imagination. The shimmer of sunlight on water combined with the desire to believe had made her see something that wasn't there. She waited, vigilant as a hawk eyeing its next meal. Her vision blurred, but she kept her gaze straight and unblinking through the glittering light. When the dolphins finally moved on, she figured that whatever she had seen—or thought she had seen—had left as well.

Paloma walked back up the beach as she tried to make sense of it all. Her father used to explain away her visions when she was young. The subconscious mind, he said, picked up on things one did not even notice taking in. She was an empathetic soul, he'd say in his quiet, thoughtful tone, an empathetic soul with a creative mind who turned both her own and other's feelings into images. And when she was even younger, he also calmed her down by telling her that the fleeting hallucinations were due to her vivid imagination, an overactive imagination, which he assured her she'd grow out of.

Then there was Justine who preached that Paloma's visions were "negative blocks" she needed to get rid of. And finally, she met Reed, who thought that "so-called" premonitions were the byproduct of mere coincidences. She shook her head. Maybe all three of them were right—or maybe all of them were wrong.

She continued on until she came to a sandy part of the beach, where a few scattered sunbathers lay before a calm inlet. Exhausted, she dropped onto the dry sand. She closed her eyes and recalled her mother-in-law's premonition about Reed's father dying in a car accident if he had gone to his father's funeral in Boston, and how she had stopped him from going—only to have him die in a head-on collision miles from home. Was Richard meant to perish at that time in his life? And if life was based on fate, then what were any of us here for? Did anything in this life matter in the long run?

Paloma held her hand against her belly. Her stomach suddenly cramped. She massaged the pain, wondering where the spirits—if there were such things—of her three would-be children were now and what they would have been like if they had made it to this world.

Once again, she caught herself. She had to follow Reed's advice and move forward. Reed was a practical man. He also loved her—and she loved him. If she could push through this, their future might work. With time, she could make him understand that adopting Tatiana's baby would not only be their answer, but also Tatiana's. After Tatiana graduated high school, she could escape Sunflower Beach to study art, and her talent would not be lost. In fact, Paloma was impressed with the teenager's style. At the high school art fair the previous year, Tatiana's paintings of the town and people milling through it looked like something you'd see in a high-end gallery.

One of her most poignant pieces was a painting of Pacific Street with a lone woman walking up the sidewalk. Even from behind, she looked like a combination of Serena, with her scraggly clothes, and Paloma, with her auburn hair. Paloma couldn't stop staring at the image. When she asked who the woman was, Tatiana merely shrugged, saying it was whoever Paloma wanted her to be. Thinking about the rueful slant of the woman's head, Paloma wondered what had been on Tatiana's mind when she had painted it.

Paloma fought back an inexplicable urge to cry. She had to rein in her emotions. She had to stay grounded. Even though Tatiana was young, maybe she really did want to keep her baby. It was foolish to daydream about adoption, selfish to even bring it up. She had to stop fantasizing of what could be and face reality. Then, without any warning, a silver-gray pattern that looked like a shimmering wall hung like a net between sand and sea. Although there wasn't a cloud in sight, nor an impending fog bank, it intensified.

Although it didn't make sense, the image seemed as real as her own thumping heart. In awe, Paloma studied the shiny pattern of light. But whatever it was, perhaps it was merely due to ordinary science. A few years back, she had watched a TV show that explained away all sorts of so-called phenomena. It described how the rare combination of weather and geographical anomalies made people think they were witnessing shadows of angels on distant hills and UFOs in the clouds. When she saw the footage, she could see why people believed these sightings were otherworldly—until the mere reality of their own magnified shadows and reflected car lights were explained.

She scanned the beach again. Someone else had to have taken notice. But even the beachgoers who weren't napping or reading but gazing directly at the horizon acted as though nothing out of the ordinary was happening. Paloma studied the colors of ocean and sand. Though she still could make out the silver-tinted net, everything around her was bathed in the yellow hues of normal sunshine.

Just when she decided that it was all too much and she'd better get home to collect herself, it shimmered so brightly she had to cover her eyes. Then, without warning, it was gone. She stood.

Telling herself that she'd better stay in the here and now, Paloma hiked up the sides of her skirt and began to jog over the sand. She'd make a doctor's appointment as soon as she got home. But when the tide washed over her feet, she stopped. She knew there wasn't anything physically wrong with her. It wasn't a brain tumor. Either she was going through something extraordinary or the schizophrenia that had flooded her mother with hallucinations was now claiming her.

Struggling for breath, she slowed down. Then a faint image of a person flickered on the outskirts of her vision. She tried to ignore it. Determined to see only what was right in front of her, she stalked up the beach, but the unformed figure followed her with a familiar persistence she could not shake. She stopped, hands gripping each other. She held her breath, trying to will it away. Yet it only ventured closer. In shock, Paloma watched as the image materialized into the woman who had brought forth equal amounts of love, loyalty—and despair.

Paloma's heart clutched. "Mom?" she heard herself whisper.

"I'm here, my darling girl."

Paloma swallowed. She reached toward her mother, but Esther evaporated. She pulled her arm away, and her mother came back. For several surreal moments, Paloma waited, her heart thudding so hard it was all she could hear.

Finally, her mother's voice reached her again. "I miss you." She could feel her mother's feelings, too, a mix of love and a strange emotion that was halfway between regret and peace.

Could she be experiencing something outside of everything that made sense? It was all so real. Regardless of all her lifelong visions—including her latest extraordinary out-of-body experience—seeing her mother hit the hardest. This apparition's need for connection, a bright heat that shot right through her chest, was as palpable as the sun's warmth on her shoulders. "I miss you, too, Mom." And in that moment, Paloma realized just how much she missed her mother, how her heart continued to ache for her since she had died.

Esther smiled, but her eyes were just as forlorn as when she cooed her long-ago lullabies to young Paloma. "I may not have much time here," she said, her smile fading. "I want to help you understand your miscarriages."

Paloma stepped closer, clasping her hands together. "Please. I want to."

Esther's image wavered. "All I can say right now is that I'm sorry." Her gaze was so adamant that Paloma imagined her mother was looking straight inside her. "So very, very sorry, my darling girl."

"I don't want you to be sorry." The need to be a child cradled in her mother's arms overpowered her. Sensing that Esther knew this, Paloma swore she could taste the red licorice candy her mother used to give her every time she visited. She held her tears, wishing she could go back in time and rewrite her mother's history—their whole family's tragic loss. "I thought of you every time I miscarried."

"I know."

And then, like a surprise punch to the gut, Paloma was certain that she knew something else, too. It had been her mother. Each loss had been her. All three of her miscarriages were the times her mother had tried to come back to her. Right before each and every one, Paloma was sure she had caught a whiff of her mother's rose perfume, tasted red licorice on her tongue, and even dreamt the night before of their last visit, when Esther pressed a hand over her own chest while grasping Paloma's hand, telling her that she'd see her again in her next life.

"But why?" Paloma asked. "Why did you try all those times only to go away?" To where, Paloma had no idea. But it must have been painful.

"No, my Paloma, it didn't hurt." Her smile was so beatific Paloma believed her. "Sometimes you have control over what happens. Sometimes you don't—even here. Each time I tried to come back to you, something outside of myself yanked me back again." Surprisingly, her smile widened. "Maybe it's because there's someone else you're supposed to connect with."

"Someone else I'm supposed to connect with?"

"It'll be okay, I promise you," Esther said. "You will find this connection—and your happiness."

Paloma wished she could grab her mother's hand, could hold on to this woman she never fully knew. "I love you, Mom." The words didn't come from her mouth but exploded with an animal-like ferocity from her heart.

"My darling Paloma, I love you, too."

"I know." Paloma said out loud. "I know you love me."

In the next instant, her mother was gone.

Paloma turned. Under an ordinary blue sky, she walked home, sorrow and loss and hope following on her heels like physical entities.

Chapter Seventeen

For a whole week after her mother's apparition had appeared—and then vanished, Paloma waited. But nothing happened. She didn't have any out-of-body experiences, witness any silver-netted skies, encounter any dead relatives, or even receive any visions. As another week passed, she told herself that she had pushed through the emotional stew that had somehow brought on the bizarre phenomena. Then one day she woke up, convinced that it was time to toss out the past and accept the future, time to get out of her own head and help Tatiana.

It was an alarmingly hot Thursday. She pushed herself up from the couch. It couldn't wait another day—or moment. She checked the time and flew out the condo. Tatiana would be on her way to work. Ignoring the pounding heat, Paloma ran up Pacific Street. Her sandals thudded against the sidewalk in an urgent rhythm that made her run even faster. A block away from the florist shop, she spotted Tatiana with a young surfer boy she recognized from the beach. They were holding hands as they sauntered down the sidewalk. Paloma froze. Could this sweet, gangly kid, whom she seen pick up trash from the beach before he hit the surf and who made sure to always bring food and water for his black lab (who faithfully waited as he watched the boy skillfully maneuver the waves), be the father of Tatiana's baby? How could she talk to Tatiana in front of him—a mere boy who may or may not be the father, and who may or may not know about the pregnancy. Tatiana spotted her before Paloma could figure out what to do.

"Hey, Paloma!" Tatiana grinned.

Paloma took in a ragged breath and walked up to them. Since Tatiana didn't say a word more, Paloma introduced herself to the boy.

He ducked his head shyly, but his smile was as bright as sunlight. "I'm Marcel."

It's nice to meet you." She turned to Tatiana. "Can we talk?"

"Can it wait? I'm heading to work."

"It can't wait—and it's personal." Paloma fixed her gaze on Marcel.

Tatiana cleared her throat. "Whatever you want to say to me, you can say in front of him."

"It's okay," said Marcel. "I'll see you after work."

"I'm going to miss you," Tatiana said, stroking his arm.

Paloma bit her lip as she recalled how her sixteen-year-old heart would jump into her throat at the slightest touch of her boyfriend, how they had spent endless hours hunting for sea glass together, how his toothy smile made her want to cry. How overpowering young love could be. How amazingly tender, too.

Tatiana glanced at Paloma, a flash of embarrassment in her eyes. But when she looked back at Marcel, her gaze melted into adoration.

He hooked a finger in Tatiana's front pocket and stared back at her. "Remember what I told you."

Tatiana nodded, beaming.

"I'm here." He held his other hand over his heart. They hugged goodbye, and then he walked up the sidewalk, sun-bleached tips of his kinky, burnt-orange hair creating a halo.

Tatiana and Paloma were left facing each other, a dense silence between them.

Paloma's hands shook, her nervousness visible, which she knew would only make Tatiana that much more guarded. Angry at her own agitation, Paloma gritted her teeth. But she would not turn back. "I want to help." Her words shook more than her hands.

Neither of them said a word. Passersby skirted around them. Paloma waited.

Finally, Tatiana drew in a deep breath. "I don't need anyone else telling me what to do. My mom has already been lecturing me nonstop."

"She's just worried about you, Tatiana. She wants to make sure you understand all the—"

"I'm going to keep my baby." Now, it was Tatiana's words that shook. "And before you ask, Marcel *is* the father."

Paloma held up her hands, hoping Tatiana wasn't basing this life-altering decision solely on rebellion. "I'm not trying to change your mind." Paloma paused as she grabbed for the right words. "But what if your mom was telling you that you *had* to keep this baby? You don't have to answer me—just think about it."

"Paloma!" Tatiana shook her head. "I'm smarter than that. I'm not going to have a baby just to go against my mom."

"What about art school?"

"Wasn't it you who told me I could work it all out?"

Paloma nodded, not sure what to say.

Tatiana smiled now. "And...didn't you also say that it *is* up to me?"

"It's just that this will be one of the biggest decisions of your life—"

"Marcel and I have already worked it out. We're going to live together as soon as we graduate. He already makes good money as a surfboard shaper. Then, in a couple of years, I'll go to art school."

Paloma looked away. Who was she to stomp all over Tatiana's plans—even if they were the daydreams of the young and inexperienced? "Have you seen a doctor yet?"

"I have to get to work...."

"You don't have to do this alone."

"I'm not. I have Marcel." Tatiana jutted her chin out, but at the same time her eyes welled up.

Then before she knew what she was doing, Paloma asked if she could go with her to her doctor's appointment. She clasped her hands, begging, but then caught herself. Her emotions were running away with her. She had better back off. "But I understand if you want to go with Marcel."

"We haven't talked about it yet." Tatiana stared at the sidewalk.

"I respect your relationship. And he seems like a good guy, but maybe it'd be nice for you to have someone else in your corner as well."

"I guess so."

"Just think about it."

Tatiana studied her and then pulled her shoulders back and grinned. Paloma smiled back, relieved to see Tatiana's old self-confidence shine through.

"Even if I let you help me, you have to remember..." Tatiana wagged a finger at her. "This is *my* life."

"Yes, of course it is." Paloma nodded. "I understand."

Chapter Eighteen

Paloma stood at the workstation powering out a luscious centerpiece for a thirtieth-anniversary gala. Even though Anca and Tatiana hadn't spoken more than a couple of sentences to each other, the three of them worked as a team, steadily building arrangement after arrangement with white Polar Star roses, Casa Blanca lilies, and French Vanilla snapdragons. Soothed by both the intoxicating scents and the hours of intense concentration, Paloma wished everything in life could turn out so sweet. When they were finally done, they helped the delivery guy load up the van, and then quietly went back into the shop to clean up.

As Paloma moved the remaining flower buckets into the cooler, Anca wiped the workstation down, and Tatiana swept up the carpet of stems, petals, and stray leather fern. When she was done, Tatiana leaned on her broom and let out a loud sigh.

"You okay?" asked Paloma.

"Marcel has to work tomorrow." Tatiana busied herself with the dustpan. "So he can't make the appointment."

Anca wiped her hands on her apron and turned to her daughter with a furrowed brow. "What appointment?"

"I already told you, Mom. It's my first prenatal."

Paloma felt a rush of blood in her ears. On one hand, she was proud of Tatiana for standing her ground—relieved, even, that she was also being up-front with Anca. Yet now it made Tatiana's decision that much more real—and, somehow, her own barrenness that much more poignant.

Anca stood stock still, pursing her lips. "It's not too late to talk about your options—"

"I've made up my mind." Tatiana looked her mother straight in the eye. "All I'm saying is that if either of you want to go with me, you can."

Anca shook her head. "Dove, I am scared for you. You do not know how dangerous childbirth can be."

"Mom, you're being ridiculous. I have more of a chance dying just crossing the street." Tatiana smirked. "Besides, you lived through two births—plus you were almost as young as me when you had Serena."

"You don't understand." Anca wrung her hands.

"Okay, so I take it you don't want to go." Tatiana directed her gaze to Paloma. "You still want to?"

"Are you sure…it's okay?" Paloma looked from mother to daughter.

Anca turned away from them and sighed. "You obviously asked her already. You might as well go, Paloma."

⌒

The exam room was swathed in seafoam green, from tiled floor, to floor-to-ceiling paint, to the examination table— even to the gown Tatiana wore.

"Is all this green supposed to be calming?" Tatiana rolled her eyes.

"I guess so...It's pretty overpowering, though."

"I know what you mean. But not as bad as all those questions. How am I supposed to know my mom's medical history?"

"Maybe she could help you with that later." Paloma still held out hope that Anca would come around.

"I doubt it." Tatiana shrugged. "And what about all those STD questions? You think they only asked me because I'm a teenager?"

"No, they asked me those same questions when I was pregnant."

Sitting on the exam table, Tatiana looked down at her folded hands. "Sorry, Paloma."

"Please don't worry." The last thing Paloma wanted was for Tatiana to feel sorry for her. She reached over and patted Tatiana's arm and smiled. "You're handling this really well."

Tatiana had undergone a pelvic exam (which Paloma had stepped out of the room for) and been poked and prodded with a variety of tests. Pleasantly surprised at Tatiana's calm demeanor through it all, Paloma saw that the teen had already matured.

Just then, a technician swooshed in, all efficiency with her tightly pulled back hair, perfectly manicured nails, and bright white sneakers. She quickly scanned Tatiana's chart and then walked over to shake her hand. "Ready to see your baby?"

Tatiana nodded and reached over to hold Paloma's hand. Then, Tatiana dutifully reclined on the exam table. The technician lifted her gown and squeezed gel on her belly.

Holding a small wand, the technician rolled it back and forth over Tatiana's brown skin. Grainy black-and-white images flashed on the screen. "You see that?"

Tatiana and Paloma stared at the inch-long being, a tadpole-shaped life that would metamorphize into a person with her own likes and dislikes, traumas and triumphs, memories and regrets. Tatiana's eyes went wide. "I'm going to be a mom."

"Let's get that heartbeat." The technician tilted her head in concentration.

The sound of tiny, galloping horses filled the room. Tatiana squeezed Paloma's hand. "Should it sound that fast?" Tatiana asked.

The technician nodded. "Everything looks good."

Paloma wiped her eyes. "It all looks good, Tatiana."

⌒

Sitting side-by-side on a lounge chair, Paloma and Reed ate take-out Chinese on their balcony. Sunset-red clouds cast a fiery glow in the evening sky. A warm wind rustled through her hair, but Paloma hardly looked up as she shoveled in mounds of the saucy food.

"Hey, slow down," Reed teased, "leave some for me."

She dropped her chopsticks, sudden tears in her eyes. "Reed…"

"What is it?"

"I went with Tatiana to her first prenatal today."

Reed set his plate down and looked at her. "Did they do an ultrasound?

Paloma nodded.

"So, you saw the baby? Heard the heartbeat?"

"I did. It was just like when we were pregnant."

"Oh, Paloma," he whispered. "I know you want to be there for her, but this is too hard on you."

She burrowed her face into his chest and sobbed. He wrapped his arms around her, telling her all would be okay, that they'd figure something out.

"Maybe..." she swallowed, "...we will." And then it happened again. With a whoosh of surreal speed, she was outside her own body. Paralyzed, she hovered over her physical self, which was lying on the deck as Reed crouched next to it. There went her reprieve from the bizarre—and the brief hope that she wasn't turning into her mother.

She watched as he checked her body's breathing and then reached for his cell. She wished he would look up and see her as Serena had, but she suddenly shot upwards, flying away like a wayward kite. As the evening air rushed past, her fear dissipated. In a flash, she was floating outside Serena's bedroom.

෴

Serena slid her window open and stared right into her. "You are pushed down, down, down, but you keep on flying up, up, up."

Paloma nodded at the simple, yet hopeful, narrative of her life.

"Well, float on in, you wild woman," Serena cooed. "You wild woman who needs to see."

Without a thought, Paloma was in Serena's room. Of all the years she'd known the Nicholson family, she'd never been in Serena's bedroom. The only furniture was a single, tightly made bed scrunched into a corner and a lone nightstand. Yet there was color; the walls were painted bright blue and the ceiling a hazy green. Paloma wondered if Anca and Leonardo had painted it to match Serena's differently hued eyes. And then there was the art. Dozens of unframed paintings lined the baseboards, huge canvases leaning against the wainscoting. Unlike Serena's seascapes, which Paloma had admired in the local galleries, these abstract works were even bolder. Geometric shapes pulled her into their complicated worlds. Serena's talent was even more extraordinary than Paloma had thought. She studied a piece before her, its colors radiating an urgent message only Serena knew.

She could tell that Serena was watching her take it all in. With a flushed expression that looked like a cross between embarrassment and giddiness, Serena glided around the maple floor, all the while keeping an eye on Paloma. Without meaning to, Paloma began to sway.

"Your work is amazing, Serena."

Serena stopped. With her feet splayed outward, she stood only inches away from Paloma without uttering a word. In the eerie silence, Serena's unnervingly calm smile widened.

Suddenly alarmed, Paloma tried to will herself away. But she was powerless. She couldn't be sure but sensed that it was Serena who was holding her there. She thought about the image of an eighteenth-century painting in one of her father's art books. It had terrified her as a young girl, but she often found herself flipping to it. The image of a fiery-eyed incubus crouched on a sleeping woman's chest reminded Paloma of how paralyzed she felt whenever her mother lost herself inside the maze of delusions. Just gazing at the picture would make Paloma feel as vulnerable as the prone woman. Now, she was experiencing an opposite, yet also similar, feeling. With the out-of-control sensation of being whisked from her own body and Serena seemingly holding her against her will, she felt defenseless—but oddly impenetrable as well. Still, she couldn't blame Serena. There was no reason to believe she would be able exert any more control over what was happening than Paloma could.

Serena suddenly backed away. "You are here now, my Paloma. You are here. It is out of our control. But now you must start to believe. You must start to believe how we both yearn to go back to the sea."

Paloma tried to think of something to say to soothe away the piercing ache that now permeated the room, but could only float before the wide-eyed Serena, as ineffectual as the air between them. Whatever the reason for this out-of-body experience, Paloma wondered if she were traveling alongside Serena, outside the fringe of everyone else's reality.

With twitchy fingers, Serena reached for her. "I can almost feel you. I can!" Serena exclaimed in an excited and hopeful voice of a girl grasping a sought-after prize at a fair. "Do not let your past paint your future. You need to get a whole new set of colors. You do."

Paloma looked at her and then said words she knew were true. "You're right, Serena. Thank you." Before Serena had time to react, Paloma zoomed back to her body at a faster-than-light speed that made Paloma wonder if everything was but a dream.

"Thank God," Reed said. "Are you okay?"

"I'm alright," she said, but her words sounded wispy, insubstantial as dandelion seeds being whisked away in the wind.

"You've never fainted before." Reed wiped his forehead. "I was just about to call 911, but luckily you came to."

"How long was I out?"

"Just seconds."

"Really?"

Reed helped her up. "Has this ever happened before?"

She didn't want to tell him how she had also "fainted" at the florist shop—let alone about her out-of-body adventures. "I'm sure it's just all these changing hormones, plus all the emotions, too." She gave him a weak smile. "And it has been a pretty emotional time."

Reed exhaled. "Yeah, it has."

Chapter Nineteen

The next morning, Paloma decided to call Patsy. She'd already researched out-of-body experiences and realized that she wasn't alone, but still, she wanted someone to talk to. And, if anyone could relate to having to deal with the bizarre, it would be her mother-in-law—even if she didn't always admit it.

"What's up?" Patsy asked.

"Not much—I just wanted to ask you a question."

"Sure. I've got about five minutes—"

"Okay," Paloma said, "It won't take long. Have you ever heard of out-of-body experiences?"

"Out-of-body experiences? You mean like when people get snatched up by aliens?"

Paloma smiled. "No, not like that."

"Why do you ask?"

"Just something I thought you'd be interested in." Paloma let out a breath, suddenly relived that she didn't divulge what had happened to her mother-in-law. Wanting to change the subject, she asked how Patsy's volunteer work at the shelter was going.

"They're begging me to increase my hours. In fact, they nicknamed me the pit-bull whisperer."

"That's quite the title." Paloma understood why Patsy had fallen in love with the misunderstood breed. Even though they were tough-muscled and ever protective of the ones they loved, Patsy often exclaimed how these "big babies" constantly nuzzled her for attention, how they were born comics, their little warthog legs flailing behind them whenever they tried to keep up with the more "refined" breeds, how they'd look into her eyes with such a soulful depth that she was sure they knew what she was thinking. "They're lucky to have you, Patsy."

"It's me who's the lucky one."

Paloma grinned into the phone, admiring Patsy's dedication. "I know you're out the door, so I won't keep you any longer—"

"Wait," Patsy said. "There's something I've been debating about whether I should tell you or not."

Paloma's heart fell to her stomach. "What is it?"

"I know I got embarrassed after I told you about my dreams, and I wrote off what I said to too many daiquiris. But I had *another* dream about you…one I get the feeling might help in some way—but then again, maybe it means nothing. Do you want to know? It's okay if you don't."

"Yes, of course." Paloma held a hand against her chest.

"Okay, here goes." Patsy exhaled. "I dreamt that you were a little girl again and you were pounding on the door of that psychic who used to work on the pier. You wanted answers. But she just stood behind her window with folded arms, looking past your furious little face like you weren't there."

Paloma's whole body went cold. "Do you remember her name?"

"Tillie, it was Tillie Summers, Ramiro Summers's mom—the guy who owns the hardware store."

Paloma ran into her bedroom. She pulled her wallet from her purse and unfolded the note she'd found at the storage facility. She stared at her mother's squiggly handwriting again: *Tell Tillie and…that I'm innocent.* She thanked Patsy and set her cell down. She sat on the edge of her bed and let herself remember.

When she was about eight, her mother was on one of her day visits from Haven House and had walked with her to the pier. Paloma begged her mother to go there, thinking that the harbor seals lounging on the nearby buoys might make her mother clap her hands like she usually did whenever she admired an animal. Whether it was a cat lounging on someone's front porch or a bird gliding through the sky, animals could open a joy in her mother that most human beings never seemed to own a key to.

Paloma recalled how Esther couldn't wait to get to the end of the pier where they could view what Paloma had assumed were not just any sea creatures, but a bloodline of seals that continued to live and play in the waters off Sunflower Beach. As she and her mother walked by, Madame Summers appeared outside her storefront. She wore a gold satin gown that shimmered so brightly it hurt Paloma's eyes. Paloma expected her to nod a noncommittal hello to them in her quiet but knowing way, as she always did whenever Paloma and her father strolled by. But instead, she ignored Paloma and stared at Esther with narrow-eyed distrust. Then she puckered her lips and, with precise aim, spit at a gap between the pier's wooden planks. Utterly surprised that a grown-up would not only have the skill but also the nerve to do such a thing, Paloma peered down at the strange, slow motion way Madame Summers's spittle glided into the waiting sea.

With a ferocious yank, her mother pulled Paloma away. Paloma stumbled alongside her as she tried to make out what her mother was reciting under her breath, a prayer-like utterance that wouldn't stop. Paloma had never heard her mother pray before, but somehow, she was sure that Esther meant to protect them, or at least herself, from Tillie Summers. Paloma stole a look over her shoulder and watched as Madame Summers marched back to her shrouded office. A dark haze of what looked like anger settled over the top of Madame Summers's blond hair. Paloma wasn't surprised to see such a thing. In fact, she'd been expecting it. She shuddered, though. For some reason, Madame Summers's anger filled her with a sudden, inexplicable fear of her own mother.

As much as she wanted to pull away, she was certain that it would make her mother cry. So, there she was, an eight-year-old girl in bright pink shorts and a purple T-shirt, locked in the handhold of her frightened mother—who now frightened her.

⌒

Paloma made her way up a narrow aisle between packed shelves toward the sound of Ramiro Summers's boisterous storytelling. Standing on the apple-green linoleum, a semicircle of customers in front of him, Ramiro was holding court. His faithful court jester, Petunia, was perched on a heart-shaped dog bed by his feet, a jaunty upturn to her so-homely-it's-cute face. Ramiro sported a pair of cuffed jeans, which accentuated his bow-legged stance, and a white T-shirt with the sleeves rolled up in vintage James Dean style. His classic nautical tattoos, inked in a crowded swirl of swallows, anchors, stars, grinning cartoon-like sharks, and even a couple of mermaids who looked like they had been modeled from pin-up girls back in the day, decorated his exposed skin. The long-ago statement of a young rebel, his tattooed mosaic was now a faded display of nostalgia.

When he saw Paloma, he paused and winked with his crinkle-eyed charm. She stood back and watched his ears wiggle at the end of some joke, which involved a bagpipe, a funeral, and a ditch digger. Everyone laughed, some people even cheered and called for more.

Ramiro held up a hand. "I'll net up another round for you tomorrow." He winked at Paloma again, and her face warmed at his attention.

He walked over, his broad-faced grin pushing away her sorrow. "Well, my dear girl, how are you?"

"I'm well…and I can see you're as wonderful as ever."

He squatted and scooped up Petunia, who had followed on his heels. "And I can see that you have quite a few question marks swimming above that brain of yours." With an impish chuckle, he set his gaze over the top of her head.

Paloma imagined that he could see actual question marks hovering over her crown. "I came in to talk with you…" She stopped, not sure how to bring up Tillie, not sure if his mother was even still alive.

"What is it?" He let Petunia lick his face and then nuzzled his chin against the top of her head.

"Ramiro, your mom Tillie…is she…?"

Ramiro laughed. "Yes, she's still hanging in there. In fact, what day is it?"

"Tuesday…why?"

"I take her out to lunch every Tuesday and Saturday, that's why." He checked his watch. "Come join us; she would love the company."

Paloma agreed, even though a surge of anxiety raced through her. But what better way to try to unravel the mystery of her mother?

Ramiro cocked his head. "Maybe she'll be able to answer your questions," he said. "There's just one thing you need to know first."

"What is it?"

"My mother is starting to show symptoms of dementia. She's mostly herself, but…"

Paloma watched his face cloud over. "I'm so sorry."

"Here's the thing," Ramiro said. "Her powers seem to be even more acute than before. It's quite amazing, actually." He held out his hand while still keeping Petunia in a protective football hold with the other. Paloma stepped arm and arm with him into the sundrenched day.

⌣

As Ramiro peeled out of the parking lot, Paloma held on to the cracked dashboard of his beloved Datsun. A relic from the seventies, the bright-orange truck epitomized Ramiro's steadfast and cheerful spirit. Still, she bit her lip as he chugged along. Seemingly unaware of traffic lights and unconcerned with lane boundaries, Ramiro's driving style didn't exactly calm the nerves. Finally, they pulled up in front of the secluded Sea Crest Retirement Community, one of the few places in Sunflower Beach that Paloma hadn't visited or even passed by before.

"I'll be right back," Ramiro said. "I'm going to escort her out and then we'll be on our way. You can watch Petunia."

Paloma looked down at the bug-eyed dog and Petunia stared back with a look of resigned patience. Ramiro hopped out of the truck and whistled "Over the Rainbow" as he sauntered up to the brick building, which looked more like an old apartment complex than the stately wood and white-trimmed establishment Paloma had envisioned.

Figuring that it would take some time for Ramiro's ninety-plus-year-old mom to make it outside, she leaned back and absently pet Petunia on the head, hoping to make sense of her conflicting emotions. With an equal mix of anticipation and dread, she wondered what it would feel like to see Tillie again—and what it was about her mother that had made Tillie Summers react with such distaste so many years ago. Perhaps Tillie hadn't understood that her mother was mentally ill and was confused by the dark thoughts she might have been tuning into. After all, the woman did claim to be a psychic. Then again, if Tillie was that gifted, wouldn't she have picked up on her mother's mental state?

Besides, most everyone in town had known that her mother had schizophrenia. The news of Annie's kidnapping had made sure of that. People were understandably curious. From there, gossip kindled and sparked in their little beach town, a fire that never completely died. Her father had protected Paloma from the majority of it, but through the years, she still overheard random comments about how crazy her mother was. Paloma exhaled so loudly she surprised herself. Petunia jerked her head up and stared at her. "It's okay." She patted the dog again. "I didn't mean to disturb you."

Ramiro and Tillie emerged from the entrance. They hobbled toward her with Ramiro's arm, a guiding force, around the old woman's shoulders. Paloma stared at Tillie. She wouldn't have recognized the bent-over woman as the Madame Summers she knew so long ago. Yes, even back then, Tillie had to have been in her late sixties—but at that time, she looked years younger than she really was. Although Tillie's hair was still blond—which, of course, had to have been due to ongoing dye jobs—her sharp black eyes had dulled, and her once-lithe body, which used to forever hold an energetic charge, was now slow and rigid. It was hard to imagine that this delicate old woman used to be the severe Madame Summers.

Gone, too, was the mysterious air she used to maintain. Perhaps it was because Paloma was a grown woman now who didn't see her through the eyes of an impressionable child, or maybe Tillie Summers didn't need to put it on anymore, now that she had stopped working as the town psychic. Or was it because of the dementia?

When Tillie and Ramiro came closer, Paloma got out so that Tillie could sit next to her son. "It's nice to see you…" Paloma had almost addressed her as Madame Summers, but stopped herself, not sure of the right protocol.

"Oh, but my dear, please call me Tillie." For a soundless moment, the three of them froze. Not a word was uttered in the pine-scented breeze. Not wanting to break the silence, Paloma studied Tillie. She told herself not to stare but couldn't help it; the intricate pattern etched across Tillie's narrow face was mesmerizing. Tillie Summers had aged even more than Paloma had first thought, but hers was a beauty that couldn't be erased. It seemed Tillie could tell what she was thinking, the way she put her hands on her hips and looked at her with a sly smile. "Yes, please call me Tillie." She held out her hand. "It has a more youthful tone to it than Mrs. Summers—or that Madame Summers I bestowed upon myself so long ago." She grinned at Paloma in a crinkle-eyed way similar to her son's. So far, Paloma would have never guessed that Tillie was showing any signs of dementia. "I'm very pleased Ramiro invited you to join us for lunch," Tillie said.

Paloma shook Tillie's hand, trying to ignore the strange coolness of her palm and the sad shakiness of her grip. "I used to see you on the pier when I was a kid."

"I know." Tillie puckered her lips, reminding Paloma about how she did the same thing before she spit on the pier all those years ago. "I saw you walk by many times when I worked as the psychic."

"You remember me?"

"Yes, when you were a little string bean of a girl and…" Tillie frowned and tilted her head, clearly struggling to find the rest of her words. Then, she smiled again, looking relieved for having been able to grab on to the memory. "Your father used to take you there on the weekends."

Perplexed that Tillie recognized her—but somehow not surprised that she had only mentioned Abel and not Esther—Paloma tried to hide her unease. "I didn't think you could tell who I was from that long ago."

Tillie averted her gaze without saying a word. Then Ramiro placed his hand on his mother's arm. "We better get going, ladies. I like to get there before the lunch crowd."

◠

At the restaurant, Ramiro asked the waitress for a booster seat. "Petunia's a little one, you know."

An elderly waitress, whose platinum wig looked like it could have been torn out of a 1950s *Look* magazine ad, nodded. "Of course, Ramiro." She winked at Tillie. "We all know that Petunia deserves the best seating arrangement."

"At least I can pretend I have a grandchild," Tillie said. She winked back at the waitress and then gazed at the snorting Petunia. "Although she's not much of a looker, is she?"

Everyone chuckled, but then Tillie caught Ramiro's arm, a sudden alarm in her eyes. "I don't have any grandchildren of the people variety, do I?"

"No, Mom, you don't," Ramiro answered. "At least not that I know of."

Paloma wasn't sure if Tillie had been merely kidding around or if her dementia caused a momentary glitch.

But Ramiro seemed unfazed as he flashed Paloma a smile and tapped her on the arm. "Please order anything you want; it's my treat."

Paloma thanked him, and then took in the comforting nostalgia of Neptune Café's décor. She swore that it hadn't changed an inch since her memories of childhood birthday parties and adolescent dates. The same frayed fishermen's nets draped across the wood paneled walls, faded plastic crabs and starfish pinned against them. The tabletops, with thick resin coated over embedded seashells, were just as shiny as ever. Even the red vinyl booths were somehow still intact, thousands of French fries probably having been fished out of their crevices over the years and spilled milkshakes having been wiped off with dishrags. Or probably the booths had been refurbished. Paloma preferred to think they were the originals, though.

Out of nowhere, Tillie started to hum the tune "My Bonnie Lies Over the Ocean." Paloma looked at her, but Tillie kept at it, a woman who didn't seem to care a hoot of what others thought of her. Ramiro ignored his mother as he cooed to Petunia. Paloma remained silent.

Then Tillie stopped singing in mid phrase. She clasped her hand on Paloma's wrist with too much force. "You must ask me your questions."

A surprised outtake of air escaped from Paloma's lungs. "My questions?"

"I see you have questions," Tillie said with a tad too much urgency.

"You do?" Even though Paloma wanted answers, she felt a sudden wariness.

"I am sure I can help you," Tillie said. "In fact, I know I can."

Paloma gave Tillie an apologetic smile. "How do you know this?"

"I just…" Tillie said, "…do."

"I'm sorry," Paloma said. "I didn't mean to offend you."

"No offence taken." Tillie turned to Ramiro and they exchanged a pointed look that made Paloma wonder what they knew that she didn't.

"But you do have some important questions?" Ramiro leaned forward, aiming his well-intentioned concern at her.

Paloma inhaled the restaurant's odor of fried fish and burnt coffee. "I do." She tried to smile, wanted to make a joke of it, but she could tell Ramiro and Tillie saw through her.

"You're in good company here." Ramiro patted Petunia, who fixed Paloma with a humanlike stare.

"Good company?" Paloma asked.

"We understand you," Tillie said. "We understand the burdens that come from your gifts."

"What do you mean?" She wasn't surprised that Ramiro and Tillie knew about her visions. After all, even Patsy had heard about them. The older she got, the more she realized what a small community Sunflower Beach was. But the fact that so many random people had heard about her "special abilities" still made her nervous.

"We want you to know you're not alone." He drummed his hands on the table, the individual letters of his "Hold Fast" tattoo marching up and down with each beat. "My mother's psychic abilities were passed down to me. I don't have visions like you do, and I don't have dreams like your mother-in-law. But I've still been given the gift of being able to help people in ways they're not even aware of. In fact, I don't even know how I do it sometimes, but somehow I do." He raised his eyebrows.

"And I can see when someone is going through something extraordinary."

"What..." Paloma said, trying to understand, "...are you talking about?"

"All in good time, Paloma," he said. "All in good time."

"All in good time?"

"Just know that it'll be okay." He patted her arm. "You'll be okay."

A strange sense of calm cooled her skin where Ramiro had touched her. She decided it was best to accept his consolatory words for now but still wondered about her mother-in-law. "How do you know," Paloma said, "about Patsy's dreams?"

He folded his arms across his chest. "That was a long time ago."

"It was me," Tillie piped in. "I remember it very clearly. Patsy didn't know who else to turn to after she had dreamt of her husband's death." Tillie flattened a veined hand across her collarbone. "It was just so awful for her that she had warned him not to go to his father's funeral and then how that poor man listened to her. And..." Tillie paused. "...how it still happened."

"Were you able to help her?" Paloma wished she could scoop the words back into her mouth, but Tillie only looked at her, a wistful smile crossing her bow-shaped mouth. "I'm sorry about the way that sounded," Paloma said.

"It's fine." Tillie nodded her head. "I understand. You're merely trying to figure out if this old woman can help *you*."

Embarrassed, Paloma studied a starfish that was forever captured inside the tabletop's resin. "*Can* you help me?"

"Paloma," Tillie's voice rose up a notch, "you don't understand. I know you don't completely trust me yet. But you can."

"What is it that I don't understand?" Paloma stared at Tillie, trying to sense if she could feel the truth behind Tillie's words. Her ears tingled, her body's way of telling her that Tillie was being honest. What Paloma wasn't sure about, though, was if Tillie's sincerity was based on reality or what she merely believed to be the truth.

"It's okay." Tillie's tone softened. "You don't have to put all your faith in me. But please know that I truly want the best for you." She hovered her hand over Paloma's but didn't actually touch her. "And I understand what you're going through."

Paloma knew she should hear her out. Maybe Tillie *would* understand. In fact, Ramiro had mentioned that Tillie's powers had grown even stronger since the dementia had started. And it'd be such a relief to open up to someone, someone who might be able to provide answers. But Paloma still wasn't sure if she should trust her. "I'm sorry." She looked first at Tillie and then at Ramiro. "I'm not ready." Even as she said the words, she wondered if she was making the right decision.

Again, Ramiro and Tillie exchanged glances that made it look like they knew something she didn't. But at this point, Paloma didn't care. Yes, she wanted help—but all she felt right now was trepidation. Since Tillie had shown such strong dislike toward Esther, it didn't seem safe to reveal herself to her. She stood.

"You must not go, dear. Now is the time for you to understand." The dullness in Tillie's eyes had cleared, replaced with a keen and slightly invasive gaze. "I mean you no harm. In fact, I'm here to guide you."

"You're here to guide me?" It sounded too out there, too much like something the supposed psychic Daphne Hollow would say. But a sudden, ravenous hunger hit Paloma so hard that all she could do was envision the fried shrimp and coleslaw platter she'd ordered. Her stomach audibly growled. Without thinking, she sat down again.

"You doubt, my dear?" Tillie raised her eyebrows.

"I wonder…" Paloma looked past Tillie. She told herself to keep the edgy-sounding suspicion from leaking out. "It just doesn't make sense how many people in our little town claim to have psychic abilities. Maybe there's something in our drinking water?" Paloma made a joke of it but still wondered at the possibility. Could there be an unknown contaminate in Sunflower Beach's water that drove people to the edge of madness? If certain meds produced such specific side effects as gambling, she wouldn't be surprised if other substances could trick the mind into thinking it had extrasensory perception.

"Paloma," Tillie said, waving her hand in the air, "some places draw more artists, some towns, more musicians; for some reason, Sunflower Beach attracts a number of people with extrasensory perception. It's a vibrational thing."

Paloma gaped at Tillie, but then Petunia suddenly cocked her head and howled. Tillie raised her eyebrows at the dog and then broke into a nervous giggle as Ramiro let out a hearty laugh. Paloma wondered at all three them: Ramiro, who sported all those nautical tattoos but was never in the navy or even sailed a boat; Tillie, who insisted that she knew how to guide her when she was in the process of losing her own memory, and there she was: a thirty-two-year-old woman who was fending off visions, out-of-body travel, and ghost visits from her long-dead mother.

Tillie patted Paloma's hand, this time making actual contact. "No matter what, we still have to try and make sense of our personal problems, our losses, our challenges." She paused and stared straight into Paloma. "And, dear…we all deserve help."

Paloma swallowed, knowing she was right.

Chapter Twenty

"I don't get it," Justine said. "Why do you think Daphne Hollow is a farce, but the ridiculous Madame Summers may have answers for you?"

It was the kind of hot, cloudless day that made everything look too sharp and bright. Justine had invited her over for a swim while Harrison was off with his babysitter. They were doing the breaststroke, but not in the leisurely way Paloma had hoped for when Justine had invited her over for a *dip in the pool.* "I didn't say that I believe Tillie has all the answers." Paloma had to catch her breath; it was exhausting trying to keep pace with her athletic friend. "But she might understand what I'm going through."

"I still don't get it. Did she ask you any questions? Did she tell you anything you didn't already know?"

Paloma pushed herself through the tepid water. She always felt like a gigantic frog when she attempted the breaststroke. Justine, however, glided by her side as gracefully as Esther Williams. Still, Paloma could sense Justine's competitive spirit tensing beneath her flexed back muscles. Why Justine felt any rivalry with her, especially in the physical fitness department, was something Paloma never understood. Although, how could she ever forget the wounded look on her friend's young face whenever Justine's ethereally thin mother, who favored short, see-through peasant dresses, chided her daughter for being too "chunky" and "cumbersome" (that is, until Justine became so emaciated in her young teenage years that her period was on and off for months at a time).

"Justine, I hope you know what great shape you're in."

"Ugh, so not true—anyway, don't try and change the subject." Justine puffed her cheeks and let out an irritated whoosh of air. "Are you sure Tillie Summers didn't say anything? Anything that would have upset you?"

"Why would you think she'd say something that would upset me?"

"Oh, well…" Justine glided forward. "You know how psychics can sometimes phrase things in a veiled way that can make people question things, how they can refer to something from the past—"

"Something from the past?" It was not at all like Justine to worry about how Paloma would react to something someone else had said, let alone how she'd feel about some of the things that spewed out of her own mouth. "What are you talking about?"

"I'm just making sure you're not going to let yourself get too vulnerable with her."

"Don't worry. I know how to protect myself." Paloma glanced at Justine, trying to decipher the fear emanating off her, a dark, choking haze that made Paloma look away. Seemingly oblivious to her own emotions, Justine's gaze remained fixed, a racehorse who could only see the lane ahead of her. They swam until they reached the other end of the pool.

Paloma gripped the edge, trying to catch her breath. "Besides, I told her that I wanted to wait until I was ready."

"Ready? Ready for what?" Justine took off. Without any observable effort, she swept her arms under the water like a bird cruising through a turquoise sky.

Paloma pushed off the edge and forced herself to catch up. "I just want some time to decide if I want to have a reading with her or not."

"Is she as absurd as she used to be?"

"What do you mean?"

"Don't you remember how she used to dress?" Gently, Justine exhaled, her lips pursed in perfect pretty-girl fashion. "All those over-the-top gowns. And then how she used to act, too? The way she always put on that mysterious air by staring at people, pretending she knew everything there was to know."

"Yeah, she was over the top." Paloma's lungs were burning, but she pushed on. "What…" Paloma inhaled, "…else do you remember about her?" It'd be a relief to know if Tillie had been as wary and hostile to others as she had to Esther.

"Just that she was silly."

"Silly?"

They were in the shallow end. Thankfully, Justine stopped swimming. She stood straight-backed with head held high, a bronzed goddess of steady gym torture and strict diet. "She was a joke." Justine jogged in place in slow-motion water resistance mode, her arms pumping up and down in the air. "Who else would traipse around the pier in all those flowing frocks like she was some mystical goddess? Who else would act like she was above everyone else because she was some so-called psychic?"

Paloma nudged Justine on the shoulder. "I could say some similar stuff about Daphne Hollow."

Justine merely rolled her eyes.

"By the way, you should know that Tillie is suffering from dementia."

"I am sorry for her," Justine said. "And I know I sound judgmental." She flexed her arms and then punched the air boxer style. "But you have to remember something, Paloma."

"Oh boy, here it comes." Paloma was only halfheartedly following Justine's moves. She couldn't wait to get out of the water and lay mute on one of Justine's padded chaise lounges while the heat lulled her to sleep.

"I don't care if you make light of this," Justine said. "You just have to remember that I'm your oldest friend and I know you better than anyone else. I can help you more than that dotty old psychic."

"I'll keep that in mind."

Justine stared at her. "I'm serious, Paloma."

"But…" Paloma tried to tame her breath. "First you get mad because I don't want to see Daphne Hollow, and now you're mad because I may get a reading from Tillie Summers. I don't get it."

Justine paused, staring into Paloma's eyes. Then she shook her head. "I just don't know why you're so hell-bent on seeking the mumbo jumbo advice of Tillie Summers—especially since you said she has dementia on top of everything else."

"You're only guessing that Tillie would throw a bunch of 'mumbo jumbo' at me. Maybe she really does have a gift."

Giving the slightest of shrugs, Justine remained silent.

Then it hit Paloma. "You had a reading from her," she said, wondering why Justine would hide it.

Justine pretended she hadn't heard as she tilted her head and jiggled her ear, draining trapped water.

"Justine, I know you heard me. Did you ever see Tillie Summers?"

Justine tipped her head on the other side. "It was a long time ago. I saw her once when I was a teenager." Justine sighed. Only Justine could make a sigh sound condescending. "Trust me: Tillie is no psychic."

"Why do you say that?"

"Her advice was as insightful as her cliché crystal ball."

"But you would have told me, Justine. Especially when we were teenagers. I know you would have."

"I didn't tell you everything."

"Come on. We hardly let a day go by without checking in with each other."

"I know I didn't share my *whole* life with you, Paloma."

An unexpected gust whipped Paloma's face. She froze, a battle-fatigued woman watching the dried oak leaves fall like dead moths into Justine's pool. As she tried to think of what to say next, the sharp odor of chlorine seemed to intensify. Without a word, she slogged through the quiet, still water toward the pool stairs. They felt so far away, much farther than they should.

"Where're you going?" Justine's words, too loud and startlingly desperate, pierced the air.

"I need time to think." As she waded through the silence, Paloma dared not look back. Waterlogged and heavy-legged, she finally stepped out of the pool. She toweled off, and then threw on an oversized T-shirt over her swimsuit. She turned around only after she had grabbed her bag off a waiting chair and clutched her keys in hand.

"There's a big fat lie that's been eating away our friendship." She didn't know why she said it, but the words flowed out, and deep down she knew that it was an unresolved truth that could no longer be avoided.

Justine froze. She stared at Paloma in shock but didn't say a word.

Heart thumping against her chest, Paloma walked away. She stepped through the French doors, through Justine's spotless house, and into the safety of her car. Paloma revved her engine and then flew down the hill. She wasn't sure exactly what their fight was about, but knew Justine was too afraid to admit whatever she'd been hiding.

Chapter Twenty-One

"You need to call me." Justine pleaded on her voicemail. Pleaded. It wasn't a word Paloma thought she'd ever attribute to Justine. Paloma curled deeper into her fetal position on the sea-green twill of her couch. Part of her wanted to call Justine back. She was tired of loss. But another part of her wondered if she was actually losing some part of herself by staying in the friendship. She thought about getting up for a glass of iced tea. But all she could do was drape her arm over her head. She closed her eyes and fell down a tunnel of exhaustion. Within minutes, though, her heart jolted as the electric current of an upcoming vision suddenly raced through her body.

In a small boat floating far out at sea, Paloma sat opposite Serena. Neither of them had oars. Paloma looked to Serena for help.

"Now, now, sweet one. I can steer this boat like the moon pulls on the tide. And if we go past the horizon, all we need to do is go deep inside." Serena gently sang in a lullaby tone Paloma knew was meant to calm them both.

The ocean seemed to glow from within. Just a few feet away, dolphins broke through the surface. Fins cutting through the sea, thousands upon thousands of them swam and leapt. Awed, Paloma saw that they stretched all the way to the horizon. Within the midst of these sleek creatures, a translucent-green tail flicked up for an instant and waved right at them in what seemed like recognition. Serena threw her head back and laughed, and then gave Paloma a sly I-told-you-so nod.

Then, all the dolphins instantly disappeared under the sheen of water. Where the ocean had once been alive, it was now dead. A severe silence hit Paloma so hard she doubled over in pain.

Serena reached her hand toward Paloma's face. She grazed her fingers gently across Paloma's cheeks in the same mournful-sweet way Paloma's father used to do when Paloma was little and he wanted to soothe away her sadness.

"That's what happens when you don't see. That's what happens. Nature rebels. Nature rebels." As Serena sang, a shaky unhappiness overtook her voice until she stopped. Paloma looked at her, willing her to go on, and when Serena's gaze became distant and unreadable, a sudden fear squeezed Paloma so violently that she thought she was going to fall overboard.

The vision went black. Trying to calm herself, Paloma stared out the window. Afternoon sunshine filtered through, a golden color that made everything in the condo glow. Paloma reached for her cell.

Tillie answered on the first ring. "I'm glad you called. I've been waiting."

For the first time that day, Paloma was able to fully inhale. "You've been waiting?"

Tillie laughed in a light, melodic way that reminded Paloma of wind chimes on a breezy day. "Before I decide to give you a reading," Tillie said, "I need to know if you'll be able to open up and trust me."

"I trust you." Yet even as she said this, she still felt a tug; should she dare mention her memory of Tillie's blatant hostility toward her mother?

"But not completely." Tillie's gentle but commanding tone caused a quick flutter at the bottom of Paloma's stomach. "I understand you have your reservations," Tillie continued. "But you need to know there's a lot more to what you've seen. You'll understand in good time."

An unexpected rush of hope gave Paloma courage. "I'd like to get answers."

"Of course. Let's meet at noon tomorrow. You know where I live. We can have a private session in my room."

Chapter Twenty-Two

Although her walls were painted Sea Crest's standard shade of Hushed Pink, Tillie had managed to personalize her room with a surprisingly youthful tone. She plastered the walls—no doubt with Ramiro's help—with a multitude of poster-sized, color-enhanced photos of flowers, wildlife, planets, and one particularly vivid shot of the Earth taken from space. Her nightstand and desk held stacks of science books with glossy images of solar systems and stars, including works by Stephen Hawking and Carl Sagan. Paloma smiled. She had expected a bunch of metaphysical books covering such topics as spirit guides and auras.

Dressed in a sapphire dress and smart navy pumps, Tillie pointed to her desk chair. "Please have a seat." Paloma turned the chair around. The seat pad was covered with gold satin, a perfect match to the gowns Tillie used to wear.

"Well, what do you think?" asked Tillie, sweeping her arm.

"Your room is very colorful." Paloma took in the purple curtains, still thick, but faded, their creases straw-colored. After all these years, could they have been the same ones that used to hang in Tillie's shop? Paloma was brought back to the day on the pier, when Tillie had glared at her mother.

Tillie snapped her fingers. "Don't let the past stop your future."

A rush of adrenaline raced through Paloma's body. "Why did you say that?" Could Tillie be reading her thoughts?

Tillie merely winked. "Now, would you please bring that other chair for me?" She pointed to a corner of the room near the window.

Paloma retrieved the wooden chair with its matching gold-satin pad and placed it a couple of feet in front of hers. What else was there to do but to see what would happen next? They sat facing each other in momentary silence.

"I can bring her to you."

"What do you mean?" Paloma had to look away from Tillie's unblinking eyes.

"Listen," Tillie said. "Just listen for a moment."

Even through the closed door, Paloma could hear the squeaky sound of someone's rubber-soled shoes retreating down the polished hallway. "I'm sorry, Tillie. All I heard was someone walking by your room."

Tillie laughed in the same twinkly way that she had before. "Yes, that was our activities director; the sound of her tennis shoes is quite annoying, isn't it?" Tillie waved her hand in the space between them Like a magician about to pull a rabbit out of a hat. "Now." Tillie took several audible breaths. "Try again, Paloma. Be as still as you can."

Paloma felt her shoulders relax and nodded.

"That's good," Tillie cooed. "Now, close your eyes."

Paloma obeyed, allowing a strange and wonderful quiet to wrap around her brain.

"That's it." Tillie's words seemed to melt into the background. "You're almost there."

It could have been ten minutes or a mere ten seconds that Paloma sat there with eyes closed to what was outside of herself, and yet at the same time, open to a whole other world inside. In a waking dream, she saw her mother nod to her, telling her without having to say the words out loud "to continue on." She saw Serena swimming out to the kelp beds, her sinewy arms cutting through the water with a vengeance. And then she saw her father. He was at his kitchen table, looking down at something he held in his hands with such sorrow in his eyes that Paloma's heart caught.

"Now, Paloma," said Tillie. "Listen."

Paloma sat as still as a rock. Ever so faintly she heard her mother sing a song from her childhood, but as hard as she tried, she couldn't make out the words. She continued to sit with eyes closed and willed her ears to hear more. Within moments, the singing grew louder, but still she could not make out what song it was. Then Tillie whispered, "It's time to open your eyes."

All she saw was Tillie staring at her with a serene smile. Like a dream, her mother's singing slithered out the closed window. Paloma looked at Tillie for an answer, but instead Tillie waved her hand in the air again. "What will help you?" Tillie asked.

Without thinking, Paloma knew exactly how to answer. "I need to see my Auntie Ruby." She didn't know where the thought came from, but knew that her aunt was the very person she needed.

"Yes," Tillie said in a hushed tone. "Yes, you do. And do you know why?"

Paloma pondered for a moment, not quite sure of the answer. "Because…" She held her hands over her face, wanting to hide her torment. Like a rogue wave, the high-rise fear of suffering the same fate as her mother had barreled in. With a pain more wrenching than her miscarriages, Paloma curled into herself, crying.

Through this, Tillie remained silent. Yet even without looking at her, Paloma could feel the patience radiating off Tillie Summers's birdlike shoulders. For some reason, this made Paloma cry even harder. How long had it been since she could be herself without having to worry about someone else's feelings? How long had it been since she wholeheartedly broke down?

After several minutes, Paloma pulled herself together. She accepted a tissue from Tillie's outstretched hand. As she blew her nose Paloma remembered how her mother's paranoia would often bleed right into her when she was little, making her afraid of things she couldn't name or see, setting her heart on an out-of-control gallop.

Tillie tilted her face with its feline-shaped eyes upward. "You need to remember this won't be easy. You'll be vulnerable."

"Vulnerable?" Paloma asked. What could Tillie mean by that? She shivered as she recalled how Justine had warned her not to become too vulnerable with Tillie. "Why would visiting my aunt make me vulnerable?"

"It isn't anything about her…." Tillie paused to stretch her spindly arms. "It's just that I believe it will spark a kind of crisis, if you will."

"Maybe I shouldn't contact her, then." What she had already been going through was troubling enough, why go any deeper?

"You have to go through this in order to fully heal."

"How do you know?"

"She's your family, Paloma. She knows your history and will help you accept what you're going through—will help you accept *you*."

Paloma nodded. It did make sense. "I need to ask you something." She fingered the tissue in her hand. "You already know I've had visions my whole life. But lately I've been going through some pretty bizarre stuff."

Tillie leaned forward. "You can tell me."

Paloma paused as her body strained to rush outside of itself. Terrified that she'd have another out-of-body experience, she clenched her hands around the edges of her chair.

"Do you want this to happen?" Tillie's voice, though only a couple of feet away sounded muffled and far away.

Paloma shook her head no. Although she was desperately fighting the urge to fly outside of herself, there was also the reassurance that Tillie Summers understood.

"You are in more control than you think," Tillie said.

But Paloma started to hyperventilate. A sharp panic invaded. If she left this time, maybe she'd never make it back. Maybe she'd be eternally adrift, a ghost trapped outside her own life.

"Paloma, take my hand."

Like a lost girl who had just been found, Paloma grasped Tillie's feathery grip.

"You will," Tillie commanded, "get through this."

"But what does all this stuff mean?" Hungry for answers, Paloma couldn't let herself give up. "It's all so confusing." She paused, trying to read what was behind Tillie's placid smile.

"I'm on your side," Tillie said. "Remember, I'm on your side."

Guilty about how she had first distrusted Tillie, Paloma nodded. "Besides my usual visions, I've seen—and heard—a ghost."

Tillie nodded. "Someone close, yes?"

The hairs prickled on the back of Paloma's neck. Still protective of her mother's memory, she hesitated.

Then, right on cue, Tillie said, "Wasn't it your own mother who has come to you?"

"Why..." Paloma tried to hide her panic, "...do you ask?"

"Because she's told me so."

Paloma stood. "She's told you so?" Now Tillie Summers conversed with spirits as well? Maybe there really was something in Sunflower Beach's water that drove people mad, that made them think they had special powers.

"Your mother is a very determined spirit." Tillie motioned for Paloma to sit back down.

Paloma lowered herself onto the satin pad. "What has she told you?" Wanting to believe, and at the same time telling herself that Tillie could be making everything up, Paloma waited.

"Although she's determined, she's grown tired. I believe she's getting ready to move on but wants to see you again. She has one last thing she wants you to know."

"One last thing." Paloma repeated the words as she recalled her own conversation with her dead mother. But if

Esther's spirit really had embodied Paloma's unborn babies, why? Why leave Paloma and Reed with not just one, but three losses? Paloma's mouth went dry; maybe it really was beyond her mother's control. Or was it some lesson that Paloma wasn't meant to comprehend yet? Or maybe this was all the stuff of hers and Tillie's combined imaginations, the human desire to pin meaning onto the sad episodes of life one had no say over.

Tillie cocked her head again, an inquisitive bird ready to catch what lay beneath the surface. "Ah, but there's more."

"Yes." Paloma shivered. Answering Tillie's questions felt like stripping off layers of clothing. But she continued on. "I've had two out-of-body experiences. And I've fought more off—just like I did in front of you a couple of minutes ago."

"But why would you fight them?"

"Why wouldn't I? I don't know if it's ever happened to you, but it's scary being so out of control." Paloma glanced at Tillie's poster of the Earth, a hearty, but doomed entity just like all the other planets and stars, humans and animals who live for a long while or a short time but eventually die one way or the other.

"Feeling out of control won't kill you."

"That's not always so." Paloma sighed, wondering at the truth of her own words. "Besides, I'm not even sure any of this is real."

Tillie crossed her arms. "What were your out-of-body episodes like?"

"I got pulled right out of myself. It all happened without my wanting it to. It was surreal and scary but also, at some points, peaceful. Still, I don't want it to happen again." Paloma paused. Could Tillie *really* understand what she was going through? "I just don't know what all this means."

"What are you so afraid of?"

"What am I afraid of?"

"It won't harm you to voice it."

Paloma slowly unwrapped Tillie's words and then, for the first time in her life, decided it was time to say it out loud: "What if I..." She paused as her throat closed in. "What if I have to face the same struggles—"

"That your mother did."

Paloma felt an immediate stab of guilt. Hadn't she just betrayed her own mother by admitting this to Tillie Summers—of all people?

"Don't worry, Paloma. She understands."

Paloma wondered again if Tillie were reading her mind but told herself that this tiny old lady was just fiercely astute, a wise woman who could so easily read facial expressions and body language that she didn't even know she was doing it. "What if I'm really losing it?" Panic coiled in her belly. "I can't deal with that pain. I just can't." A memory of her mother flailing around on the kitchen floor slammed into Paloma's brain. Esther was crying hysterically and pulling at her own hair as she screeched about what the voices were telling her to do. What had those voices said? Paloma tried to remember. But nothing came.

"Keep still. I'm going to lead you to the memory you seek," Tillie whispered.

Paloma closed her eyes. Sooner than she thought possible, a dreamlike gauze settled over her mind, but her heart was still trembling. "I'm not sure I want to remember."

"You're safe here," Tillie said, her tone as cool as a breeze.

Like Alice falling down the rabbit hole, Paloma's memory tumbled down a staircase of years. At the bottom landing, she was brought back. Esther was writhing on the kitchen floor. Then Paloma saw herself, a little girl with terror in her eyes as she clenched her knees to her chest. She was perched on one of the dining chairs, afraid to run out of the room lest her mother grab one of her ankles and take her down. Her loving mother who had become the feared monster, the creature who was waiting to drag her into its nightmare. The creature you stayed as far away from as you could.

"What did she say?" Tillie asked, her question riding alongside Paloma's memory.

Her mother's words crashed into Paloma's skull without warning. "I must drown myself," her mother screamed. "They're commanding me. I must do it. I must. I must."

Imprisoned within the glossy white walls and dark oak cabinets of their kitchen, Paloma watched her mother's frantic eyes track something Paloma could not see. Her mother darted to a corner and cowered. As she hugged her body even tighter into itself, Paloma widened her gaze. Maybe if she concentrated with all her might, she could see what her mother was so afraid of and then try to stop it from hurting her. But as hard as Paloma stared into the empty air, nothing materialized. Her mother crumpled to the floor.

Paloma wished she could gather the courage to get up and comfort her but could only sit tight as she held back tears. She knew that whenever she cried, Esther would hide her own face behind unsteady palms—which somehow transformed from the smooth hands of a young mother into the shaky claws of an old, pain-ridden lady. But even as she commanded herself not to cry, Paloma felt the heat of her tears.

Somehow through all of her pain and paranoia, her mother saw. "You cannot cry!" The demand was like a knife cutting the space between them.

"I'm sorry, Mommy," Paloma whispered. She knew that it wasn't because her mother was angry. It was worse than that. Even before she started preschool, Paloma knew that her own crying scared her mother. And that was the last thing Paloma wanted to have happen. When Esther became afraid of her own daughter's pain, the voices grew even more menacing. Dark, taunting voices that her mother couldn't ignore—and sometimes even obeyed. Paloma never knew what she should say when this happened. What she yearned to do, though, was run away and never return. But then, she was just a kid. Where would she go? Besides, she loved her mother with all her heart. No matter what, she loved her—and her mother loved her, too.

Then Esther looked up and with an odd, faraway light in her eyes, stared right through Paloma. "I need to die. I need to die."

Paloma's heart collapsed. "Please don't, Mommy," Paloma whispered. "I love you."

Just then, her father's keys could be heard in the front door lock, a jangle of clicking metal with the agitated concern of someone trying to get in the house as fast as he could. Finally, Paloma heard the door bang open. Her father ran into the kitchen and took Esther in his arms. He rocked her in his arms like a baby, which reassured and scared Paloma at the same time. "Hush," her father said into Esther's ear, "you must have lost your meds again." He gently caressed the auburn waves of her mother's hair away from her face. "*Mija*, you go along to your room now."

As much as she had been waiting for release, Paloma couldn't move.

Her father, who was busy tending to her mother, didn't seem to notice. So, Paloma sat there and watched him try to soothe away the unspeakable demons that lived inside her mother's head.

Within the walls of Tillie's colorful room, Paloma opened her eyes but could only see a flash of white—and then total darkness.

Chapter Twenty-Three

Paloma groped the empty air with outstretched hands. She heard Tillie trying to calm her but was too terrified to respond.

Finally, Tillie caught her arm. "Breathe."

Paloma could only take a quick gasp.

"It's okay, Paloma. Take another breath."

Paloma did as she was told as she grabbed on to Tillie's words.

"I know you're going to be okay." Tillie patted Paloma's hand. "But you need to tell yourself that *you* know you're going to be okay."

Paloma said the words out loud, trying to believe them.

"You can see," Tillie said. "Look around and see."

Paloma widened her eyes, but all was still dark. Panicked, she wondered if she'd somehow been blinded for life. "I can't, Tillie."

"Listen to me," Tillie commanded, "and look."

Paloma clenched her fist and concentrated. Slowly but surely, Tillie's face and the surrounding room emerged. Paloma exhaled, relieved yet still unnerved.

Tillie smiled. "See. Everything is a transition. You'll be okay."

"But why..." Paloma saw that everything before her—the windowpane, the books, even Tillie herself—somehow looked more solid than before. She blinked. "Why did that happen?"

Tillie shrugged. "I can't say why."

"But I just lost my sight. I don't know why, you don't know why—but you were sure that I would be okay."

"I was sure," said Tillie, "that you'd be okay. What I want to know is what you remembered right before it happened."

Paloma shook her head. "My poor mother was so tormented."

Tillie leaned over and placed her hand on Paloma's shoulder. "You are not your mother. You will not fall over the edge—and, dear Paloma, even if you did, there are safety nets."

"What do you mean?" Paloma glanced down at Tillie's round-toed pumps.

"Even if you did inherent your mother's schizophrenia—which I highly doubt—treatment options are better than ever before, and people with this disease get better over time, not worse. You would still live and work and love."

"But my mother—"

"Just as I said before: You are not your mother."

"But I am her daughter."

"Just know that she was her own person. You are yours. And what you're going through right now is not to be feared."

"Then what am I going through?"

"Trust me," Tillie said with an authoritative air. "It's spiritual in nature, nothing to fear, but nothing to write off, either." She gave Paloma's shoulder a slight nudge. "In the end, it'll all make sense and you'll be more than okay."

"But how could you know this isn't something to be afraid of?" Paloma was suddenly leery of Tillie again, though she knew it wasn't fair. The woman was only trying to help. But no one could ever know for sure what was going to happen. Psychic or not, how could she be so sure? "Maybe all you're trying to do is give me a sense of hope, even though it may be a false one."

"A false sense of hope?"

"I know you have the best of intentions, Tillie…but I'm not sure that all will be okay."

Tillie stared at her. "Take a moment. If you go way down deep, I think you'll feel it."

Paloma looked out the window. A sparrow flitted past— the same species of the dead baby bird she'd seen floating down a creek in her pre-miscarriage vision. "I don't know. I don't know anything, anymore." She wanted to believe Tillie Summers had the answers. It would be so much easier.

Tillie rubbed her hands together. "Remember when we first started, and you heard your mother singing?"

"Yes."

"Well, I heard it, too."

Paloma shrugged, not sure how to answer.

"Please look at me." Tillie waited until Paloma met her gaze. "You never told me that you heard it. Do you realize that?"

"I guess so." Now Paloma was even more confused. Maybe Tillie really could read her thoughts. Or had she somehow used mind control to make Paloma think she heard the sound of Esther's singing? Or perhaps it was a shared delusion. Paloma didn't know what to say. She bit her lip as she realized how irrational these thoughts would sound to the most rational people in her life—people like her father, Anca, and Reed, who would try to to explain all of this within the parameters of psychology, common sense, and science.

"I want to give you answers." Tillie looked at her evenly. "Answers you so deserve."

"What about all my miscarriages then?"

Tillie slid her chair even closer. "Did your mother's spirit speak to you about them?"

"She said that all three of my miscarriages were her trying to come back to me."

"Your mother told you that she tried to come back to you?"

"Yes, but she said that she couldn't be born into this world anymore."

Tillie stood and grabbed Paloma's hand. "Come over here." She led Paloma to the window.

"You see that?" Tillie asked.

Paloma followed Tillie's gaze. All she saw were two pine trees, their branches thick and rough against the blue sky.

"Your mother is out there." Tillie pointed to a spot between the pines.

Paloma started to make out a dim image of her mother flickering in and out of her peripheral vision. Maybe she *had* let herself get too vulnerable, had been too open to Tillie's suggestions. Or maybe it was real. But what did *real* mean anyway? "What does she want?"

Tillie gave her a winsome smile. "Watch her," she said. "Watch. She's trying to get through to you."

As before, Paloma couldn't make out her mother's spirit if she looked at her straight on, but if she turned her head just the right way, the image grew more substantial. She positioned her body at an angle until her mother came into focus.

Esther held her arms out with palms up. With a fierce yearning that made her heart beat too fast, Paloma imagined running to where her mother floated over the pine needles. She imagined that they could touch hands, that her mother would be able to give her all the hope she ever needed. But that was ridiculous. Her mother couldn't really be there. But then, either in the physical world or the spiritual one, dealing with mental illness or not, who was ever a hundred percent there, who could truly provide all that was needed?

And just like that, Esther vanished. Startled, Paloma gasped. She clutched Tillie's arm.

"Yes, that really was your mother." Tillie let Paloma lean into her, a diminutive but surprisingly solid support.

"Tillie…is there something you know about my mother? Something you should tell me?"

"What are you asking?"

Paloma inhaled Tillie's fear, a strange odor that smelled of rotten fruit, which reminded Paloma of the decayed-peach stench that had permeated Justine's kitchen. "Why did you hate my mother?" The words sputtered out of her mouth, spiky-sounding in their accusation.

"Paloma…"

"Be honest, Tillie. I need to know."

Tillie's shoulders caved. "I might have been very wrong about my judgments of her," she said. "I came to understand that she was ill. At the time, I didn't fully realize this."

All at once, Paloma knew. It was about Annie. Tillie thought Esther had something to do with the disappearance of Esther's own daughter, the little girl that should have been Paloma's big sister for the rest of her life. "You think my mother was guilty?" She looked down at her purse, debating whether or not she should show Tillie her mother's note.

"She was your mother and you loved her." Tillie sighed, a resigned breath that said it all.

Paloma felt her face flush with shame, even though she knew she had nothing to be embarrassed about. "My mother was mentally ill." Paloma paused. Why was it so hard to utter the words "mentally ill" when they were attached to her mother? It was as if by saying them, Paloma became disoriented and at any moment could inadvertently fall into a hole that people with sane mothers knew how to avoid— yet, at the same time, it also made her proud. Wasn't Esther that much stronger to have lived with such a challenging condition—and wasn't Paloma herself that much more resilient? She straightened her back. "In fact, she was severely ill. If you picked up on anything, it was probably because the voices in her head made her think she did it."

"You're right. That is why I said that I could be very wrong."

"Could be wrong?" Paloma said. "How about that you *know* you were wrong? You must have known the police found strands of both my mother's and sister's hair in the kidnapper's van."

Tillie simply shook her head.

"I've come to you for answers, answers you said that you wanted to give me. Please be honest."

Tillie's gaze darted around the room, her hand covering her mouth with shaky hesitancy. "I'm sorry."

"What are you sorry for?"

"It's difficult to explain…."

"Tell me," Paloma said. This odd little woman stirred such a tide of conflicting thoughts and emotions that she wished she had never seen her again. But it was too late now.

"I may be a psychic, but I'm like any other person. I'm proud of the ways I've helped others—but also have to live with the mistakes that hurt them, too."

"Did you hurt my mother?"

"I…" Tillie smoothed her fingertips across the windowpane, a regretful-looking gesture that made Paloma wonder how much of the past she wished she could change. "Your mother came to me for a reading after your sister disappeared—"

"But she became catatonic after my sister's kidnapping. My father told me."

"Not right after it. She came to me first."

"What happened?"

Tillie held her hand across her chest and patted herself in a self-soothing way that looked like she was trying to hold back a surge of anger or guilt—or maybe both. "She was too paranoid to listen to my advice. She…" Tillie patted herself again.

"She what?"

"She said that she had to…" Tillie sighed. "That she had to hide little Annie in order to protect her from the bad men. I understood that your mother was distraught. I also understood she was in shock, but there was something behind it. Something about the way she begged for my guidance on what to do next, about how she wanted me to understand that she wasn't guilty."

"She wasn't guilty," Paloma said. "She was innocent…an innocent woman who was falling into mental illness."

"She shared something else." Tillie's voice dropped into a hoarse whisper.

Paloma clasped her hand around Tillie's forearm. "Tell me."

"You have to understand I was sworn to secrecy."

"She's dead now," Paloma said. "My mother is dead. She's gone." Paloma sensed that her words were somehow showing her mother the possibility of a more peaceful place than the one she'd been hovering in, somewhere far off and forgiving. "You need to realize that it's okay to tell me now."

Tillie looked at her, an ancient woman with the open-faced expression of a child trying to decide what was fair. She clicked her tongue and for a moment didn't say a word, and then, reluctantly, the words came out. "You're right."

Paloma waited, afraid to say anything that would make Tillie reconsider.

Tillie closed her eyes for a moment and nodded. Then she looked down at her clasped hands. "Your mother said something very strange about how she did something good, even though others would think it was bad. She swore me to secrecy because she said that she never wanted the evil men to be able to find Annie again." Tillie rubbed her brow. "Her exact words were…"

"What were they, Tillie? Please try and remember."

"You may not believe me, but I remember exactly what she said. Her words took me so aback that I actually repeated them to myself after she left. It's just hard to think about, even now. But I suppose it's time to tell you." Tillie straightened her shoulders and exhaled. "What she said was..." Tillie met Paloma's gaze head-on, "...that she had to let your sister fall far away into the sea."

"She said that she had to let my sister fall into the sea? What did she mean by that?"

"I think..." Tillie faltered, but then she set her jaw in a sharp determination. "I cannot say what I am not sure of."

Paloma didn't like the insinuation. "What I am sure of is this: My mother was struggling with reality, and two men really did kidnap my sister." Paloma gritted her teeth, hoping to make Tillie understand. "What I'm not sure of...is what happened to Annie after that."

Tillie's face softened. "Yes, you're right. We don't know for sure what happened, but I still have something else to tell you."

Paloma clenched her mouth shut and waited, Tillie's concern fluttering around her like a netted butterfly.

"The advice I gave your mother was that she needed to tell the police exactly what she told me. You see, I couldn't be sure what really happened, and I didn't know what else to do. But after I told her this, she fell completely over the edge, screeching about how she wasn't guilty of anything and that if I really was a psychic, I should know without a doubt how innocent she was. When I tried to calm her down, telling her that the police would only be able to help if she told them the complete truth, she fled, more hysterical than any deranged person you've seen ranting on the street. I've always felt guilty about my part in all of this."

"I don't understand," Paloma said. "Why should you feel guilty for trying to convince her to do the very thing that might have helped?"

"But I should have read her better. I should have realized that she needed me to tell her that I was on her side." Tillie's eyes shifted to the past. "Because right after I told her that, your mother drowned herself—"

"No, she didn't." Alarmed that Tillie was suffering from the effects of dementia, Paloma wondered if she could trust anything she said. "My mother died years later of pneumonia."

"You didn't let me finish. Your mother had drowned herself but was brought back to life. She had gone under for quite some time. A surfer saw it happen. He paddled out as fast as he could, dived under where he'd seen her go down, and somehow found her. It really was a miracle."

"Miracle?" Paloma repeated the word, wondering how many millions of people in the world were praying for one at that very moment.

"Yes, it was. After that, the young man wrestled her lifeless body onto his board and paddled her to shore. I heard that people waiting on the beach were sure that she was dead. Her skin, I was told, had turned a mottled shade of blue but, unbelievably, he was able to resuscitate her."

Paloma gasped for breath.

"Are you okay?" Tillie's wrinkled forehead furrowed deeper with concern.

"I'm fine." Paloma didn't tell her that her own lungs had suddenly squeezed shut. She inhaled, barely able to breathe. "Please go on."

"Are you sure?"

"I need to know. It's worse if I have to imagine," Paloma said. "Please go on."

"I understand…" Tillie paused.

"Tillie, you were saying?"

"Oh, yes, I remember…" Tillie answered in a small voice that seemed to float in the air between them. "After your mother was rescued, she told anyone who would listen that she had seen a glimpse of what was on the other side of death. When people asked what it was, she just shook her head with such a savage look in her eyes that people turned away. I guess you know the rest of the story. Soon after the kidnapping, she became catatonic, and when she finally broke out of that, she was diagnosed with schizophrenia—although I'm sure she was already struggling with it before the kidnapping."

"What makes you say that?"

"Looking back, I realize she was keeping it down the best she could, but then the tragedy surrounding Annie must have opened up the floodgates."

"I wonder why my father never told me about the near drowning." Paloma looked pointedly at Tillie. "And why hasn't anyone else ever mentioned this to me?"

"I'm sure your father was trying to protect you from the knowledge that your own mother had come so close to committing suicide—and the other people who knew about it at the time wanted to steer you away from the pain. When a mother tries to kill herself, whether successfully or not, her child is bound to suffer a huge sense of betrayal."

Paloma thought about how she had already felt betrayed as a child due to the fact that her mother was mentally ill and her sister had been kidnapped. Even though she had been taught at an early age that Esther couldn't stop her own mental illness nor Annie's disappearance—and then had come to know that this, of course, was true—she still lived with a general sense that life itself had betrayed her. "But I overheard so much mean-spirited gossip about my mom over the years, I'm sure that her trying to drown herself would have reached my ears as well."

"Maybe it did, and you tuned it out."

Paloma shook her head. Could Tillie have dreamt this all up? Maybe her dementia was far worse than Ramiro knew.

"You had so much weighing on you at such a tender age," Tillie said.

"I guess so." The memory of Esther losing it on the kitchen floor seemed even more poignant. Her mother had said that the voices told her to drown herself, that it was the only way she'd be able to cleanse herself. Paloma glanced at her belly and realized Tillie might be right. Her father would protect her from this awful truth—and maybe she *had* blocked out some of the most unnerving accounts surrounding her mother. How she wished she could fly into the past as the adult she was now and save her sister from the kidnappers. If her mother had never suffered the unbearable loss of that tragedy, maybe she wouldn't have plunged into the depths of mental illness, and Paloma would have grown up having a big sister who would always be there, would always love her. Maybe her mother could have lived a happy life, playing with her and Annie in the surf and building sandcastles on the shore with them until they left their childhood. And then? Then Paloma would have moved on without being haunted by the past—and Annie would have had a future.

Tillie broke into Paloma's thoughts. "I'll never get over the feeling that I should have been able to lead your mother down a different path."

As much as Paloma related to the way regretful thinking could sometimes give a false sense of control (hadn't she just been doing it herself?) and even a false comfort in which one would be able to change things given the chance, she knew that Tillie wouldn't have been able to make any difference in the tragic outcomes of her mother's life and her sister's childhood. "None of what happened was your fault."

"If I had been more sympathetic instead of fearful, if I hadn't told her to go straight to the police and tell them exactly what she told me…" Tillie wiped her eyes. "If I had tried harder to understand her, then I might have been able to heal her. I had always prided myself on being able to help people."

Paloma pondered Tillie's words. Then she remembered Tillie's red-faced judgment of her mother. "If you felt so guilty, then why were you so rude to her on the pier that day she and I passed by you?"

Tillie hesitated and then, finally, spoke. "You're not going to like what I have to say." She dabbed her brow with a tissue. "But I'm going to be frank with you. Although I had learned about your mother's mental state…" Tillie clenched the tissue, her knucklebones jutting from the mottled skin of her fist. "I still wasn't sure if she had something to do with Annie's disappearance."

"But you weren't sure and you already felt guilty. It doesn't seem right. You should have given her the benefit of the doubt."

"Looking back, I agree," Tillie said. "But this was an innocent little girl. I just couldn't let go of the feeling that Annie would have been alive and well today if…"

"If what?"

"I really don't know." Tillie's head sagged. "After all these years, I really don't know."

"Now it's time I shared something with you." Paloma picked up her purse and fished for her wallet. She opened it and then slowly unfolded her mother's note. She handed it to Tillie.

With whispery reluctance, Tillie read it out loud: "Tell Tillie and…that I'm innocent." Tillie put her hand over her mouth and looked at Paloma. "I am so very sorry."

"It's okay, Tillie. Please know that I forgive you. You did what you thought best at the time. But I do want to know the other person's name she scribbled out."

Tillie pursed her lips. "I wouldn't know."

"Are you sure?"

"I'm too worn out." She sighed. "Please understand." A rush of air blew through the room, even though the window was closed. Tillie enveloped Paloma's hand in hers. Although Paloma felt conflicting currents of hurt and empathy, she couldn't pull away. Instead, she allowed the heat of Tillie's regret to penetrate her skin. Sensing that Tillie had carried guilt that was not only unwarranted but had also hurt her in ways that even Tillie herself wasn't aware of, Paloma began to understand how they both had suffered.

"But I want to repeat something I do know, Paloma. You are not your mother—and you will not suffer the same way she did. I am sure of that. One day you'll know that, too."

"I hope you're right." What more was there to say? She wished that she could be half as sure of Tillie's words as Tillie seemed to be. She turned to go.

"Wait," Tillie said. "Go to the spot where we saw your mother standing, and you will see."

"I'll see?"

"Something that is both mundane and miraculous."

"What do you mean?"

Tillie looked right through her. "I'm sorry, my dear...."
Her face went slack, her gaze falling into another world.

"I'll go, Tillie." Paloma bit her lip. "Thank you."

Chapter Twenty-Four

Once outside, Paloma inhaled the smell of dried grass and dirt. She slowly walked to the spot where she had seen her mother's spirit—or whatever the strange, flickering image of her mother could be called. She pondered Tillie's doubts regarding her mother's innocence. A shiver ran through her, though beads of sweat crawled down her back. With arms crossed, Paloma stood under the trees, absently looking at the scattered pine needles near her feet. She didn't know what to believe. Then she sensed a slight displacement near her feet.

Although she seldom ran across them, she wasn't at all surprised to see a snake. She carefully backed away and then stood as still as the cloudless sky above. It was just an ordinary garter snake, but it was beautiful. It sported yellow and white stripes down its back with matching stripes running down either side. She eyed it. The dark head with jet black eyes seemed to stare right back at her, a tunnel into the instinctual.

She—for some reason Paloma assumed the snake was a she—flicked her red tongue singed at the end with black. Paloma found that she wasn't at all repulsed as she would have been in the past. She watched the lone creature, thinking how this limbless reptile sliding between untamed nature and domestic landscapes understood things she'd never be able to comprehend.

"What do you have to tell me, snake?" Paloma gingerly followed its fluid movement.

"If you don't acknowledge your powers, then you might indeed go insane."

Startled, Paloma turned to see that Ramiro was behind her. He tipped his fisherman's hat in hello while Petunia tugged on her leash. The pug bull strained forward, pulling her whole body to get to the curious, earthbound creature ahead.

"What are you doing here, Ramiro?"

"Sorry to have snuck up on you," he said. "I just wanted to get a good look at whatever it was you were following. You looked so intent that my curiosity got the better of me." Ramiro eyed the snake and paused. "Snakes are quite mystifying, aren't they? Do you know that they've evolved a second way to hear? They're able to do this through their jawbones by picking up sound waves carried underground."

Paloma considered this. For some inexplicable reason, this intricate fact put her problems in perspective. Feeling like Alice falling down the rabbit hole again, Paloma drew in a deep breath. Then she turned her gaze back to the snake. Yes, it was sad that she had suffered through three miscarriages. And, of course, it was devastating to have had a mother who not only struggled with her sanity but also died young, and a sister who was kidnapped before Paloma was old enough to know her—but there were so many other people who had gone through far worse. And, yet, the world moved on. Mystery and life could still be found, even though cruel events forever scarred the psyche. She looked at Ramiro. "There are so many things right in front of us we're unaware of, so many things that make life worthwhile, aren't there?"

"You got it."

Paloma's lungs expanded in the same way they used to when she was a little kid and her Aunt Ruby would praise her crayon drawings with such enthusiasm that Paloma actually believed her.

"Are you thinking about someone you miss?"

How could he have guessed? "It seems your gifts are stronger than you know, Ramiro; I am." She tried to swallow the knotted lump that had formed in the back of her throat. "In fact, I realized in my session with your mother that I need to see this person."

"I'd make a wager," Ramiro said, "that most everyone's gifts are stronger than they know." Petunia ventured closer to the snake. "No pretty girl, you cannot play with the serpent." Now that Petunia had heard the word no, she pulled her little muscle-bound frame with even more vigor. Ramiro tugged her leash again. "Just cause it's not poisonous, girl, doesn't mean it won't bite."

Upon hearing this, Paloma felt a piercing bite on her ankle. She gasped. The pain grew so fierce, she leaned forward, an instant vertigo blurring her vision.

"You okay?" Ramiro held a hand carefully under her arm.

She rubbed her ankle. Despite the pain, nothing had happened; there was no mark and no bleeding. "I guess I'm fine..." The snake merely continued on, ignoring Paloma,

Ramiro, and Petunia who didn't make any difference in its world—because, of course, they didn't.

All three of them remained silent as they watched the snake undulating through the pines. Then, for the briefest of moments, Paloma felt that everything was going to be okay. Everything.

"Ramiro?" She looked at him as she noticed both the worry lines on his brow and the creases of laughter around his eyes.

"What is it?"

"What did you mean about me not acknowledging my powers?"

He patted her on the back like a proud coach. "I said that if you don't acknowledge your gifts, you might go a bit bonkers."

"But what do you mean by that?" Silently, too, she wondered why he happened to be there right after her reading with Tillie.

"What I mean is that when people push down their gifts, it can fester into all sorts of gruesome stuff." Ramiro made an exaggerated face, his eyes widening in mock horror and his lips gnarling in a gnome-like grimace. This comic expression along with his enormous Alfred E. Neuman ears made Paloma smile. Ramiro gave her a knowing nod. "And what I'm doing here is that my mother called telling me that she'd need some fresh air after your session, and would I please come with Petunia for an afternoon stroll."

"How'd you know...?"

Ramiro tapped his forehead. "Remember, my girl, you said so yourself: I have gifts buzzing around this noggin as well. Ramiro cocked his head and gave her a smile that held both tenderness and mirth. "I know it can be hard. But you must stay true to yourself."

Paloma glanced at his tattoos. How much pain did he endure to have each and every one of the images inked into his skin? "I don't know, Ramiro. In fact..."

"In fact, what, my dear?"

She wasn't sure how to articulate the dread. After all this time, she was still afraid that her visions didn't just predict future events but could *cause* them. "I just want to live a normal life."

"A normal life?" Ramiro shook his head. "You can still have a so-called normal life, and you can still find meaning working as a floral designer, but your true happiness will also depend upon tuning into your own gifts, learning how to help others."

"Do your gifts allow you to help people?"

Ramiro nodded. "I used to be like you. I was afraid. But after I finally accepted my abilities, I was able to do good. Instead of hanging the psychic banner over my head like my mother did, I decided that I'd weave my gifts into the very fabric of my life. I learned how to help others by tuning in to their needs during casual conversation. It's as simple as that."

"As simple as that?"

"After I opened my hardware store, I connected with even more people. Most of the time I don't even know what their exact issues are, but like a magician, I'm able to pull out the right joke or quote from my hat for the right person. It's my calling, you could say. In fact, my greatest pleasure in life is helping people laugh at their fears."

Paloma remembered how she had stood at her window and watched Ramiro walk Petunia, how she had thought that it was the down-to-earth characters like him who could very well be the truest healers.

"So you see, you have a future of possibilities ahead of you," he said. "A future that might not be the one you planned—but a decidedly rich one."

Paloma looked Ramiro straight in the eye. She swore that he resembled a sprite or elf of fairytale lore, laughing at all the mundane stuff of human foibles while at the same time wanting to heal those he felt deserved his magic. She raised her eyebrows. "You really are special, you know that?"

"I'm no more special than anyone else."

"I think you are."

"And so," Ramiro said, "we all are."

Paloma studied his thuggish nose and his wonderful, wonderful ears, which stuck out like tiny wings ready to take flight. "I do appreciate everything you and your mother are doing for me. I just don't know if I can live up to your expectations."

"No worries. Whether you know it or not, this will be your time to get past limitations."

Paloma thought about her out-of-body experiences. "Trust me, I've been working on that."

Ramiro whipped off his hat, waved it like a flag over his nutshell-brown head, and let out a belly laugh. "Well, then you have a good start, don't you?"

"I do." Paloma glanced at Tillie's window. Although she couldn't see her, she was sure that Tillie was observing them, maybe even guessing at their conversation. Or...was she merely looking at her son, who was conversing with the lady she recognized as the string bean of a kid from the pier all those years before? Or maybe all Paloma was to Tillie in this very moment was a familiar-looking person who Tillie's memory couldn't categorize. Paloma crouched down to pet Petunia. She wanted to ask Ramiro about how the dementia was affecting his mother and how much more the doctors were expecting it to progress but thought better of it. "I guess I should get going," she said, still feeling Tillie's gaze on them. "I'm sure your mom is ready to take that walk with you."

"You're right. I should get on with it." With a nod, Ramiro waved goodbye and trotted off with Petunia. But then he stopped mid step and called out, "It's time to look up to the sky, Paloma." He winked and then quickly turned back, continuing on his way without further explanation.

Paloma looked upward but saw nothing out of the ordinary. Yet, her heart began to race, and a cold sweat washed over her. Holding her hands against her temples, she told herself that it was time to leave. But then she heard it. A faint lullaby drifting down. Paloma peered through the tree branches at the cerulean sky until her eyes watered. Still, nothing. But the whisper-thin song told her to wait. Finally, the wavery image of her mother hovered above the trees. Paloma held her breath. Esther stopped singing. She gazed down at Paloma, her translucent body looking as if it were made of air and water. Paloma reached her arms overhead, hoping to draw her mother to the ground. But Esther merely smiled.

"Please know, my darling girl..." Esther paused, her windblown form swaying in the air. "...that your visions will never cause things to happen—unless you choose to make them."

Paloma stared up at her ghost mother, her desire to believe so intense that she could feel it burn all the way into her belly.

"This is the one present I can give you." Esther's eyes glowed. "You no longer have to be afraid of your gifts."

Relief flooded through Paloma's veins. She dropped to her knees in gratitude. And then, slowly but surely, Esther flew away, her long, auburn hair trailing behind her like the final streak of a sunset. Paloma watched it fade until the last trace of her mother vanished from sight.

Chapter Twenty-Five

Reed looked at her with clenched jawed scrutiny. "You saw Tillie Summers today? That crackpot who used to work on the pier as a so-called psychic?"

"I knew I shouldn't have told you." Paloma turned back to chopping a spindly carrot and then threw the pieces into their dinner salad. Clenching her teeth, she opened a can of tuna. It didn't seem right having to hold back so much from her own husband. "There's a lot more to Tillie Summers than you can imagine."

Reed gripped the neck of his beer bottle. "I didn't mean to…" He scratched his head. "I mean, I understand you're searching for answers."

"I know you don't want to believe it, but some people *really* do have a gift."

"Don't you think…" Reed's shoulders sagged as he let out a sigh "…that it'd be more productive to talk to a licensed therapist?"

"Not about this." Reed's skepticism hit her right in the gut; at the same time, her mother's parting words about why she didn't have to fear her gifts brought on an exquisite weightlessness. And in an instant, Paloma finally knew without a doubt that her visions *were* real—even if she didn't always like them, even if she didn't always know how to handle them. "I believe in my own gifts."

Reed studied her with his careful eyebrows-lowered, lips-pursed expression. "You *are* very perceptive—and some of those scenarios you've come up with do *seem* to predict actual events." He paused, elevated the beer to his mouth and took a long, audible gulp. "But none of those things mean you—or anyone else—have true psychic abilities."

A heated anger rushed through Paloma's body. "First of all, what you call those scenarios are actual premonitions. I don't make them up; they come to me." She stood before him and looked him square in the eye. "It's time you realize how your own fear has been blinding you." What she didn't say was what she knew his fear was about: the power of the unknown.

Before Reed could answer, someone pounded on their front door. Guessing it was Tatiana, Paloma told Reed they'd pick up the conversation later. Paloma swung the door open to see the puffy-faced teen standing on the welcome mat. Tatiana didn't say a word, but her red, swollen eyes and disheveled hair put Paloma on alert.

"What's happened?" Paloma glanced at the teen's belly.

Tatiana took in a huge lungful of air. "I need to talk to someone."

"Come inside." Paloma closed the door and led Tatiana into the living room.

Reed peeked in from the kitchen door and nodded at Paloma. She raised her eyebrows and nodded back, thankful that he understood Tatiana's need for privacy.

Paloma settled next to her on the couch. "What's going on?"

Clamping her hands against her belly, Tatiana looked down. "It's Marcel."

"Is he okay?"

"He promised me that we'd raise our baby together, that he'd never leave." Tatiana intertwined her fingers into a tight ball. "And now he wants to take a year off to live in Hawaii after graduation, all because his stupid surfer friend can get him a job renting out surfboards at some stupid-ass tourist resort."

"I'm so sorry." Paloma held a hand over her own chest as Tatiana's heartache bore into her. "He didn't invite you along?"

"He said he'd be living with a bunch of guys, but if I wanted to go I could. I begged him that we should get our own place there. I told him how he could surf, and I could paint, and we'd have this mellow year together with our baby. But he just kept saying how we couldn't afford not to live with a bunch of people—and that he really wanted to do this." Tatiana squeezed her eyes shut. "How could I have been so stupid?"

"You weren't stupid. Marcel is a sweet guy and there's nothing wrong with you hoping for the best. He's just young and afraid."

"I'm the same age, you know."

"But you're the one who's pregnant." Paloma squeezed Tatiana's hand.

"Yeah." Tatiana sighed. "I guess that's the big difference between us." She managed a small smile.

"Still, once he gets over whatever he's going through, he may very well change his mind."

"I don't know." Tatiana shrugged nonchalantly, but Paloma saw the weight of worry perched on her young shoulders. "He expects me to wait for him, but how am I supposed to know if he'll ever come back?"

"You won't, that's true—but hopefully he will."

"Either way, though," Tatiana shook her head, "I don't know if I want to wait."

Paloma bit her lip. "I understand…."

Tatiana's face crumpled and she turned away. "I'm not so sure about anything now."

"You're not sure about anything?" Paloma swallowed. "What about the baby? You're still sure about the baby, right?"

Tatiana's back straightened and a sharp silence filled the room. Suddenly, she shot up. "I'm going to L.A. for a couple of days with a friend." She wiped her nose on the end of her sleeve. "Her big sister lives there and has been through almost the same thing as me. I'm going to talk to her."

Paloma clutched a pillow to her stomach. "What did she do?"

Tatiana looked down at Paloma, a strange, flinty look in her eyes. "I'll be back soon."

"Wait." Paloma stood, heartbeat thumping and stomach fluttering. "Let's talk about this—"

"There's nothing more to say." Tatiana turned to go.

Paloma grabbed Tatiana's arm; it was now or never. "Reed and I—"

"What?" Tatiana eyed the door.

"Reed and I could adopt your baby." Paloma's body shook at the weight of her own words.

Tatiana jerked her head back. "Adopt my baby?"

"It could be an open adoption. You'd be able to see her anytime—"

"You better…" Tatiana narrowed her eyes, "…place your dreams on something else."

"Please," Paloma begged. "Just think about it."

Tatiana gave her a sad, sorry shake of her head and walked out the door.

Chapter Twenty-Six

As soon as Tatiana left, Reed came into the living room and held out his arms. From the downcast expression on his face, she knew he had heard what had just happened. Paloma leaned into him and heaved a long, heavy sigh.

"I hope you understand," she murmured as she pressed her head against his chest.

"Understand?" He pulled back with both his hands on her shoulders.

"For trying to talk Tatiana into adopting without checking with you."

"Look," he rubbed the back of his neck, "I get why you did it. And I get why you think that an open adoption with Tatiana would be a good idea, but—"

"But what?" She hoped that maybe, just maybe, Reed was opening up to the possibility.

"You need to remember that even though Tatiana is young, this is her decision."

"I know that, and I'm not going to try and talk her into something she doesn't want to do. But Tatiana is headstrong and rash and needs to fully consider this option. If she could understand that we'd welcome her involvement, that we'd want her child knowing she was the birth mother, then she might realize how wonderful this could be."

"There would be unforeseen problems—"

"There's unforeseen problems in every family," Paloma countered, sure that this was just Reed's way of stalling.

An abrupt thud of the front door's knob hit against the wall. Paloma was sure it was Tatiana, probably coming back to retrieve something she'd left behind. But then the scent of gardenia permeated the air.

Serena flew into the living room. Her eyes alight with anger, nostrils flaring like a runaway horse. "My sister will keep her baby. My sister knows what to do. She will keep her baby." Serena's voice hit a fever pitch. "Keep her baby!" She glared at Paloma. "You do not know what I know."

Paloma held up a hand as she tried to ward off Serena's accusing stare, while at the same time wanting to understand. "What is it? What do you know, Serena?"

Serena closed her eyes, and then let out a strangled sob. Shocked, yet also strangely prepared for the sudden outburst of tears, Paloma embraced Serena, who seemed to hold something deep and true inside herself that no one else was able to comprehend.

Serena abruptly backed away. Then, without a word more, she bolted out the door and vanished as suddenly as she had appeared.

Reed shook his head. "You weren't setting all your hopes on this, were you?"

"Reed, you have to know that I truly believed that Tatiana was hell-bent on keeping her baby. It wasn't until tonight, when she acted like she might go into a whole other direction, that I even mentioned the possibility of adoption." Paloma collapsed back on the couch. "I just don't know how Serena seemed to know—"

"I think." Reed exhaled. "It's time for us to try again."

"Reed..."

"What is it?"

She ignored the hopeful glint in his eyes. "What if..." she said carefully. "What if Tatiana changes her mind about adopting?"

He pressed his hands together. "Think about it," he finally said. "What if Tatiana agreed, thinking how great it would be to go off to art school and at the same time knowing that she'd be in her child's life anytime she wanted. What then?"

"What would be so bad about that?"

"Bottom line? The different fallouts from Tatiana's possible change of mind to Serena's adamant desire that her sister raise her own baby could lead to the biggest heartbreak of our lives."

"Heartbreak?" But merely repeating the word made her think.

"What if Tatiana wanted her child back when she was older? Even if it were a legal adoption, what would we do? And then you have to consider your Serena."

"My Serena?"

"She's always been your Serena. She's always followed you around, has always acted like she somehow—"

"Somehow what?"

He shrugged. "I don't know, like she owns you."

"That's not true." But she understood. There was an odd feeling of proprietorship that Serena seemed to claim on her, that she could take care of Paloma better than anyone else and so appointed herself as a watchful entity.

"It is—and you also saw how mad she just got." Reed pushed on. "Can you imagine raising a child while always looking over our shoulders to see if Serena is stalking us, always worried that she might do something crazy?"

Paloma averted her eyes. Could he be right? Serena had stormed into their house like an enraged hellcat, but then she also broke down in Paloma's arms afterwards, an inconsolable woman whose despair did not seem to include any strain of vindictiveness. "Things are just stirred up right now. I'm sure that Serena would learn to accept the—"

"Accept the fact that we had taken her own niece or nephew away? She just made herself more than clear on this, and Tatiana doesn't seem to know what she wants. So as much as this may sound like a good idea to you, it would be an emotional land mine, something that could rip everyone wide open. We can't take that chance. Not on a child's life." He pressed his lips into a determined line. "It wouldn't be fair."

Paloma stood. It was time. "I'm going to visit my aunt." Without a word more, she went straight into the bedroom to pack.

Reed followed on her heels. "What are you talking about?"

"My Aunt Ruby. I need to see her."

"This is crazy, Paloma. You need to calm down."

Paloma clenched her fists at her side, ignoring him.

"Anyway, I didn't even know you had an aunt."

"I do," she said. "She was my mother's sister. We lost contact." The more she talked, the more Ruby solidified into a real person. "She and my mother got into a horrible fight. She had pressed my mom about what had happened during Annie's abduction. My mom became paranoid and started yelling at her, accusing her of hiding Annie from her." Paloma remembered the horror-stricken look on her aunt's face and the hard-eyed rage on her mother's. Even though she was just a little kid at the time, Paloma knew that her auntie had nothing to do with it. In fact, she felt sorry for her as she wished—like she had so many times before and after that—that if only her mother could be cured, then all their lives would be healed as well.

"You lost contact with her," Reed raised his eyebrows in disbelief, "but you know where she lives?"

"I know it was Santa Barbara." Paloma pulled out a drawer and threw a couple of T-shirts on the bed.

"When was the last time you saw her?"

"When I was a kid."

"Surely, through all these years, she would have contacted you."

"Maybe she tried." Paloma skirted by him to retrieve her toothbrush and grab a quick moment to gather her wits.

"Paloma," he called after her, his uneasy hitch hitting her between the shoulder blades.

"What?" She marched back into the bedroom.

"I know you must be reeling with what just happened with Tatiana—not to mention, Serena. But suddenly deciding to visit some long-lost relative isn't the answer."

"I'm doing this whether you think it's a good idea or not." She squared her shoulders. "Anyway, you need…" she tried to keep her tone neutral so he wouldn't label her as hysterical, "...to stop trying to control me."

"What?"

"Nothing."

He narrowed his eyes and studied her, and in that moment, Paloma could tell that he both loved and feared her. She clamped her mouth shut, worried that she was about to lose it. But what was on the tip of her venomous tongue? She could not say.

Reed backed away. "What's wrong?"

Paloma didn't answer. But what she wanted to yell out was that she wasn't the only one who had problems, that he had plenty of issues, too. What about the boxed-in way he was living his life, only seeing half the truth? She unclenched her fist.

"I need to tell you something." Reed's authoritative tone seemed to echo off their bedroom walls. "Your father and I..." Reed held his hands in a pleading, palms-up way, which inflamed Paloma even more. "We think you should seek professional help."

She froze. She knew she looked like a madwoman, her eyes wide with anger, the pissed-off furrows on her brow more pronounced than ever, the veins in her neck bulging with ugly clarity. Her mother had the same look whenever Paloma's father tried to challenge her reality. But she was not her mother. She was not.

"I am worried about you," Reed said. "Very worried." He actually looked scared, and for some unfathomable reason this made her happy.

Then she heard Serena's voice floating through the condo. Knowing that Serena had gone back to her usual post on the sidewalk below brought on a sudden relief—and a strange rebellion toward Reed. She imagined flying into the kitchen and flinging open the cupboards as she grabbed all their plates, glasses, cups, and bowls and tossing them out the window. Yet even through her pent-up anger, hearing Serena sing about mermaids serenading sailors into their watery world brought on a wonderful empowerment.

Being drawn like the very souls Serena was crooning about, Paloma glided from the bedroom to the living room so she could better hear Serena's words drift through the balcony's screen door. Reed followed her, but she would not turn to look at him.

His hand brushed the back of her shoulder, but she shrugged it off. "Your dad and I realize you've had a lot to deal with and your grief is completely understandable, but you need help." He paused far too long; a pause that made Paloma's neck hairs rise. "Abel gave me a couple of referrals."

She crossed her arms. She would not allow the destructive images to leak out and become reality. She would not bash everything in sight. She would not spit in her husband's face. In all her life, she had never entertained these kinds of thoughts, thoughts that made her want to seriously wreak havoc on something—or someone. It scared her. Tillie was wrong. She probably was her mother's daughter, a woman who was going to fly away from reality.

She finally turned and faced him, but still averted her eyes. "Just let me be for a while, Reed."

"We do need to talk," he said. Then he shook his head and ambled into the kitchen.

Paloma tried to concentrate on Serena's singing, but an image of her mother with a shrieking Annie in her arms caught her. What if her mother had been locked in such a delusional state that she thought that it was perfectly reasonable to traipse into the ocean with her frightened two-year-old trapped in her arms? What if her mother had then shoved Annie under the sea and continued to push down on her daughter's desperate thrashing? What if her mother was so out of her mind that she didn't let up until Annie's fight for air stilled? Paloma shook her head, telling herself that these thoughts were conjured from the fearful depths of her imagination, not from reality itself.

As Reed rummaged around for something in the kitchen, she told herself to stop imagining nightmare scenarios about her mother and Annie and instead concentrate on the mystery of her aunt. That was where she'd find her true answers. Once, and only once, Paloma and her father had driven to Santa Barbara to visit her. Paloma remembered that he made her promise not to speak about it to her mother because Esther couldn't bear even the slightest mention of her one and only sister since their falling-out.

Paloma also recalled that her father scheduled the visit during one of the times when Esther had gone missing. Haven House, an unlocked psychiatric center, couldn't always contain Esther's restless spirit. No one had ever been able to corner Esther during those rare but nerve-racking sojourns, even though some neighbors swore they had seen her traipsing up the beach at dawn. Although Esther always made her way back, promising once more to take her meds and engage in the program, she seemed to fight a feral yearning after each disappearance, a yearning that made her despair grow into an even more menacing entity.

Auntie Ruby had greeted them at the door, her broad face as friendly as could be. Her crooked smile mimicked Esther's off-kilter grin, yet at the same time, it was different in that it didn't turn into tight-lipped paranoia. Ruby wore a black crop top and knee-length leggings. Her capable arms and squat calves, which bulged from her leggings like sculpted marble, made her look as though she could pull the whole world to the other side of the solar system if she wanted. That and her frizzy, blond hair, which reached all the way to her belly button, made Paloma want to skip down the street with her hand in hand, leaving her father behind with his sorrowful eyes and hunched-over back.

Soon after they entered Ruby's yellow and white-trimmed cottage, her father's face grew even sterner than it had been at the doorway. With narrowed eyes and pinched mouth, his daily mask of contemplative concern had been ripped off and replaced with one of distrust. Paloma sensed it was a warning, but of what she couldn't guess.

He sent her into the sunlit kitchen to play with Auntie Ruby's orange tabby, and Paloma readily agreed, hoping that whatever her father and aunt needed to talk about wouldn't take too long. She couldn't wait to spend some time with the aunt she hardly knew but loved all the same. Patiently, she stroked the cat and closed her eyes as she listened to his purr. But when she heard her father yell (he never yelled!), she set the startled tabby on the table and ran into the living room to see what was wrong and if she could stop him from shouting— just as she was sometimes able to halt her mother's rantings.

Yet neither her father nor aunt seemed to hear her ask what they were fighting about. After a tense pause, her father gently, yet adamantly, led her by the arm all the way back to the car. She couldn't remember what they had talked about on the long drive home. But she did remember that she never saw her aunt again, and anytime she asked her father about her, he explained that Ruby was a very busy woman—and then he'd maneuver the conversation in another direction, until Paloma would forget that she had even asked about Ruby. After so many years, Paloma learned that it wasn't worth bringing Auntie Ruby up at all.

Now she wished she had. She did know that her aunt had been married and divorced at least three times—once before the visit and twice years after—because she'd heard an old friend of Ruby's joking with someone at the bakery about how many husbands and lovers the "free-spirited" Ruby had gone through. Even though Paloma remembered that Ruby had changed her maiden name when she first married, she couldn't recall Ruby's married name and didn't know any of the surnames that may have followed. Paloma shut her eyes and focused. There had to be something more that could help her find her aunt. And then, a postcard-like image of an abundant rose garden popped into her memory. Paloma recalled that she and her father had driven right by it to get to Auntie Ruby's cottage.

Suddenly, Reed stalked back into the living room. He grabbed her shoulders, and she jerked away. "I'm here, Paloma. Where are you?"

"I'm fine," she said, backing farther away. "I just need to reconnect with my aunt."

"I don't think that's a good idea."

For some reason, Paloma found herself staring at his ankles. She grimaced as she noticed that they were too narrow for a man of his breadth and height. An abrupt silence crashed through the living room. Reed stuck by her side as Paloma stepped onto the balcony. She peered over the edge but could only make out the bottom of Serena's bedraggled skirt and tense muscles of her bare feet. "Don't go, Serena," Paloma called out. "Please sing another song." In her peripheral vision, she saw Reed's face burn with embarrassment, but she didn't care.

Serena's toes tapped an odd-looking code on the sidewalk, and then she belted out a mournful yet melodic song. Relief flooded Paloma. She turned to Reed. "Thank goodness she's singing again."

Reed gaped at her. "What are you talking about?"

"Nothing, Reed."

"You have to understand—"

"What do I have to understand?"

"There's this distance between you and me that never allows us to get any closer." Reed sighed. "I could run twenty feet toward you, but you'd push me back forty. I just can't reach you."

"Maybe that's all part of my grieving process," Paloma said. "Anyway, what about you?"

"Me?" Reed blinked in surprise.

"Yes, you. What about your grief? This was your baby, too—your third loss as well." She paused as she realized how sad it was that instead of consoling each other, they'd spent most of their time combating one another. "You wanted our babies just as much as I did. How are you dealing with it?"

"I've cried plenty."

"You have?"

Reed leaned his back against the balcony's railing. "I let it out when I'm alone in the car."

"Alone in the car?" This didn't sound like the Reed she knew.

"You know those nights we hear Chance howling for food, and I go down to feed him?"

Paloma nodded. Now that she thought about it, it always seemed to take an inordinate amount of time.

"After he eats, I stand around for a while until he finally slinks away. Don't ask me why, but it's not until the very moment his tail disappears around the corner that I'm able to really feel what's inside. Hell if I know why, but it's the only way I can finally let it out." Reed shrugged. "And then I get in the car and sob. I just lose it. I think about our babies. I think about my dad's death, my mom's loss, even about how pointless life seems sometimes."

"I'm so sorry." She breathed in the evening air. "I had no idea." She really hadn't known how much pain he'd been in and it made her realize that she was just as guilty as he in the unraveling of their marriage. "Do you ever think about us?" she asked.

"I do," he said. "I just don't know how to get back to where we were."

She knew exactly what he meant. They used to fit so well. There were times when doing the most ordinary things together made her feel a connection that she hadn't shared with anyone else. Even while doing dishes, they'd fantasize about things, like the most out-of-the-way places they'd visit together and then, later, all the amazing national parks they'd take their future kids to. Though they never made it to the exotic locales they daydreamed about (there was never enough time nor money), they were able to imagine together, to enjoy each other while muddling through their ordinary existence. This was their life before miscarriages, the life when they still celebrated their time together and could still hear their yet-to-be-born children's laughter floating over the horizon.

"I don't know either," she said.

"It's not over," Reed said. "This doesn't mean we're over."

"No, we're not," she said. Although Reed had become an expert at floating on the surface, she understood now how much she had simplified him. It wasn't fair to either of them.

"I know we see things differently," he said. "But I still love you."

Reed was trying. He really was. "I love you, too." She bit her lip and looked away. "But I still need to see my aunt. In fact, as soon as I'm done packing, I'm going to hop in the car and drive up there." Before he could reply, she clasped her hand around his arm. "Really, I'm going to be okay."

Reed's face adjusted itself into the tight-jawed, furrowed-browed expression of the concerned, yet discontented, husband. "I am worried about you."

"I'm a grown woman. If I want to take a trip by myself, it doesn't mean I've lost it."

"I never said that."

How quickly they had shrunk back into their warring corners. "No, of course you didn't." Paloma's anger flared so bright and hot again that she had to stop herself from shouting, *but you thought it, didn't you?*

All Reed did in that moment was shrug. A shrug that told her that he did, indeed, think she was losing it, and that if she left, he and her father would only dissect her emotional instability even more. But if she didn't leave, she knew things would only get worse. With a surge of energy, she marched back into their bedroom and pulled her duffel bag from under her bed.

At the doorway, Reed stood, a tense soldier carefully eyeing territory known to contain land mines. "Please don't go."

She turned her back to him as she started to fold the pile of clothes that she'd thrown on the bed. Then she placed a T-shirt in the bottom of the bag, the musty smell of long-stored canvas stirring an even bigger desire to leave.

Reed crossed over the threshold of their bedroom door and stood before her. "Why don't you wait till I can go with you?"

Paloma looked past him. "I have to do this now, and I have to do it alone."

"I don't understand."

"No, of course you don't," she said.

"Paloma…"

"What?" She had to get out of there. She really did. If she didn't leave now, she *was* going to lose it.

He studied her face with too much concern on his. "Surely, your aunt would have tried to get in touch with you—"

"That's the thing," Paloma said. "I don't understand why she never contacted me again—and I really don't have a very good answer why it's taken me so long either. But it's time now."

"You should get online and research her first, or at least ask your dad—"

"That's not going to work. My dad never wanted to discuss her with me. And I'm not even sure what her last name is now.

As implausible as it seems, I'm going to look for her in my own way."

"You sure you don't want me to go along? I could call in sick to work tomorrow and we could find a nice hotel to stay at."

"Please try and understand," she said. "I need to do this by myself."

"How are you," he let out a resigned breath, "going to find her?"

"All I remember is that my father and I drove by a huge rose garden right before we got to her house. As crazy as this may sound to you, I have a strong sense she still lives there. If I go to the same rose garden tomorrow morning, I'm pretty sure I'll remember where her house is."

"I still don't get it," Reed said. "Why would you have lost contact with your only living relative?"

Paloma knew it was a reasonable question. Even if her father didn't approve, it did seem odd that a grown woman didn't seek out her own niece. After all, Paloma had not only lost her only sibling, but then later, her mother, too. Paloma reached for the most likely explanation she could offer. "My dad and aunt had also gotten into a big fight."

"What was it about?"

"I don't know."

Reed swallowed. "I just wish you'd think about getting some help first."

"This will be my help." She looked him in the eye. "I'm going to get answers only Ruby can provide. And as impulsive as this seems to you, I'm leaving now."

"Why tonight and not tomorrow?"

"If I don't go now, I feel as if I might never make it."

"Let me at least call a hotel for you—"

"I'll handle it myself." She picked up her bag.

"But you haven't had time to make a reservation."

"I'll find someplace when I get there."

"But what if there aren't any vacancies—"

"Reed." She looked at him evenly. "I'm going."

"Promise to call me once you're there?"

"It's going to be okay," she said. "I will be okay." She hugged him goodbye and swooped out the door.

Chapter Twenty-Seven

Paloma stepped onto the sidewalk and eyed Serena. With her wild hair and furious eyes, Serena was still standing under Paloma's window. Now silent, Serena focused her blazing intent on Paloma. It wasn't personal, Paloma knew, but something beyond the usual symptoms of Serena's mental state. Something much bigger was biting at Serena's heels. All at once, Paloma feared for Serena's life as she recalled a recent vision where they were facing each other on the beach. Serena's skin had abruptly turned milky blue and her eyes a muted white. As the vision unfolded, Serena staggered blindly into the ocean. Paloma raced after her, but somehow Serena remained out of reach. Paloma ran as fast as she could through the water, but a rogue wave towered overhead and forced her under. She held her breath, squeezed her eyes shut, and swam with all her might underneath the wave's pull. She finally emerged, gasping for air. Her throat raw with saltwater, she searched the water's windblown surface. But Serena was nowhere in sight.

As she stood in front of the real-life Serena, Paloma took in a deep breath. How would Serena react to this nightmarish prediction? But she had to say something. "I know what a strong swimmer you are." Paloma paused, not wanting to scare her, but nonetheless heeding the duty to warn. She grappled with how she would explain her vision. But then, catching the anxiety behind Serena's tight glare, it didn't seem like a good idea to share it at all.

"I'm very strong in the water," Serena burst into a loud, operatic outcry. "I will never be weak. Never. Never. Never."

"Yes, I understand," Paloma said. "But the ocean can be even stronger than we are. Sometimes there're huge waves and powerful rip currents we cannot fight. We have to be extra careful sometimes."

"Careful?" Serena's face darkened. "I do not need to be careful. No, I do not." She stared at Paloma and then shook her head in such a vigorous manner that Paloma felt a wave of vertigo just watching her. Then she abruptly stopped, gritted her teeth, and muttered something dark and guttural.

"What did you say?" Paloma asked.

"I said what I said," Serena snapped back in such a way that Paloma, for the first time in her life, felt a pinch of trepidation toward her. Not that Serena would ever intend to harm anyone, but that her angst, which emanated from her body with the sweaty, dank stench of dread, could somehow cause physical destruction to the things, and people, surrounding her. Serena opened and shut her mouth in such a way that it looked like she had taken a bite out of the air. "But care does need to be taken," she yelled. "Care has to be taken. Or we will all be forsaken."

Paloma wished she could reach out and tame Serena's turbulent thoughts. But she could only try to understand, only try to make sense of the unseen so that Serena would know that she was on her side. "Why, Serena?"

"All the mermaids are dying." At this, Serena's eyes watered. She didn't make a sound, but tears rolled down her cheeks. "Every one of them, in every single sea."

Paloma dropped her duffel bag and gave Serena a careful hug that she hoped would provide her unpredictable friend—yes, she had come to realize, after all these years, that Serena *was* her friend—comfort rather than alarm. Under the loose denim shirt and beneath the rigid muscles, Paloma could feel Serena's bones, which she imagined as spindly, parched driftwood that could crack at the slightest pressure. "I'm so sorry," Paloma said. "I can see how upset you are."

All at once, Serena pulled back, her posture having changed from hunched-over sorrow to upright outrage. She sneered at Paloma's duffel bag, anger flashing in her eyes again. "When you get back, they will all be gone. Gone, gone, gone." Serena's face fell into her hands.

Paloma inhaled the tepid air. She thought about how the once commonplace sand dollars, cowry shells, and starfish of her youth had practically disappeared from the shoreline, and how, in many places, the ocean *was* dying. "I'm just going away for a couple of days, Serena. I'm sure they'll be okay."

"No, they won't," Serena said, her tone little-girl despondent yet still madwoman adamant. "You'll see. You'll see. The sea is dying. The sea is dying. Just like you. Just like me." At this, Serena jabbed a finger into the hollow of her own neck.

Paloma winced, the transferred pain, a shock-like stab piercing her own collarbone. "We aren't dying," Paloma said, hoping to pull Serena out of her anguish. "It'll be okay. When I get back, we'll go for another swim."

"Just go. Leave me and go." Serena stalked off, but then turned and pointed a shaky finger at Paloma. "You can't stop it even if you did stay. We are women between two worlds. We can't stop what is meant to be."

"Serena, I care about you."

A mountainous silence embraced them, and it seemed to Paloma that the two of them were separate from everything but each other. She watched Serena eye her with suspicion, and yet she could see, a spark of hope, too.

"I really do care," Paloma said. "I want you to stay safe."

"But what about the baby? Don't you want the baby to stay safe, too?"

"Tatiana's baby?" Paloma uttered, feeling the spike of her own heartbeat. "What are you saying?"

"I'm going to make sure that she's going to keep her. She's going to keep her safe. You will see. You will see."

Dumbfounded, Paloma searched for the right words.

Then Serena looked past her—no, more like through her—and began to hum. With her palms pressed up to the sky, Serena started in on a wistful tune that made Paloma's throat constrict. This time, it was a song about the demise of a sailing ship crushed against a jagged shore. There were no survivors except for one woman who was treading the stormy sea as she desperately clasped her baby girl. But then one brutal swell separated mother and daughter forevermore.

When Serena finished, she looked straight into Paloma's eyes. "There is but one hope, Paloma. One hope. Do not let men's fear of your power stop you. Do not. Do not let them stop you."

Paloma nodded. "I won't, Serena." Slowly, Paloma reached down and grabbed her bag. "And don't let anyone stop *you*, Serena."

Serena gave her a slow, sad smile. "I will try, my Paloma. I will try."

Chapter Twenty-Eight

Paloma made it to Santa Barbara a few minutes before midnight. She veered her car off at the first beach exit. Although she knew this wasn't the way to her aunt's house, if she stayed close to the coast, there'd be a better chance of finding a hotel. She slowed her car below the posted speed limit, appreciating the glints of moonshine bouncing off the night's laminate-black ocean. She smiled. How gratifying it was to be alone, to travel down a road she couldn't remember being on before. Moments later she saw that there was, indeed, a strip of hotels on her right. If only Reed could see how easy this was. Yet, as she drove on, the no vacancy signs told her otherwise. She sighed. Why had she been so hell bent on having to make the trip tonight anyway? And was she really going to find her aunt? She shook her head as she realized that her father would have tried to talk her out of it had he known. Perhaps that was what the rush was all about: getting to Santa Barbara before he knew and tried to pull her back from going, before she thought about it too much and pulled *herself* back from going.

She continued, starving for sleep yet at the same time as calm as the stately palm trees lining the beachfront promenade. Even if she didn't find a hotel, she wasn't afraid. It was a relief to be untethered, if only for a short while. She rolled down her window and sang "Over the Rainbow" as she pictured Ramiro Summers's hearty grin.

Once she was past the line of hotels and restaurants, she pulled into a beach parking lot. After she texted Reed that she had made it and all was okay (but didn't mention how she was about to hunker down for the night in the car), she turned off her cell and clambered to the back seat. As exhausted as she was, she could not settle down from the drive. She tried to curl into a comfortable position that could lull her asleep, but her body was still wired from all the miles that had sped by. Finally, after an hour or so, she took one last look at the muted stars from her fogged-up window and drifted off.

When the first light of day wedged itself into the car, Paloma woke in cramped-backed and sour-mouthed grogginess. She inched herself to awareness from the dazed state of a night drenched with dreams. She tried to recall them all but could only remember that in the very last one, she was swimming in the sea with Serena, who whispered the words: *I am the girl who floated underwater.* Serena then dove beneath the ocean's surface and sent Paloma a final goodbye from the flip of her green tail before it dipped into the sea after her. Paloma wondered what the dream was trying to tell her. But its details evaporated into the air as she watched the sunrise. And then she drove toward the morning's soft, yellow-wheat dawn.

〜

After a breakfast of cinnamon oatmeal and black tea in the comfortable anonymity of a bustling harbor-side diner, Paloma drove straight to what, thanks to a brochure she picked up outside the diner, she learned was called the Mission Rose Garden. She parked her car and breathed in the fragrance of rose petals and mowed grass. The garden was almost as large as she had remembered, its August bloom fading but still impressive. The roses brought to mind the colors of saltwater taffy, standing with their strawberry-pink, tangerine-cream, and vanilla-colored heads soaking up the morning's light. Just like a postcard, a sea of grass stretched directly behind it. Across the street, the Santa Barbara Mission, with its red-tiled roof, stone facade, and two bell towers, was perched against the crisp blue sky.

Paloma was tempted to take a stroll among the rose beds, but instead, revved up her engine and drove up a small side street, convinced that her aunt's cottage would appear. Within minutes, she saw it, just like she hoped she would. Although it was now painted forest green instead of its long-ago yellow, Paloma recognized the brass weather vane in the shape of a dolphin, which she only remembered now upon seeing it. How odd memory could be. If this weather vane had been taken down, she would never have recalled it. Yet there it stood, a testament that forgotten things could be found. For several moments, she remained fixed inside the confines of her car as she stared at the corroded sculpture. Then a movement behind one of the front windows caught her eye. A woman was opening her curtains, her stocky silhouette moving efficiently. Paloma clasped her hands to her chest.

It all seemed too easy, too simple. She was just going to knock on the door, and then her long-lost aunt would welcome her in? If Ruby hadn't contacted her after all these years, maybe she didn't want to be found. Yet what alternative was there but to drive away? And if she did that, then she'd forever wish she hadn't.

Drawing in a painful, pinching breath, Paloma stepped out of her car. She could see that whoever stood on the other side of the window was now watching her, tense-shouldered with expectation.

There was nothing else to do but to find her way up the stepping-stones to the arched doorway. And there she stood, knowing there was no need to knock. The door opened and a woman with frizzy gray hair and light blue eyes stared at her. She wore pink sweats and a black tank top, an older woman with burly arms and thick legs, a woman who could still move the Earth, if given the chance.

"Paloma?" the woman asked.

"Auntie Ruby?" Paloma said, sounding so much more matter-of-fact than the inward sprint of her heart.

Without a word, Ruby hugged her so tightly that Paloma had to pull back in order to catch her breath. "I knew it was you," Ruby said. "The second you got out of your car, I knew it was you! I'd recognize that wild mane anywhere."

Overcome with emotion, all Paloma could do was nod.

"Come on in, then," Ruby said as if it had all been planned and it hadn't been decades since they last saw each other.

Paloma's stomach fluttered with anticipation as she entered her aunt's living room. Filled with lively 1950s décor, it wasn't at all how Paloma remembered. Her aunt motioned her over to a red davenport with throw pillows sporting a pattern of dominoes, cards, bowling balls and pins. "You like all the kitsch?" Ruby asked. "After my last divorce, I decided to go Technicolor."

Paloma wondered if there were even more ex-husbands than the three she had heard about, but decided it wasn't the right time to ask.

Aunt Ruby sat cross-legged on the couch just inches from her. "I know why you're here." She cocked her head and studied Paloma's face.

"You do?" There was something so relatable about her aunt, something that went beyond Paloma's childhood memory of her, even beyond the familial resemblance that brought to mind her mother's crooked smile and round blue eyes.

"You need to know about your mom," Ruby said.

"Yes." Paloma noticed the uneasy way Ruby clenched and unclenched her hands.

Ruby abruptly stopped and uncrossed her legs, hugging her knees to her chest. "You know you look so much like her," Ruby said, her words trailing away in whispery reminiscence. "If you could travel back in time to when your mom was your age, you two would look like twins."

Paloma shook her head. "Really? I don't see it." No one had ever told her that she looked like her mother, and she wondered if her aunt's nostalgia was coloring her perception. "Besides our hair and eye color, my mother and I are very different. She had those high cheekbones and striking looks. I'm full-faced and ordinary."

Ruby gave her an odd smirk. "Oh, but I'm sure you are far from ordinary, Paloma."

"What do you mean?"

"My goodness, we need to catch up!" Ruby affectionately patted Paloma's arm. "Tell me all the details. Married? Kids? Work?"

"I'm married to a man named Reed, and I'm a floral designer." Paloma swallowed. "Not much else to report, I'm afraid. What about you?"

"Divorced four times and never want to get married again. Never had kids. Website designer." Ruby looked at her watch. "In fact, I'm supposed to be meeting a client soon—but it can wait. She grabbed her cell off the side table, sent a text, and then looked expectantly at Paloma. "Amazing timing on your part, by the way. If you had shown up even five minutes later, I'd already be gone."

"I'm glad I made it." Paloma smiled, grateful that she'd been so adamant about leaving Sunflower Beach when she had. She might very well have turned around and never come back if her aunt hadn't been there to usher her in. "The last time I saw you was when my father and I visited all those years ago."

Ruby slapped herself on the forehead. "But where are my manners? Let me get you a cup of tea."

Paloma shook her head, but her aunt was already up, a too-bright smile plastered on her face, a smile that couldn't hide Ruby's sudden trepidation. "You still live in Sunflower Beach?"

"I do. I drove up last night and had breakfast at the harbor café this morning, so there's no need—"

"No worries," Ruby sang out, disappearing into her kitchen.

What was her aunt so afraid of? Paloma bit her lip and stared at a porcelain figure standing on the side table. It was a little boy wearing a blue hat inscribed with the words "I Am A Sailor Boy." His impish grin reminded Paloma of Ramiro Summers, and for several minutes, as she took in the rest of the living room and wondered about her aunt's life, she forgot why she was there. But when Ruby brought in a tray with teapot, cups, and snickerdoodle cookies—the same kind that little Harrison had shared with her in Justine's immaculate living room—Paloma snapped to attention.

As her aunt set the clattering tray on the coffee table, Paloma's cheeks burned. She knew she had to ask. "What happened to you? Why didn't you ever reach out to me?"

Ruby plopped back down on the davenport. "I'm sorry, Paloma. It's complicated—"

"I'm better with the truth," Paloma said. "And I'm far better being told the truth sooner rather than later."

"I understand." Ruby poured two cups of tea into bright-red mugs and placed Paloma's on a matching saucer in front of her. "I'm the same way, so was your mom."

"So you understand."

"I do." Ruby's chin trembled. "I really wanted to be there for you, Paloma. I did. But it was impossible. Your father forbade it."

"He forbade it?" Even though Paloma had guessed at his resistance regarding her aunt, the word "forbade" was so absolute. She knew her father was a man who felt it was his responsibility to steer others in the right direction but forbidding her own aunt to see her did not sound like the ethical father figure she grew up with.

"Paloma, he did tell you how your sister, Annie, was kidnapped?"

"Of course." Paloma's mouth went dry. "Why do you ask?"

Ruby squeezed her eyes shut the same way Paloma's mother used to do before she had to explain something that was difficult to say—and even harder to hear. Then with a hesitant shake of her head, she gazed into her cup of Earl Grey tea. "I'm aware there were actual kidnappers. The police found their van in Chula Vista and figured that they'd fled over the border into Mexico. I was also told that strands from Esther's and Annie's hair were inside the van."

"I know all of this."

"Yes, I was hoping you would know at least part of it." Ruby blew on her tea but then set it down again without taking a sip. "You see, I understand that there was an attempted kidnapping—"

"Attempted?" Paloma's heart hammered against her chest. "What are you saying?"

"The police tried to find witnesses, but it was too early, just at the break of dawn. Plus, the ocean happened to be exceptionally flat that day, so there weren't even any surfers around. Detectives questioned your mom, and she *did* have a nasty bruise where one of the kidnappers had jammed the gun into her stomach." At this point, Aunt Ruby glanced at Paloma's belly, and Paloma hunched forward.

"So why are you saying it was an *attempted* kidnapping?"

Ruby held Paloma's hand. "There is a lot more to this than you know."

"You don't think my mother had anything to do with Annie's disappearance?" Paloma remembered the reluctant way in which Tillie Summers had finally shared how she wondered about Esther's guilt, how Esther had confessed that she did something good that others would think was bad, and how she had to let "Annie fall far away into the sea."

"Listen, Paloma." Ruby cleared her throat. "Your mom suffered from schizophrenia, so it could be very true that what she said was really due to a hallucination."

"You think she hurt Annie?" Paloma blurted out.

"I…" Ruby's mouth twisted, and Paloma could see she was trying to stop herself from crying. "No, I don't think she hurt Annie. But I do know what your mother shared with me. She told me that what really happened was that she was able to kick one of the kidnapper's right in the groin while the other one was starting up the engine. And then, during the escape, she had mistakenly banged Annie's temple against the inside of the van before she jumped out with her."

"You're saying that she got out with Annie?"

"Yes, Annie was still in her arms," Ruby answered, her voice suddenly hoarse.

"But she always said that the kidnappers drove away with Annie."

Ruby shook her head. "And she also swore on her very soul that she was afraid she might have lost her."

"Lost her?"

"Your mother was racked with guilt." Ruby cleared her throat. "But she did say that after the kidnappers had sped off, she decided that Annie had become their prey—and there was no stopping them from coming back and stealing her away for good."

Paloma nodded as she recalled Tillie telling her that Esther had said she didn't want the *bad men* to ever find Annie again. "What did she say happened after that?"

"Your mom…" Aunt Ruby lowered her gaze. "She said that she had to make little Annie disappear into the sea."

"I'm sure that was just another one of her hallucinations." Paloma didn't dare tell her that Esther had uttered the same confession to Tillie.

"Maybe so." Aunt Ruby's eyes welled up. "But your dad ushered her out of the room with way too much urgency, lecturing her about how she wasn't remembering things the right way—that what she had told the police was what really happened." Like leaves shuddering in the breeze, Ruby's hands fluttered as she reached for her tea. "He just looked so scared—"

"Do you remember what she told the police?"

Ruby set the mug down again without taking a sip. "Don't you already know?"

"I know only what my father told me."

"If you really think this will help." Ruby studied Paloma's face.

"Wouldn't you want to know everything if it had been your mother and sister?"

Ruby shrank into the cushion and nodded. "Yes, I would. You're right. You deserve to know."

"I want to hear it from you," Paloma said. "I want to know if it's the same story I remember."

"Where do you want me to start?"

Paloma flattened her palms against her temples. "Where it's important."

"Your mother told the police…" Ruby squeezed her eyes shut for a moment and frowned, a pained expression that held the weight of her memory. "She told the police that a man jabbed a gun into her stomach and forced her and Annie into the van before she could react. Once inside, she said that there was another man behind the wheel—and then the one with the gun wrenched Annie out of her arms. She froze and watched in shock while Annie shrieked so loudly that the man purposely banged the side of Annie's head against the inside of the van. Then he slid the door open and shoved Esther onto the pavement. The van sped off so fast that when the cops went to verify your mom's story, they had no problem finding the tread marks."

"Then why don't you believe that's what really happened?" Paloma said, fear closing in around her throat. "Maybe my mother had such horrible survivor's guilt after she told the police the real story that she made herself believe she was the one who had hurt Annie." She suddenly remembered the scribbled note in her wallet and reached for her purse. "There's something you need to take a look at." She took it out and handed it to her aunt.

Ruby peered at it, reading it out loud: "Tell Tillie and… that I'm innocent."

"I believe that scratched-out name is yours, isn't it?" Paloma stared pointedly at her aunt.

"Paloma," Ruby whispered as she handed the note back. "What I believe is that your father loved your mother so much that he wanted to protect her from her own truth."

Paloma gripped one of the pillows. The room tilted and her insides jolted so hard she was sure that she was on the verge of another out-of-body experience.

Ruby placed a hand on Paloma's shoulder. "Don't leave now. You have control over this."

With a shudder, Paloma came back to herself. "How did you know?"

"You were about to leave your body, weren't you?"

Paloma flinched. "But I don't understand how you—"

"It runs in our family. Your mother, God rest her soul, had even more of the gift than I do. She didn't just have visions; she could leave her body at will and come back in a matter of seconds."

"She could?" A wave of fear swelled in Paloma's stomach. She *was* her mother's daughter.

"Your mom didn't want you or your father to know," Ruby said. "After she fell in love with him, she tried to will it away, and when she couldn't, she tried to ignore it. I think, though, what really happened is that the more she tried to push it down, the harder it hit—so hard that it bled right into her reality."

"Do you think that's why she became schizophrenic?"

Ruby paused, and Paloma knew she was struggling to say the right thing. "I don't think so."

"But why her—and not you...or me?"

"I think it's a matter of genes. Then some major crisis happens, and it's like the cork explodes off the bottle and the genie bursts out. In your mom's case, the crisis happened to be very traumatic."

For several moments, neither of them spoke. Then Ruby broke the silence.

"Schizophrenia does run in our family as well," she said. "I was told that your great-grandma Hanna suffered from it so severely that they locked her away."

"They locked her away?" A smothering pain in Paloma's chest and arms pressed into her; she could feel the very same restraints that she somehow knew had bound her great-grandmother.

"I'm afraid they did. Things have gotten a lot better now, even though there's still a stigma surrounding mental illness."

Paloma stood and walked over to the nearest painting. Trying to gather her thoughts, she pretended to study the 1950s atom-and-kidney-shaped abstract. "What you said about my father..." Paloma turned to face Ruby as she clenched her hands behind her back. "You said that he loved my mother so much that he wanted to protect her from her own truth."

Ruby looked down and slowly nodded.

All at once, Paloma knew that her mother's stories were built on both fact and fiction. She pictured how her father used to soothe Esther, pressing her head against his chest as his gaze landed someplace too far and complex for Paloma to follow. No matter what had happened, though, Paloma understood that his was an absolute truth. He knew to his very core that Esther's actions were never based on any ill intent. And that is why he continued to love her, continued to protect her, even in death.

Ruby gave her a confused smile similar to the ones that used to cross Esther's lips. "I hope you understand, Paloma. I couldn't visit you. He didn't want me to trigger her. And when I asked to see you after she died, he told me that it would only confuse you. Your dad was just taking care of your mom—and her memory—the best way he knew how."

"But why didn't you contact me after I turned eighteen?"

"I should have." Ruby patted the seat next to her. "But I was still afraid that it would upset your dad."

Paloma crossed over to the davenport and sat back down. Without saying a word, Aunt Ruby turned her left hand over to show Paloma her exposed wrist. On it was the exact "Hold Fast" tattoo with the same bold red-and-black font that graced Ramiro Summers's knuckles.

Chapter Twenty-Nine

The next morning, Paloma woke up to find herself tucked into a queen-sized bed, covered with a light blue bedspread, inside a small, clean room. For a moment, she couldn't remember where she was, yet she knew she was safe. Then she stared at her duffle bag resting on the pine floor and remembered that she had spent the night in her aunt's guest room. She drew in a breath, recalling how her aunt had shared that she was the one who gave Ramiro Summers his "Hold Fast" tattoo, as she had trained to be a tattoo artist for a time—to name just one of the many careers she had pursued over the years. It wasn't until Ramiro and Ruby had gone their separate ways that Ruby decided to get the same words inked on the inside of her wrist. It didn't surprise Paloma that Ramiro and Ruby had been an item, for there was a similarity between these two friendly, yet intense, souls. But she wondered at the meaning of the matching tattoos.

An insistent chirp interrupted Paloma's thoughts. She gazed out the window and eyed a mockingbird perched on the highest branch of what she knew to be a gold medallion tree, its sunset-yellow blooms hanging like bouquets. The slender bird cocked its head, looking straight at her while it serenaded her with another interlude before launching into the cornflower-blue sky. Paloma watched the bird's retreat, her mind suddenly ablaze with thoughts of Serena. What was Serena doing at this very moment? Was she going for a morning swim? Was she safe?

Paloma shook her head, then forced herself out of bed. She threw on a T-shirt and jeans. Following the aroma of toasted onion bagels and hazelnut coffee, she hurried toward the kitchen, emptiness gnawing her insides and a disconcerting rush of anticipation constricting her chest.

Ruby greeted her with her lopsided grin, bringing to mind Ruby's younger, blond-haired self, whose stout sureness had seemed in direct opposition to Esther's gaunt-faced unpredictability. "I'm making us my favorite comfort food: lox, bagels, and cream cheese." She poured a mug of coffee and proceeded to stir in a heaping spoonful of sugar followed by three tablespoons of cream. She handed it to Paloma and winked. "That's how your mother liked her coffee."

Paloma accepted the mug and held it between her palms. "It's how I like mine, too."

"I had a feeling."

Ruby led her to the backyard. They ate their breakfast picnic style on a vintage tablecloth; its faded cherry-and-leaf print a reminder of more hopeful times. Although the sun gazed down from a spotless sky, the sunshine wasn't as glaringly sharp as it was in Sunflower Beach. Relieved, Paloma inhaled the spicy-green scent of her aunt's nearby herb garden.

"You know," Ruby said. "I can tell you've suffered much sorrow in your life—even beyond the loss of your sister and the early death of your mom."

Paloma nodded, not sure how to answer. Did her aunt really possess the psychic gift she claimed ran through their family? Could she be picking up on the miscarriages, which Paloma hadn't opened up about yet? Or was Ruby merely noticing the unhappy creases etched on Paloma's brow? Eyeing the grass, Paloma thought about Annie. "Tell me more about my sister." And that's when the very air between them changed into something that felt as tangible as the earth beneath them, solid and yet unpredictable, a sleeping giant under the threadbare tablecloth.

Ruby set her plate down and wiped her hands on the sides of her cargo shorts. She neither smiled nor frowned, and for what seemed like an impossibly long time, didn't say a word. Finally, she tilted her head and, with a maternal touch of hand on Paloma's shoulder, nodded. "It's time I tell you everything." She paused as she frowned at their breakfast remains. "But let's gather up our dishes first and head to the house."

~

For several moments, Paloma remained mute. She couldn't look at her aunt. Instead, she studied a lone ant traveling across Ruby's countertop, seemingly in search of its colony. It moved in an erratic way that conveyed fear and what seemed to Paloma, loss.

"Please say something." Ruby sponged off a plate. "I need to know you're not angry with me." She handed the dish to Paloma, as if they had always been in each other's lives, relatives who were used to cleaning up together after family gatherings.

Her throat constricting with both fear and love, Paloma reached for the plate and stacked it in the dishwasher. "I just don't know what to say."

"I know this is a shock for you, but I really believe…" Ruby backed away from the sink and went to sit on one of the chrome chairs surrounding her kitchen table. She turned her wrist over and stared at her "Hold Fast" tattoo. "Just think about it. Serena is the same age as Annie would be had she survived. She has the same olive skin as you and your mother, the same black hair as your father. Her one blue eye is the same shade as yours—and the other one could have changed color due to the side of her head getting banged in the van."

"I've never heard of such a thing."

"I looked it up. Head trauma can change someone's eye color."

"Come on, Ruby. This is just too crazy. Your theory that Anca and Leonardo somehow found Annie and then raised her under the name Serena doesn't fit. And as far as her eye color goes, Leonardo has blue eyes, and Anca told me that the lone green eye runs in her family."

"And I bet you never saw any pictures of Anca's relatives," Ruby said.

Paloma shrugged.

"Did you know that Anca was adopted?"

"No—what does that have to do with any of this?"

"Quite a lot, actually." Ruby drew in a breath as she caressed her tattooed wrist. "Anca was adopted from a

Romanian orphanage when she was three. I used to be friends with her mother before she passed. She had told me that it was a terrible place, that she could tell that Anca had been severely neglected—or worse. I'm guessing that Anca's instincts kicked in when she saw that Annie had been abandoned and, acting on pure instinct, she just scooped her up."

"She still would have reported it to the authorities once she got Annie home," Paloma said. "I know Anca and Leonardo; they wouldn't do something like that. And, besides, Serena looks like their biological daughter."

Running her fingers through the gray tangle of her frizzy mane, Ruby sighed. "You just assume that Serena is Anca and Leonardo's biological daughter. I bet you if you really looked at the girl, you would see that she's your sister."

"That girl, as you call her, is now a grown woman," Paloma said. She was about to tell her aunt that Serena struggled with severe mental illness but refrained. This fact would only fuel Ruby's fire. "You haven't seen her in years. And besides, Anca and her family didn't move to Sunflower Beach until Serena was in sixth grade. I remember."

"And I remember that Anca had a mom in Sunflower Beach that she used to visit, and then she suddenly stopped after Annie's disappearance. It wasn't until after her mother's death that she showed up again. After it was a long enough time for people to assume that Serena was her own daughter, a girl whose one eye conveniently changed color, which made any resemblance to the memory of two-year-old Annie even more remote. It was good timing for her, being able to move her family to Sunflower Beach to live in the house she inherited while taking over her mother's florist shop."

"You're reading into things that mean nothing. Nothing at all." Paloma's legs felt hollow. "Anyway, why would you notice when—and if—Anca stopped visiting her mother?"

"I lived just a couple of houses away, remember?"

Paloma's head throbbed. Her aunt was being ridiculous. Now she understood her father's anger toward her. "Aunt Ruby, you haven't thought this through. How would Annie end up in Anca's hands after my mother had supposedly fought off and then escaped with her from the kidnappers? How would Anca and Leonardo be able to raise Annie and get her into the school system without a formal adoption? They couldn't just spirit her away for all those years and then come back to Sunflower Beach without anyone being the wiser. None of this makes sense."

"But it does," Ruby said. "First of all, she could have easily paid someone to create a fake birth certificate for Annie, stating her name as Serena Nicholson. And secondly, but more importantly, I have a very strong feeling that Anca saw what happened after your mom escaped out of the van with Annie, plus she often took break-of-dawn walks before she headed to the shop."

Paloma turned away from her aunt. If she had known that Ruby would be throwing this at her, she would never have made the trip. She looked out the kitchen window as she planned her goodbye. The urgency of Ruby's belief pushed against her skull, though, a pressure that made it difficult to turn back around. But she forced herself. "A strong feeling?"

"I know you're having a hard time believing me," Ruby said. "I understand that it's an awful lot to take in."

Paloma leaned against the counter. She stared at her aunt's hands, palms pushed flat against the Formica table but fingers still trembling. Paloma could tell that her aunt was more nervous than she let on. But how could she believe this preposterous theory? "So you're saying that my mother abandoned Annie and then Anca found her?

"Yes."

"You think," Paloma swallowed, "that Anca saved Annie from my mother, don't you?"

"Your mom was ill. She didn't know what was right or wrong. And whatever happened that day, Anca and Leonardo ended up raising Annie as their own daughter. I know it sounds far-fetched—"

"Beyond far-fetched," Paloma snapped. "And what about my dad? Don't you think he'd recognize Annie when they moved to Sunflower Beach? She couldn't have changed that much."

"Sometimes what's right in front of our faces are the things that are easiest to push away," Ruby said. "Especially when it's too painful."

"But Anca and Leonardo are good people. They wouldn't have just stolen my sister without thinking about how devastating this would be for my dad."

"Anca didn't know your dad—or you, back then. They just came to visit her mom from time to time. What I think happened is that Anca assumed little Annie was going to be thrown into the system, and she so desperately wanted a child herself—plus you know how Leonardo does whatever it takes to please her."

"Then what about you?" Paloma clenched her hand against her stomach.

"What about me?"

"If you had guessed this all along, why didn't you say anything? Do anything?"

"It didn't come to me right away."

"Why do you feel this need to believe that Serena is Annie? I've long since accepted that my sister is dead, that she died a long time ago. Let it rest, Ruby. Let Annie rest."

Her aunt shook her head. "You don't understand. It's time to accept the truth."

Paloma didn't know what to say. Serena did seem to carry something inside herself that grew from a profoundly sad place. And Paloma did sense it the most when she saw her following young families with babies. During those times, Serena's sorrow was so overpowering that it infiltrated Paloma, making her want to cry and scream at the same time.

⌐

The next morning, Paloma found her aunt in the kitchen, sipping coffee. A small, old-fashioned suitcase sat at her aunt's feet.

Paloma settled on the chair across from her. "Are you going somewhere?"

"Yes." Ruby nodded. "My friend has a cabin off Paradise Road and I'm going to stay with her for the next couple of days."

"I understand," Paloma said, even though she didn't. "I guess I'll gather up my stuff and head home, then."

"No, it's important you stay here." Ruby leaned across the table and squeezed Paloma's hand. "I'm doing this because you need time to be alone."

"What?"

Ruby held a hand under Paloma's chin. "Please keep an open mind."

"My mind is as open as the sky," Paloma said, thinking how impossible it would be to not have an open mind after what she'd been through this summer.

"Have you ever heard of a spiritual crisis?"

Paloma hugged herself. When she had researched the term "out-of-body experience," the term *spiritual crisis* had popped up. She hadn't clicked on it for fear it would lead her down an even more confusing path. She had also overheard her father confer with a colleague years ago about a client who claimed she was going through one. Given the client's symptoms, Abel was sure that it really was a nervous breakdown, as he explained that people sometimes deluded themselves with metaphysical labels in order to dodge the painful origins of their problems.

"I know you've been holding back on telling me what you've been going through, Paloma."

"I'm sorry, I didn't mean to—"

Ruby held up a hand. "It's okay. I understand. I went through some pretty rough stuff myself when I was about your age, stuff that led to my own spiritual crisis, and then breakthrough."

"What happened?"

"I suspect," Ruby said, "that it was similar to what's been happening to you. It's scary because you're not sure if any of it is real or not, right?"

Paloma stared at her aunt. "You went through this, too?"

"I did. It started after my first divorce. Oftentimes it's sparked by loss. But loss is just the precursor. Now you have to let it overtake you. It's like letting a fever burn through you before you can heal." Ruby smiled at her. "But don't worry. I know how fearful you are about suffering the same fate as your mom. But I'm here to tell you that you're on a different path. Remember I've gone through this, too—and I've never been diagnosed with any serious mental disorder. Eccentric, yes, maybe a tad neurotic, too—but I wouldn't have it any other way."

"But what purpose does this all serve?"

"The purpose is to open you up so that you can fully accept your gifts."

"But why do I have to be alone?"

"You have to stay in it before you can fully understand."

"Stay in it?"

"You'll see more of the truth. It's not going to be easy. But I know you can do it." Ruby paused and then laid her wrist on the table, showing her tattoo. "I got this after I went through my own breakthrough. It's an old sailor's term that they used to get tattooed on their knuckles, reminding them to hold fast on to the lines during rough seas so they wouldn't be thrown overboard. I got it to remind myself to hold fast on to my gifts so I wouldn't end up drowning in my own disbelief."

"Did Ramiro Summers go through the same thing? Is that why you gave him *his* "Hold Fast" tattoo?"

Ruby merely smiled, grabbed her suitcase, and stood. "It may help you to think about what you're *really* yearning for, Paloma."

"What I'm really yearning for?"

"Don't worry," Ruby whispered, "it will come to you."

Chapter Thirty

Ruby hugged her with such ferocity that it seemed to Paloma they were parting for decades again rather than just a few days. Then, without a word more, her aunt walked out the door and Paloma was alone.

Immediately, she slipped into a strange, flighty state that made her feel like she was about to blow away. To keep herself together, she came up with a mental to-do list: delete emails off her phone, finish the novel she had brought, take a walk through the neighborhood. Yet she froze, her mind racing faster than she could rein it in. What *had* happened to Annie? And why in the world did Ruby tell her to think about what she was really yearning for? Paloma stood stock still in the center of her aunt's living room. She knew that if someone was peering through the window, they would think her a deranged soul, paralyzed in an eerie pose. Maybe she even looked like her mother did when she became catatonic. But movement took energy, and she was stuck at level zero. Though maybe if she tried harder, she could summon enough strength to at least seek refuge on the couch. She'd feel safer if she could curl into herself. But it was only ten in the morning.

Although depleted, she knew she didn't need sleep, and that even if she could make it over to the couch, coaxing herself into a hazy veil of slumber would only make her feel more lost upon awakening.

Then her cell rang, releasing her. With a charge of newfound energy, she sprang into action. She grabbed her phone off the coffee table and without looking to see who called, turned it off and slid it between two dream interpretation books sitting on the lowest level of Ruby's bookshelf. Then she flew through the house, closing all windows, shutting the bedroom and bathroom blinds, and pulling the kitchen and living room curtains closed, making sure there were no gaps. Now privacy was hers.

Still unsettled, she paced the house until she stood in the middle of Ruby's living room again. This time she allowed herself to remain still, trying to picture the mother of her past and the sister she never knew. She pondered Ruby's claim that Serena could be Annie. She shivered, trying to throw off the thought. What was she supposed to do if it were true? But it couldn't be.

She should have never visited her aunt. It sure as hell didn't provide any real answers, only more questions—reckless questions that could only hurt people. The smartest thing to do would be to go back home. Forget all this nonsense. She'd follow her father and Reed's advice and see a psychiatrist. She'd stay in the real world. She'd been a fool taking in Ramiro, Tillie, and Ruby's talk of psychic abilities. A desperate fool. But then, when she tried to move her legs, they would not obey. As unyielding as her body had been before, this time was worse. She was frozen inside her own skin, and nothing could release her. She wanted to scream but realized no one would be able to help. Hyperventilating, she waited for release.

Then something in her brain crashed. Like a crack of thunder, it roared inside her ears. She clamped her hands against her head as she pleaded out loud for it to stop. But her only answer was a blinding flash of light that cut into her thoughts. Now she had gone beyond anything she'd known before. She had flown over the edge. And yet, still, all trepidation had retreated. For too long, she'd been balancing on a tightrope between reality and visions, between what she thought was real and what she had told herself couldn't possibly be. It was finally time to surrender.

Like a deep snowfall, silence settled over her, enfolding her in a hushed world where nothing bad could happen. Her mind became calm. Still unable to move, she stood without thoughts of past or future. She stood without emotion. She grew cooler by the minute. Her body became both stronger and lighter. Time shifted in such a way that she wasn't sure if mere minutes were sifting by or if they had formed into something as large as an hour—or could it be even several hours? Her vision dimmed, making everything appear behind the milky fluttering of a moth's wings. Sound became muted, the loud tick of Ruby's wall clock now barely audible. Still standing, she imagined that she was floating between what she knew this world to be and a malleable place where all possibilities existed.

After an indeterminate amount of time, her body finally gave in to her desire to move, and she swayed to a sudden, far-off melody. She couldn't be sure if it was seeping through the closed windows or perhaps was playing in her head, a long-forgotten melody from childhood. A tingle grazed her crown and then sent a pulse down her spine. She didn't fight the sensation. Surprised at her own calm, she wondered if she had already been through the worse of it, if whatever this was might be easier than what Tillie and Ruby had predicted. But just as soon as this thought settled in, the room became electrified with a charge similar to what would hit before her most violent visions.

Before she knew it, a rock-hard shock slammed her back onto the floor. She struggled to get up, but her body convulsed with such violence that she wondered if she'd somehow been electrocuted. Pushing her hands against the floor, she willed her body to stop. But it wouldn't. All she could do was shut her eyes and hope it would end soon. How long could she last like this, her body flailing against the floor like a hooked fish begging for release? How long could her brain withstand the fierce shaking? Maybe she was dying. If this were meant to be the end, why fight it? With that thought, she let her body ride the convulsions like waves.

Slowly the tremors subsided. Paloma lay motionless. Sweat ran down her body, making the floor underneath her slick with it. Yet she shivered, her fingers blue and limbs numb. The only thing she was capable of doing was focusing on her ragged breathing. Within minutes, she gave herself over to the vulnerability of sleep.

She later jolted awake in utter darkness. Sprawled against the floor, she recalled her last feverish dream, in which a sea lion was circling around a small creature it was trying to protect as it barked in alarm to an upcoming rowboat.

Without understanding why, Paloma started crying, tears pouring down her cheeks. She let herself cry far longer than she ever had before. When she was finally spent of tears, she sat up and then gingerly stood on shaky legs. Or was it the ground that was shaky? She couldn't be sure.

She shuffled in the direction of the kitchen. Her body had been pummeled and her brain shell-shocked. With each step, she winced from jolts of pain that surged from her head down to her feet. She had to stop. The pain made each breath a concentrated effort. But the worst of it was the slithering sensation inside her skull. What was happening to her? Was this the same thing her aunt had experienced? But maybe it was exactly what her mother had gone through. Maybe she was utterly losing it. Paloma clasped her hands against her head, willing it to stop, but it only grew worse. What could she do but go on, though?

She grasped the edge of the wall and inched her way toward the smell of discarded coffee grinds and ripe bananas. Finally, she stepped over the threshold. The stove's clock glowed at 11:59. Holding on to the counter, she realized that it had been over twelve hours since her aunt had left. She pulled the kitchen curtain open. The night's inky-blue light spilled through, landing on her outstretched arms. She squinted, wondering if any of this was real.

ᕲ

The next morning, Paloma found herself tucked between the flannel sheets of Ruby's guest bed. She couldn't remember the nighttime trek from kitchen to bedroom but figured that this was all a part of whatever strange transformation she was going through. She threw off the covers but didn't move. The twisting inside her brain had intensified, while at the same time, everything around her blurred. She clapped her hands, testing her hearing. Like her eyesight, it had also diminished even more than it had the day before. As her mind continued to whirl inside her head, the external world misted over. Were these strange symptoms ever going to end?

She got out of bed and reached for her jeans and T-shirt but shook her head. Her skin needed to breathe. Naked, she shambled into the kitchen. She wasn't the least bit hungry, though, and her usual craving for caffeine was absent. What was she to do with herself? Grateful now that her aunt had left her on her own, Paloma decided that the only thing she could do was to keep giving in to whatever bizarre state this was.

She glided from room to room, a fog-like fugue drifting through her. By midday, she was roaming around in a vaporous landscape, where waking and dreaming melded together. Was she really walking down her aunt's hall or was she stepping along the rose garden's pathways? Was she even at her aunt's house or was she home dreaming all of this up? She stopped in front of a mirror and nodded at her reflection, then floated into the guest room.

Though her sight was still hazy, Paloma eyed the chenille bedspread, her jeans strewn on the floor, the day's light trying to sneak through the curtains. Her skin tingled, just like it did before all her visions. She waited as the fringes of an inner image started to form. First it was just the outline of a house, a silhouette of a tree, the swath of a pristine sky. Then she saw Justine's childhood home zoom into view. Similar to Paloma's other visions, this one continued without her consent—yet instead of glimpsing into the future, this one flew into the past. It was Justine as a young teenager, exiting her pink bathroom. Justine then entered her bedroom and sat at her makeup table. She brushed her hair and heaved a sigh, and in the next instant, she bent her head down and sobbed. On her table was a small picture of a newborn baby. Paloma saw her own young teenage self entering Justine's room. Justine jerked her head up, pushed the photo under her jewelry box, and rearranged her face to its regular expression of haughty perkiness.

Justine then gripped Paloma's wrist, making her vow that neither of them were ever going to have children. Paloma nodded her head, not wanting to upset her friend and, at the same time, wishing she had summoned up the courage to say no.

The vision dimmed. Paloma drew in a deep breath. She finally uncovered what Justine had been hiding all these years. She wished she could have been there for the young Justine, a girl who never allowed herself any self-pity, never wanted to admit her own pain—a girl who dealt with something so devastating that she didn't even share it with her best friend.

Paloma racked her brain, trying to figure out a time when the teenaged Justine would have been able to hide a pregnancy, would have given birth without Paloma ever knowing. And then she recalled that in ninth grade, Justine had metamorphized from a rail-thin teenager who wore skin-tight tops and cut-offs to a curvy young woman who favored loose, bohemian blouses and baggy jeans—and how she had disappeared that summer to visit her cousins in Arizona.

As Paloma tried to pull back more memories, her crown crackled with electricity. She prepared herself for yet another vision. She held her breath, waiting. Within moments, she saw a lanky teenage boy surrounded by friends and family as he blew out eighteen birthday candles. He had only one wish. Paloma could not only read his life, but his very thoughts: Although he was well-loved and had enjoyed a happy childhood, he desperately wanted to know his birth mother. And now he was old enough. Before the vision retreated, Paloma could see that his eyes were the same amber color of Justine's.

After the vision dissolved, Paloma held a hand across her chest. One way or another, she was going to have to find a way to share it with Justine. Hopefully it would not only mend what had been broken in their friendship but, more importantly, would give Justine some much-needed peace—and perhaps hope as well. Paloma smiled at the thought.

As she pictured the different ways Justine was going to react, her stomach suddenly growled, reminding her of her physical body. She thought about getting up and making her way into the kitchen. But even though she hadn't eaten a bite since her aunt had left the previous day, she winced at the thought of food. Staring at the ceiling, she thought about how Ruby would be coming back the next day. What was going to happen between now and then? Before she could think about it any further, she fell into a cavern of sleep.

Chapter Thirty-One

Paloma did not wake until the next day. She arose slowly, in thick, gradual increments. She finally stood and stretched her arms to release the discomforting sensation that her skin had grown too tight.

She walked as fast as her somnolent legs could carry her to Ruby's bathroom. Sitting on the side of the turquoise tub, she drew herself a bath and threw in a handful of nearby bath salts that had a handwritten note, "For Paloma," taped on top. Once in the verbena-scented water, she relaxed. Hypnotized by the sound of the dripping faucet, she noticed that the movement inside her brain grew more urgent. She closed her eyes, wanting to focus, wanting to understand. Then a vision suddenly flew into her swirling mind. Once it landed, her brain finally became still.

A flat sea reflected the overhead sun as it blinded her with its blades of light. She was three years old, pretending to dig in the sand, but really watching her mother and father. She held her hand over her brow and squinted. Her parents were only a few feet away, but the glare made it hard to see what was happening on their faces. She did know that her father was holding her mother back from entering the water. She also knew that her mother was crying so hard that she might fall down. Paloma wanted to get up and squeeze her arms around her mother's legs, but she couldn't move. Finally, her father was able to soothe her mother's sobs. Limp as a washed-ashore sea bird, her mother fell into his arms. He picked her up and carried her to their blanket.

Like a baby, Paloma crawled to her mother and tried to curl into her lap. But her mother held her hand up. Paloma stopped.

"I'm sorry, my darling girl, but I don't deserve you," her mother said.

Paloma did not know what this meant but could feel— even though she was only three years old—that her mother needed her. "I love you, Mommy."

Her father scooped Paloma up and held her against his chest. "She knows you love her, *mija*," he whispered in her ear. "And she loves you very much, too."

Paloma closed her eyes and leaned her head against the crook of his neck. Her mother started to sing one of Paloma's favorite songs, "My Bonnie Lies Over the Ocean," but replaced Bonnie with the name Annie.

Paloma held back from crying as she listened to her mother's singing. Still in the tub, the adult Paloma couldn't be sure if this vision was a buried memory or something she had manufactured. But one thing she did remember now: Her mother sang that song a number of times, always replacing the name Bonnie with Annie, always making Paloma yearn for her mother's attention, even when she was right there.

Just as Paloma thought she'd come back to herself, her body prickled in anticipation of yet another vision. Oddly, she was still seeing the one with her mother and father on the beach, lying in the sunlight next to her mother's prone body as her father read. Suddenly, both the three-year-old Paloma on the beach and her adult self in the tub saw the same thing.

Paloma's mother raced to one of the small rowboats left between sand dunes by nearby homeowners, and then plopped two-year-old Annie on the weathered seat. With a fierce yank, her mother then grabbed the boat's line and pulled it to the ocean. She shoved the boat into the water and jumped in. Annie sat so still that she looked like a doll that'd been propped up, her glassy eyes staring straight ahead, but at the same time, incapable of taking anything in. Her mother furiously rowed past the bobbing kelp beds. She stopped. A wrecked look on her face made Paloma know that her mother believed this was her only answer. She quickly scanned the shore and kissed Annie on the forehead.

Then Esther slipped into the sea, a soundless sob contorting her face. She swam with head out of water toward the beach. She didn't look back at little Annie, who waited in the boat like an abandoned pup.

And then there was Anca. Anca, who crouched behind one of the other boats and waited until Esther raced off, her sobs wafting over the waves. But as Anca rowed out to sea to collect her, Annie tumbled overboard. Without a sound, without a struggle, Annie sank beneath the surface. Anca cried out as she continued to row. With tears streaming down her face, she was about to dive in after Annie. But just then, a sea lion surfaced, buoying the little girl safely on its back.

With her mouth open in shock, Anca watched as the sea lion glided over to the boat. Anca reached over and grabbed the water-drenched Annie in her arms. The sea lion, with its huge, unblinking eyes stared solemnly at Anca and then dove underwater as Anca held Annie and cried with relief. Anca and Annie had no idea that Esther had run back and was about to dive in the ocean. Encapsulated in the vision, Paloma knew without a doubt that despite Esther's fears that the "bad men" would come back for Annie, she had decided to retrieve her, decided that she couldn't let her darling Annie float out to the mermaids, even if she thought it was the only way to keep her alive. And when she saw that Anca had saved her, she slowly walked away.

Replaying the vision, Paloma cried until the pounding of her heart stilled. Then she got out of the tub, wrapped herself in a robe, and waited for her aunt. When Ruby returned home shortly afterwards, Paloma fell into her arms. As vulnerable and open as a newborn, Paloma knew what she'd been yearning for—and yet denying herself of—for all these years: the solid grasp of a mother figure. As Auntie Ruby continued to hold her, the sadness lodged inside Paloma's chest—an ever-thickening mass that had been there ever since Paloma could remember—quietly began to dissolve.

Chapter Thirty-Two

Ruby grabbed Paloma's duffel bag. "Come on," she called. "We need to get there by dawn."

In Ruby's brightly lit kitchen, Paloma rubbed her hands together. She looked out at the pitch-black sky waiting outside the window, anticipation coursing through her veins. "It's four in the morning. I'm sure we'll make it." She was still wrapping her mind around how everything led up to this particular date. It was surreal—but, then again, what wasn't? "But why is it so important to get back on the exact anniversary of Annie's disappearance?"

"Because," Ruby said gently, "…because you're worried about Serena."

Paloma nodded. "You're right." She followed Ruby outside and then settled in the driver's seat of her own car.

After they turned onto the highway, a shudder ran through her body. She thought it might be signaling an upcoming vision, yet nothing materialized—except her ever-increasing fear surrounding Serena. She drew in a deep breath and told Ruby about the adult Annie had become, which Ruby took in with quiet aplomb. When Paloma was through, Ruby replied how she wasn't surprised; since Serena was, indeed, Annie, it all made sense.

When Ruby wanted to know more about Serena's family and the little sister she grew up with, Paloma paused, wondering what had happened when Tatiana visited Los Angeles. Had she been talked out of having the baby? Was she still pregnant? Paloma shared it all with Ruby: the miscarriages, Tatiana's pregnancy, Anca's fear about Tatiana giving birth, Paloma's misguided hope about an open adoption, even the vision regarding Justine. Again, Ruby took everything in with silence. When Paloma was through, she looked at her aunt, hoping for answers.

Ruby exhaled. "I don't want to comment on what may or may not happen, but I do know something else from the past you probably don't." Ruby tipped her water bottle back and took in a thirsty-sounding gulp.

"What is it?"

"Anca's adopted mother told me that Anca's birth mother died right after Anca was born—and her birth mother had only been seventeen."

Paloma swallowed. It seemed everyone she knew was affected by their own family history—even, at times, repeating it generations later, whether they knew it or not. "That explains a lot."

"I'm sure Tatiana will find her way." Ruby patted Paloma's hand and then leaned her head against the closed window.

As her aunt drifted off, Paloma continued to drive toward a future that was as unpredictable as anyone else's in the world. The road flashed by, and then she found herself parking the car in the same spot where the kidnappers' van had peeled away so many years ago. Even though the tire marks had long since vanished, a clump of ever-expanding Mexican fan palms on the strip of nearby grass remained. Ruby woke with a start and then clasped her hand on Paloma's forearm. "We still have time," she said. "Let's catch the sunrise."

They got out of the car and stood, watching the day open into the translucent yellow of a newborn sky.

"It's time," Ruby whispered.

Without a word, they made their way through a pebbly path between beach cottages and then over the rise of sand dunes. An insistent wind whisked by. They continued on, miniature sand storms prickling their ankles. Once they made their way down the other side of the dunes, they stopped. Nestled at the base were two time-worn rowboats, one a scattered skeleton of ripped-up planks and cracked-in-half seat, the other, trying to survive with its once-white paint worn down to a gray, weathered wood, and rusted-beyond-repair oarlocks. Paloma bent down and touched the splintered seat, wondering if this was the very boat her mother had rowed Annie out to sea on. Ruby took Paloma's hand and beckoned her forward.

A few moments later, they planted their feet on the flat plain of beach. Gazing at the whitecaps of an already choppy sea, Ruby sighed. "Strange how we never really know," she said, "of all the sad and desperate thoughts running through the minds of our loved ones."

"I'm not sure we even know what flows inside ourselves some of the time." Paloma noticed the faint scent of gardenia floating through the air—so faint in fact, she wondered if she had imagined it. Yet all at once, she overlapped Serena's face with her vision of two-year-old Annie's wide-eyed fear before she fell overboard and the peaceful, secretive smile when the sea lion delivered her to Anca. Paloma realized that Serena's mind had transformed Esther's well-meaning—yet still devastating—abandonment into her own myth: A mermaid mother who had not only saved her but also continued to watch her beyond the waves was more reassuring than the truth of a human mother who had cast her away.

An even stronger wind blasted by. Paloma squinted. She was sure she saw a splash near the kelp beds. Although she told herself that it was most likely a pelican diving for its meal, she sensed it was Serena. She waited. Then she saw someone with long, black hair emerge from the surface, only to disappear again. Her heart flew into her throat. Serena *was* out there. Without thinking, Paloma whipped off her shorts and T-shirt and threw them on the sand. She stood in her underwear and bra under the morning's crisp light, inhaling her strength.

"What are you doing?" Ruby asked, yet at the same time, she pulled Paloma toward the ocean.

"I'm going to her."

Ruby nodded with a mixed expression of sorrow and joy.

Paloma raced into the water. In the suspended world that was Serena's, she pushed toward the boundary of waiting kelp beds. Terrified that Serena might drown, Paloma swam so hard, her lungs felt like they had lost their capacity to recognize air. She stopped and scanned the surface as she struggled to breath. There was no sign of Serena. Paloma frantically kicked her legs as hard as she could. Every few seconds, she stopped, only to find herself fighting to hold her head above the ever-powerful current. Yet she pushed on, swimming until the lone figure of her aunt Ruby waiting on the shore looked as if it were a dream.

Farther out to sea than she'd ever ventured on her own, Paloma treaded water. Crests of windblown ocean slapped her face. Her fingers paralyzed with cold and her body past the point of numbness, her limbs were too weak to work much longer. It was a very real possibility that right then and there, the sea would decide to swallow her. But all at once she could see her father inside the walls of her childhood home. He picked up the one photo of their family of four before Annie was lost and Esther fell under the spell of mental illness.

With Paloma in her father's arms and Annie in her mother's, Esther and Abel grinned at the camera as if their future were as clear and bright as the sunny sky that crowned their heads. The solemn Abel now hugged the framed picture to his chest and with his sad, rumpled smile, bowed his head.

With renewed strength, Paloma inhaled as much air as she could, then submerged herself and pushed onward. She knew Serena was near. In the murky saltwater, Paloma spotted a lithe body, like liquid itself, undulating with the current. Mesmerized, she wished that she could turn into one of the mythical mermaids Serena so adored, but then, instead, she shot up, gasping for air. Her eyes stinging, she waited. Then, right beyond the rise and fall of the sea, there was Serena. Exhausted and elated, Paloma swam toward her.

"You okay?" Paloma asked.

"I am always okay in the sea," Serena answered. "I am safe here. I am safe even when I want to dive into the darkness. I am safe."

"Will you swim with me, Serena?" Paloma undulated her arms just beneath the surface, keeping her head above the choppy water as best she could. "Will you swim back to shore with me now?"

For a moment, Serena didn't answer. Then she nodded. "You do know that I was the girl who floated underwater?"

Paloma smiled, picturing Annie's extraordinary rescue. "I know, Serena. I know you were that girl."

～

After they made their way to shore, Serena gave Paloma a brusque hug. Her scent of sea and gardenia melded into Paloma's wet skin, and before Paloma could say a word, Serena turned. With her long, wet hair flying behind her, Serena traipsed through the tide. Paloma watched her skip up the beach, relief anchoring itself deep inside her belly.

Ruby ran up to her. "You must be freezing." She draped a blanket, which she had insisted on toting all the way from the car, over Paloma's shoulders.

"Thank you." Paloma gripped the blanket closer, rivulets of saltwater dripping down her back. "Thank you for helping me understand."

"Just remember..." Ruby smiled, her eyes brimming with tears. "I'm here for you now—just as you'll be for your sister."

Paloma squeezed her aunt's hand in hers. "I know."

Chapter Thirty-Three

Later that morning, after Paloma had dried off and changed back into her clothes and then wolfed down a peanut butter-and-honey sandwich Ruby had brought, she and Ruby lounged side-by-side on an oversized beach towel. Paloma sighed, filled with both emotions and memories. She was about to doze off when Ruby looked toward the dunes. "There's someone up there. Someone who's been watching you."

Paloma turned to see a lean woman in shorts and a white tank top looking their way. "That's my friend Justine."

"I believe," Ruby said, tilting her head, "that you two need to talk."

Paloma paused, looking back at the ocean, the very same body of water where her mother had left Annie, thinking it was the safest place to hide her daughter from the bad men, a beautiful vastness that held so many secrets beneath its shimmering cover.

"She's waiting, you know," Ruby said.

"I've been, too."

They walked to her as Justine hiked down the dunes toward them. When they were finally within speaking distance, Paloma saw the upset on Justine's downturned mouth. "What are you doing here?" Paloma asked. Justine's disquiet clamped itself against Paloma's heart, a dense guilt, which Paloma could tell had cemented with time.

"I saw your car. Reed told me you were visiting your aunt." She looked at Ruby. "And you must be the aunt in question. I'm Justine."

"I am that very aunt," Ruby replied. "And I look forward to getting to know you." Ruby looked at Justine, then at Paloma. "But I'll let you two talk first." She smiled and then sauntered down to the shore.

"What's going on?" Justine rubbed her brow.

"We drove back this morning. We wanted to commemorate the day Annie disappeared." Paloma bit her lip. It wasn't time to divulge the strange and wonderful knowledge that Annie was Serena.

"Paloma, I get why you're here…but what about your aunt?"

"It's a long story." Paloma clamped her hands together. "I'll tell you later. But right now, we need to talk."

"What is it?" Justine stepped closer and stared into Paloma's eyes. "Are you okay?"

"I need to share something important—something you need to know." Paloma took her by the hand and led her to a nearby rock. They sat side by side like they did when they were kids drying off on the rock's sunbaked warmth. Paloma inhaled, wondering where to start.

"Just tell me already," Justine nudged her.

"Justine, did you…" Paloma averted her gaze. "Did you have a baby when you were younger—before you had Harrison?"

"What?" Justine shot to her feet. "What are you talking about?"

"I had a vision. I believe you had a baby…a boy. He's going to be eighteen this year."

Justine's hand flew to her mouth. She paced for a bit with the twitchy look of a wild animal looking to escape. Finally, she sat back down. She shook her head. "This is unbelievable."

"Tell me," Paloma said, "what happened."

"I was fifteen. I didn't even know the guy—he was some friend of a friend visiting from another city, I don't even remember. But it was all a huge mistake, a mistake that gave me no choice." Justine's chin quivered as she hunched into herself.

"What do you mean?" Paloma had never seen her friend look so vulnerable.

"Remember how chunky I'd been as a kid and then how skinny I got by the time we hit middle school? Remember how you were worried about me being anorexic?"

"I do." Paloma was surprised Justine could remember her concern, as she dared to voice it only once—and Justine's response was to quickly change the subject.

"The weight loss had made me used to my periods being sporadic, so by the time I got a test, it was too late." Justine stared at her hands. "My mom carted me off to my cousins in Arizona. I thought about keeping him, I really did…but everyone expected me to give him up, and I figured it was best for him." Justine sighed. "But even now there's a big chunk of my heart that's still gone. There's never a day I don't miss him—that I don't replay over and over again how his tiny hand held onto my pinky, begging me to never let him go."

"I'm so sorry, Justine. I had no idea—"

"I wanted to tell you—especially after I got back. But then it would have made it that much more real. I was in this zombie-like state of denial and anger—and I made you responsible."

"You made me responsible?"

Justine gazed down at the sand, but then she lifted her head, tears welling up in her eyes. "I know it doesn't make any sense. I know it wasn't fair. But we had always had each other's backs, and when you didn't show up at that party where I got way too drunk and decided to lose my virginity in the bathroom with a random guy, I blamed you. It wasn't right, but I ended up directing my rage at you."

Paloma's throat went dry. It all made sense. "Is that why you had that session with Tillie Summers?"

Justine nodded. "She told me that I was wrong for holding it back from you, that I had to tell you why I made you promise about never having kids—and that I should tell you that you needed to break that promise. But I was still too pissed off at what happened, still wanting to put the blame on you instead of my own dumb-ass decisions—and on the young, fumbling guy who didn't even realize the condom broke."

"Justine, that silly promise is not why I miscarried. You *have* to know that."

"But it was wrong of me. I've been so unfair to you. And as time went on, it just got harder and harder to tell you." Justine reached for her. "I'm sorry." Justine's apology pressed into Paloma, as smooth and warm as a beach stone.

"Please know there's nothing at all to forgive—I'm just sorry I didn't clue into your pain back then." Paloma squeezed

Justine's hand. "But…there's something else I need to let you know now—something about your son."

Justine's eyes went wide with alarm. "Is he okay?"

"Yes, he is. It's just that he wants to meet you, but you have to wait till after his eighteenth birthday—something about not wanting to upset his adoptive mom."

Justine gasped. "Every time…" she whispered, "…Every single time I'd dared to think what it would be like to finally see him again, I always figured that he'd be happier if I let him be, that he'd never want to know me." She pressed her hands against her chest. "But are you saying there's a chance? A chance that I'll get to know my first-born son, a chance that Harrison will know his big brother?"

Paloma nodded. Her visions did have meaning, could help others.

Chapter Thirty-Four

A s dusk settled its tranquil blue light into the corners of
their condo, Paloma and Reed finished dinner. "You
haven't told me much about your visit with your aunt," Reed
said. "There's got to be more than you two having a picnic
on her lawn and her insisting you drive back together on the
anniversary of your sister's disappearance."

"There's so much more." Paloma stood, taking his hand
in hers. "Let's go for a walk."

They left the dishes and strode out into the evening.
Thankfully, the weather had turned. The whole neighborhood
seemed to breathe a sigh of relief. "You seem different," Reed
said. "What happened?"

Paloma looked up at the sky, knowing there were some
things she needed to store under her own thoughts, memories
that were to be opened for her examination and no one else's—
just like the baby clothes her father had given her before the
first miscarriage and the worn shirt from her dead mother,
which covered them. No one else would ever need to open
that box, no one else would fully understand the emotions
that wafted from it. "It'll be okay, Reed. I'm okay."

Reed nodded. "Paloma?"

"What?"

"I'm sorry we haven't found an answer yet."

"I know." Paloma squeezed his hand, steadying herself. "I have something to tell you," she said. "Something you're going to have a hard time believing."

"I might surprise you."

Paloma looked at him, hoping he was right. "I know you won't want to believe it; I didn't at first."

"Whatever it is, you can tell me."

Paloma listened to the sounds of clattering silverware someone was loading into a kitchen drawer, the drone of another neighbor's TV, a mother calling out to her teenage son to make sure to wear his seatbelt. Normal, everyday sounds that belied the very strange and beautiful currents that ran through people's lives. She turned to Reed. "Serena Nicholson is my sister."

He took a step back. "What?"

"Serena is Annie."

"That can't be." He raked his fingers through his hair.

"It's true." She stared at a perfect half-moon hanging on the horizon. "I'll explain it all to you." They continued on, Reed asking her the same questions she had hammered her aunt with.

Paloma felt Reed's disbelief cut through her. Would he ever be able to accept this incredible turn of events? Just as she was about to lose hope, Chance appeared. The tomcat slinked his scrappy body toward them. When Chance came closer, he looked only at Reed and yowled with an insistency that made Paloma smile.

"There, there, guy. I got you," Reed cooed. He picked up Chance and cradled him in his arms.

Paloma held out a hesitant hand. She dared to pet Chance's spiky fur. "I didn't think he'd let anyone cuddle him."

"I'm pretty sure I'm the only one." They stood for several moments listening to Chance's gravely purr until Reed let him go. They watched him turn the corner. "I can't tell you if I believe this or not, but I'm wondering," Reed said, "what you want to do about Serena?"

"I want to be her sister," Paloma answered, a shiver of appreciation running down her spine. "I want to be there for her in a way I never was before. I just need time to figure out how." Her world was finally rotating into what it was meant to be.

"I understand," Reed said. "If this is true, it's huge."

"It's hitting me more and more."

"Is there anything else I should know?"

Paloma smiled. "Not right now—but I can tell you that I was finally able to open my eyes."

"Open your eyes?"

"Yes," Paloma said, slipping her arm through his as they continued down the sidewalk. "I'm not afraid of seeing things as they are anymore."

Chapter Thirty-Five

A month before the baby was due, Paloma was at work with Anca and Tatiana. In comfortable silence, they worked on getting out two dozen wedding centerpieces, arranging a medley of soft pink roses, hydrangeas, creamy-white dahlias, and sprigs of pale-green seeded eucalyptus. Paloma glanced over at Anca who, after a long heart-to-heart with Ruby, had finally accepted Tatiana's pregnancy in full proud-grandmother measure, even bragging to customers about how she couldn't wait to spoil her granddaughter and throwing not just one, but two baby showers for her young daughter. In fact, the bigger Tatiana got, the more Anca's face glowed with anticipation.

Just when they finished the last centerpiece, Serena sailed in. Never having known Serena to step foot inside the shop, Paloma looked to Anca and Tatiana for a clue, but their speechless faces registered her same surprise. Serena sauntered over to them, hiding something behind her back.

"Are you not feeling well?" Anca asked, her eyes squinting with concern.

"I am," Serena looked at Anca, "very well, thank you." She then turned to Paloma. "I am holding something for your heart to know." From around her back, she produced a battered leather journal, it's once-red cover faded into a gentle rose-colored hue.

Paloma gasped. "Serena, where'd you find that?"

"I was a girl on the beach when our mermaid mother sent it."

"Our mother?"

"She wrapped it up in clear, clear bubbles and buried it under a rowboat. It was her gift to me. But now it wants you."

With a pounding heart, Paloma opened it. As she flipped through the pages, though, she saw that all her mother's long-ago words had faded into undecipherable lines of barely-there blue ink.

Serena smiled. "Look at the last page, my sister. Look at the very last page."

In black marker pen, Paloma read her mother's last entry: "I want to swim and swim until I see my mermaid daughters. I want them to find each other and rise above every wave. I want them to know I love them above all else."

Choking back tears, Paloma hugged her sister.

Serena patted her back. "All is in place now. All is in place."

Serena then walked over to wide-eyed Tatiana and caressed the huge ball of her little sister's stomach. "Her name shall be Bonnie," Serena announced. "It will be a name that no one will be able to toss to sea."

Tatiana looked down at Serena's hand, then at Anca, and finally at Paloma. "That is a beautiful name, Serena." She held both hands around her belly.

Surrounded by the multitude of flowers, which seemed to glow in the afternoon light flooding through the store's window, Paloma breathed in the vibrant scent of eucalyptus combined with the gentle fragrance of English roses. As they gazed at Tatiana's belly, the three Nicholson women also looked as if they were aglow. Watching them, Paloma knew this would be a moment she'd never forget, a moment that told her she was now moored to other people's lives, as they were to hers.

Smiling, Serena stepped over to her. Without a word, she guided Paloma closer to Tatiana. "You can feel the baby, too, Paloma," she said. Paloma looked to Tatiana for affirmation, and then rested her hand over the unseen daughter who would soon fill all of their futures. "She will love you, too," Serena said. Right on cue, a tiny, determined foot answered, pushing its confirmation against Paloma's palm. Her eyes stung as though she were swimming under the ocean. Yet when she took in the faces of the women surrounding her, her vision remained clear. For a moment more, she held her hand on Tatiana's stomach, remembering her mother as the wind outside ruffled through the trees, and leaf shadows danced upon the inside walls of their world.

THE END

Acknowledgements

Huge gratitude to editors Ashley Brown, Sophia Dembling, Maria Gordon, Grace Safford, and Benjamin Sutherland; you not only helped me to shape *Floating Underwater* through its many revisions, but also taught me to become a more in-depth and thoughtful writer.

I'm eternally grateful for my alpha readers, Anne Diamond and Carol Talley, who read and provided feedback on both my debut novel as well as this most current labor of love. A big appreciation also goes out to Eve for her amazing insights and to Stephela for all the years of wisdom.

Thank you to Amber McCullough, Spiritual Counselor and Energy Healer for answering my myriad of questions about spirituality, including out of body experiences, ghost sightings, and metaphysical awakenings. You provided a wealth of information! A very special thank you, as well, to detective Dave who provided vital details regarding crime scenes and physical evidence.

And, of course, an ocean of gratitude to my family who have been there through all the ups and downs of life as well as the trials and tribulations of my writing journey. Your love keeps me going.

And finally, a gigantic thank you to my readers. I am forever grateful for your support. Through all my doubts, through all the rejections, your encouragement keeps me writing.

Book Club Discussion and Reader Questions

1. Paloma feels she is a "hostage of her own mind" while experiencing a vision. Do you think you'd feel the same way if you had ongoing premonitions? Why or why not?

2. At different times throughout the novel, Paloma notes that her husband, Reed, is fearful of her power. Why do you think Reed is so afraid of his wife's gifts?

3. Frequently reminding herself that the past does not have to affect her present, Paloma fights ongoing dread. Do you believe personal history often colors a person's present state of being?

4. Paloma asks Reed if he thinks it's at all possible that there's such a thing as an inner knowing that can't be explained. He responds, saying that random coincidences may make it seem that way. Do you think Reed has a point?

5. Serena tells Paloma that mermaids are only part women, the other part being of the sea, saying that this is "part of who we were, who we are…and who we'll be." Why do you think Serena says this to Paloma?

6. When Paloma is in the midst of an out-of-body experience, she wonders if she could become eternally adrift. In what ways was Paloma "adrift" in her own life?

7. Paloma's childhood friend Justine can be bossy and controlling as well as thoughtful and caring. Did you like or dislike Justine and why?

8. Paloma tells Justine that she does believe there are true healers, yet there are still con artists as well as people "who talk themselves into believing that they're gifted but are as receptive as a loaf of bread." What do you think of this statement?

9. What scene was the most memorable for you and why?

10. How did you feel about the ending? What do you think will happen next to the main characters?

CPSIA information can be obtained
at www.ICGtesting.com
Printed in the USA
LVHW110129240322
714225LV00002B/367